A SISTERHOOD
of SILENCE

Vigilante Justice in a Cornish
Seaside Town

JULIE EVANS

For my best friend Allison and all the Sisters out there.
Together we are powerful.

ABOUT JULIE EVANS

 After training as a lawyer, Julie returned to her native Cornwall to establish her own law firm and to raise her three children. After years building a successful legal practice it was time for a new adventure and she decided to write the stories she had formulated in her head over the years about her community and the lives of those who find themselves on the wrong side of the law.

Julie's novels in her CORNISH CRIME series. *RAGE, A SISTERHOOD OF SILENCE* and *THE BITTER FRUIT BENEATH* are available to buy now on Amazon.

Book Four: *A BAPTISM OF FIRE* is due to be released later this year.

If you would like to read more about Julie, visit her website www.cornishcrimeauthor.com where you will be given the opportunity to join her readers' club and receive free downloads and inside information exclusively available to members, including a FREE novella in the **CORNISH CRIME** series, *THE ROSARY PEA What's Your Poison?*

ONE

Sister One
Carly

The blindfold slips, and sky squints through broken planks; chinks of blue like precious jewels. I can't tell if it's the same sky of three minutes, three hours, or three days ago. Time has lost its shape in the darkness.

Plastic sheets flap and flutter like giant moths in the shuttered light through which I can make out wooden planks and concrete beams balanced against earth walls running with water. I listen to the constant drip, drip, drip and the metallic groan of unknown objects shifting below, knowing if I move, I'll plummet after them. I keep still, arms locked by my sides, wrapped in my canvas cocoon, pins and needles turning my feet to ice.

Flexing my fingers, I claw at my thighs. The torn skin burns, but I dig deeper because the pain lets me know I'm still alive. I worry about bugs for a second crawling over me but then reassure myself no creature would choose to live here; the sulphurous air keeps them away. I feel a rush of strange disappointment as I face the fact I am truly alone here.

At least I have the words for company. The letters race through my brain like tiny ants, their spidery legs connecting to make the words. I keep them safe, so they have time to multiply. I will not release them to the void to echo and die. I will never abandon them to the darkness. Blinking the weight of raindrops from my lashes, I let the cool droplets trickle down my throat and taste the bitter tang of copper coins on my swollen tongue.

I don't know how I got here. I remember only the muffled voice of a faceless man, who spoke of me when he taunted, "She can't speak, she can't scream, poor cow."

It's true, I've never spoken, never screamed, I've been silent all my life, but my silence is not my sentence, it's my refuge; my special gift.

My name is Carly Taylor, I'm eighteen, and just like the words of that song Mum loves to sing at Karaoke, 'this could be the day that I die.'

TWO

Carly hadn't come home.

'She's meant to be helping me with this quiz tonight,' John Taylor moaned, shuffling the stack of sticky beer mats before scattering them on the newly arranged tables.

'She took her paints down the beach this afternoon. You know what she's like; she gets carried away and forgets the time,' replied Alice, his wife, stretching up to wipe the optics with a damp cloth.

'You mind the bar, love; I'll go look for her,' said John.

'She won't want you fetching her home like some kid; she's eighteen, not ten. Look, I'll help you set up; she won't be long,' she reassured, but as dusk bruised the horizon she relented and let him go.

The evening trade was brisk; competitive spirits high, but Alice, distracted and hesitant in her delivery, had to repeat several questions as her eyes bounced between the clock and the door. She was over halfway through, about to begin the literature section by the time John wandered back through the bar; alone.

'Last question,' said Alice, microphone hovering as she raked his face for an explanation.

'But there's five more to go,' protested a voice from the back.

'Are you bloody deaf? She said last question,' John barked over the heads of the quizzers; huddled together in teams of four; pens poised like missiles.

The place fell silent.

Alice, gripping the microphone tighter, tried to control the quiver in her voice as concern crept up the dial to dread. She could barely read the words on the sheet printed off the internet that morning.

'Who wrote; "'Tis better to have loved and lost than never to have loved at all"?'

The quote caught in her throat like a warning.

John placed a steadying hand on her shoulder. 'I found this on the beach,' he whispered, reaching into his back pocket and unfolding a crumpled sheet of paper. 'It was flapping around by the quay wall where she usually sits.'

Alice looked down at the sketch in her hand; two Kittiwakes, black-tipped wings tilted as they surfed invisible thermals. One of Carly's favourite subjects. Her eyes shone with tears as John turned and yanked the rope to the ship's bell above the bar. 'Time, gentlemen, please.'

'But it's only ten o'clock?' protested Harry Dyer, one of their regulars, as John bundled him and the other stragglers out onto the pavement, bolting the door behind them.

'You don't think she's slipped ... off the quay or the rocks and not been able to cry for help ... hit her head; been washed out by the tide?' Alice asked, fiddling with the St Christopher around her neck.

'I don't know, love, but I'm calling the police right now.'

Alice hovered at his elbow as he made the call. 'Mind you tell them about our Carly's problem, else they won't raise a finger til she's been gone twenty-four hours.'

John's chest tightened as he tried not to imagine all the things that could happen in twenty-four hours to a girl like Carly. His hand shook as he handed Alice the phone.

'I can't ... you do it, love.'

He could hear her talking to the woman on the other end but couldn't seem to focus on the words. His mind was elsewhere, remembering the day Carly was born, how he'd kissed her velvety cheek and known he'd never be the same again. How, as the months passed, it became obvious his child was different from other toddlers. Carly didn't speak; not a word.

'Your daughter's an elective mute,' the specialist said, 'she has chosen not to speak; not to us, not to you; not to anyone. It may change over time; some EMs choose to communicate with one or two people, but often, they never talk at all.'

The sadness was paralysing, and for a while, he and Alice lost their voices too; a self-imposed gagging order as if not talking about Carly's disability meant it wasn't real.

Then finally, one morning, he'd woken up; truth lashing like a whip, inflicting such pain it almost finished him. He'd fought through the grief for Alice's sake, and finally, in time, he'd begun to believe the positive spin he conjured for her.

'Look, it's no secret, people can be ignorant bastards about disability, but at least here, in Penzance, everyone will be kind to her for our sake, and she need never leave; she'll be safe here with us,' he'd promised, and he'd been right. The town accepted Carly, and tourists foolish enough to comment on his golden-haired child's silence found themselves barred from the pub. John made it his life's mission to keep his only child safe, and it had worked until now.

Now in her late teens, Carly was a beauty, and John knew it was only a matter of time before she'd be plagued by every spotty youth from miles around. He could have coped with that but not this; this was theft. She had been taken from right under his nose.

***

The police arrived within the hour.

'I've told her time and time again to take her phone, so she can text, but as usual, there it is on her dressing table,' said Alice to the young female PC searching Carly's room.

'Don't worry, Mrs. Taylor, I'm sure she's fine. We've all been there; met up with friends and forgotten the time. Do you know the password ... for her phone or her laptop?'

'No ... no I don't,' replied Alice, remembering all those police dramas on the telly where they find out about the secret life of some run-away from their internet use.'

'You don't think she's been talking to someone online? She looks so much younger than she is. You don't think she's been groomed by some ... ?' Alice couldn't bear to say the word.

'Please try not to worry yourself. We can't assume anything at the moment. It's just useful to check her contacts. Could you take a look to make sure she hasn't packed a bag?'

Alice turned and opened the wardrobe door. Everything was just as it had been the day before when she'd hung up Carly's ironing.

'It's all there; nothing missing,' she said, relieved, before wondering if it was a good thing or not? If she'd packed a bag, it meant she'd planned this; if not, it could mean something far worse? She began to sob.

'Why don't you go downstairs and sit with your husband? Have a cup of tea. I can manage here.'

Alice did as she suggested. She sat with John, drinking tea, listening for the key in the lock that never turned.

THREE

The clock ticked as hope, like a thief, scuttled to the darkest corners of the room, and no amount of coaxing could prize it out as it became clear Carly hadn't gone to a party; or met some boy, or been rushed to A and E.

By the time dawn crept silently along the quayside, John knew what had to be done. Trying not to wake Alice, who'd succumbed to tear-stained sleep only an hour before, he lifted his car keys from the bedside table.

His mobile rang. It was his friend Ross Trenear; a DI in the Devon and Cornwall police force. Ross sounded groggy, hadn't slept much either, keeping them updated throughout the night.

'Just calling to give you the heads-up, mate. We've called in the CCTV from the arcade and the shops along the quay. The RNLI is on standby and the helicopter has been out searching the cliffs since first light, but still no news I'm afraid.'

'I'm going around to Fielding's.' John blurted.

'You can't do that?'

Ross sounded panicky.

'Watch me.'

'Slow down ... use your head. You can't go accusing someone like Jem Fielding on a hunch. You trust me, don't you; let us deal with this. Stay put. I'm coming over. for Christ's sake don't do anything stupid.'

John cut him off. Ross was like a brother; of course, he trusted him. They'd grown up together; compared bruised knees and broken hearts. He was Carly's godfather, but he was also a policeman, and they had rules. They needed warrants and reasonable suspicion; he didn't; the twist in his gut was all he needed.

Alice stirred. He sat down on the bed next to her.

'I'm going out for a bit, love,' he said, gently tucking a damp curl behind her ear. 'I won't be long.'

'But where are you going?'

Her voice held the flutter of a sob he could hardly bear.

'Out in the car. I know the police are looking, but they can't cover everywhere. I can't sit here doing nothing.'

'Then I'll come too.'

She swung her legs over the edge of the bed to get up, and John thought she might topple; she looked so frail. He's heard you could age overnight when terrible things happened, but he'd never seen it close up. He helped her back into bed.

'No, you stay here in case Carly comes home. Why don't you call Karenza to come over and sit with you.'

Karenza was Ross's ex-wife. He'd introduced Ross to the daughter of Gil Martin a friend of his father's and head of the local licenced victuallers association twenty years before when they were all still at school. The two couples had been firm friends ever since. He and Alice had been determined not to take sides when they split up. He was glad they hadn't, as he watched his wife shakily lift her mobile and make the call.

Downstairs was unusually tidy. He'd busied himself until three in the morning, washing glasses; wiping tables, anything to distract. They wouldn't be opening today.

He'd been born upstairs. He knew every pitted quarry tile, every tar-blackened beam, but today it felt alien, hollow like him; the familiar yeasty tang of stale beer, prodding his tonsils to heave. He needed air.

Pulling back the heavy bolt, he stood on the threshold, letting the watery light flood the bar as he sucked in a lungful of salt-scoured air before lighting a cigarette and setting off down the side of the pub, past the stacks of empty steel barrels in the alley to his car. Head down, he refused to succumb to the urge to glance up at Carly's window; the longing for her to be there, when logic said she wasn't.

He paused for only a second to think of what this might mean to Alice if it went wrong before twisting the key in the ignition and heading east out of Penzance, past the harbour lined with tubs of starry flowered Agapanthus, tracing Mounts Bay towards Marazion where Fielding lived. On any other day, his eyes would have been drawn across the sand towards St Michael's Mount. He would have looked to see if its granite feet were paddling yet or if the causeway was still open.

Like every Cornishman, he danced to the rhythm of the Atlantic but not today; today, his feet felt heavy, his vision landlocked.

Rounding the corner, he caught sight of Fielding's house between the trees. Shielded behind high hedges at the end of a long drive, the massive electronic gates complete with CCTV and intercom kept out unwanted guests. Leaning against the bonnet of his car, determined to do the same, was Ross.

John pulled up sharply; the relentless thrum of the engine adding to his anxiety.

Ross looked up, his stern policeman's stare melting, as he flicked his cigarette to the ground and walked towards him; arms outstretched in a gesture acknowledging the inevitability of his presence there. John revved the engine, and for one brief moment thought Ross flinched as he spun the car into a sharp U-turn and, pressing his foot down hard on the accelerator, sped off back the way he'd come.

He knew why Ross had stopped him; knew he meant well, but this wasn't Dodge; Ross wasn't the sheriff. It wasn't his child missing. He knew if it had been, his friend would have had those gates off their bloody hinges.

He'd go over Ross's head; tell the police everything. After all, it wasn't like they didn't know all about Jerome Fielding the same way Ross knew about him. Hadn't Ross been the one to warn him about Jem in the first place three years previously, just after he'd been elected as Chairman of the Penzance Round Table. They were busy fundraising for a local children's charity. Fielding had waded in with a massive donation, wanting free publicity for his nightclubs in return. He'd mentioned this in passing to Ross after five-a-side one evening and remembered how taken aback he'd been by his friend's response.

'He's bad news. Steer clear, that's my advice, no matter what he's offering.'

'Is it about the clubs? I know he employs lap dancers in some of them, but to be honest, beggars can't be choosers. Loads of companies aren't squeaky clean; it doesn't mean the big charities won't take their money, so why should the little ones like us be any different?'

'This isn't about ethical trading or political correctness. Just find a way of turning him down. Trust me, the man's toxic.'

A few pints and a good deal of persuasion later, Ross eventually told him what he knew about Fielding.

He'd arrived in the county in the early noughties in the guise of a property developer. The police suspected this was a front for laundering money, earned through drug trafficking, pimping and protection pay-outs. Modern-day piracy without the swashbuckling charm.

'Why aren't you lot doing something about it if you know what he's up to?'

'We've tried. We were alerted because of his connections with known criminal gangs. He had a couple of convictions when younger; you know, joyriding, carrying an offensive weapon, affray; minor stuff compared to what he's up to now. Let's just say he's friends with some really bad bastards, although neither our lot nor other forces up the line have had any luck pinning anything on him. We've been close a couple of times, but he's been tipped off, or people retract their statements at the last minute. He's got the luck of the devil.'

'But this is Penzance, not New York; it's Cornwall; people talk.'

'Whispers without proof are hearsay. He's tooled up with the best lawyers crooked money can buy and takes a good deal of trouble not to get his own hands dirty ... well, you get the picture.'

He'd got the picture alright and refused the donation, telling Jem the committee was not comfortable with a strip club owner being out there as the main sponsor of a children's charity. To his surprise, Jem hadn't sounded the least bit offended on the phone. He merely confirmed he wasn't interested in donating without the free publicity and to John's relief, withdrew the offer. Their paths may never have crossed again had Fielding not had his eye on his and Alice's pub.

Fielding needed premises for a new lap dancing club; somewhere with an entertainment licence, easy to shoe-horn through the planning process. The pub had a large cellar with a quick rear exit running down to the quay, which he intended to convert for private dances. It was part of a much bigger scheme to develop the old waterfront into a marina, with luxury apartments, a hotel and a casino. That meant getting rid of some of the current inhabitants, whether they liked it or not.

John didn't like it and wasn't afraid to say so. Every time Jem approached him, he'd turned him down flat.

Their final conversation had been a month or so before Carly disappeared.

'Come on, John, be reasonable. How long do you expect to be able to keep this place going? I know you got the tourists in the summer, but you need more than the motley crew who come in for a couple of pints of an evening during the winter months to keep your head above water. Times are changing, punters want tapas and gin cocktails,' counselled Jem, like a Dragon from the Den.

'Not here they don't. Anyway, that's my business. I've told you a dozen times, I'm not interested. This was my father's place before he retired and I won't be selling until I do the same, and that's a good few year yet.'

'Yeah, well, you might find it's sooner rather than later,' Jem sniped, his annoyance beginning to surface.

'What are you saying; are you threatening me?'

'Of course not, why would you think that? Jem grinned. 'I'm just saying shit happens. I'm being over-generous here. I'm offering you a way out, a bit of security for the future.'

'No, the answer's no. It'll always be no. So why don't *you* do yourself a favour and stop bloody asking.'

Jem had stopped asking. The almost daily calls ceased, and he'd put the whole episode to the back of his mind as he and Alice worked relentlessly through yet another busy summer season, but now Jem's words flooded back. He replayed every syllable; every gesture in an attempt to decipher any hidden meaning, any clue which might tell him where Carly was.

By the time he reached the station, his temper was at boiling point;

'I know Fielding's got her. I'm telling you it's him. He threatened me and now he's done this,' John shouted, banging his fist down on the counter so the desk sergeant had to retrieve his pen from the floor.

'Sir, if you could please calm down. I've told you to take a seat, and an officer will be with you in a moment to take all the details. Anything you want to tell us can be said then, in private.' The officer raised his eyebrows, scanning the waiting room as bums began to shuffle in their seats.

'My daughter's missing. She's a vulnerable teenager, and she's missing. Do you think I'm going to keep quiet about that; stand here twiddling my thumbs while you lot do your paperwork when I know who's taken her?'

The officer motioned to a young female PC working behind the desk. Getting the hint, she jumped to her feet and opened the side door to the interview rooms.

'Mr. Taylor, if you come with me, I'll take your statement now.'

John followed her and an hour later emerged, having told her all about his history with Jem.

Later that evening, John got the call.

The accusation had fallen at the first hurdle. There were several dozen people, including the local MP, willing to confirm Fielding was at a charity golf tournament in Newquay when Carly went missing.

'But don't you see. He won't have done it himself. He would have got someone to do it for him. You have to search his house ... or his clubs; yeah she might be there.'

'I'm afraid we can't do that, Mr. Taylor, without reasonable suspicion that a crime has been committed. You have to leave this to us. We are doing everything we can to find your daughter. I'm sending over a family liaison officer to sit with you. In the meantime, I strongly recommend you get some sleep and put any ideas you have about Mr. Fielding out of your head. It will only serve to confuse matters and ... it's a dangerous thing to do; accuse someone like him without proof. Do you understand?'

Slamming the phone down, John sank to his knees.

'Don't do anything stupid,' Ross had said, but the warning had come too late. He'd already done the stupid thing. He'd not taken Fielding seriously, thinking he could deal with the likes of him. He'd been wrong, and now he was paying the price.

***

In the days that followed, flyers were posted and announcements made in the media, urging anyone with information to come forward.

On day four, encouraged by Ross, John and Alice appeared on local TV. Staring like zombies into the cameras; grey-faced and drawn, they tried to explain Carly's disability and how it felt to miss her silence.

Droves of people contacted the police with information.

Sightings of a girl resembling Carly getting onto a train in Plymouth. Another, boarding the boat to the Scilly Isles; most ruled out as innocent misidentifications.

Others were not so benign; false leads by sad, damaged individuals peddling viperous allegations. One witness claimed she'd seen John on the cliff with his daughter in the hours before her disappearance and the local radio station received no less than four locks of auburn hair claiming to be Carley's; three of animal origin and one snipped from a nylon wig.

He and Alice reeled at the cruelty. Floundering in a deluge of misinformation and speculation, they barely tread water. Alice became more and more withdrawn. He'd wake in the night to the sound of her sobbing. Like a favourite dress, washed too often, she'd lost her vibrancy. At times she seemed transparent; barely there at all.

Ross came daily; Karenza too, to sit with her, and despite his agony, in those endless afternoons, John recognised something pass between the two of them; a sideways glance now and then; unfinished business.

FOUR

Meg Trembath's eight-year-old grandson stood over her; floppy blonde fringe falling in his eyes.

'Are you alright, Nan?'

'I'm fine,' she lied, 'but where's Ginny? There's sheep in the fields off the path. If she gets in with them, there'll be hell to pay ... go ... go after her.'

She pointed to where she'd seen the young Spaniel scramble through the bracken.

'Go on, Charlie!' she urged, reaching in her pocket for a dog treat, "ere take a biscuit and get her to come to you, then grab her lead.'

She hadn't seen the rabbit hop onto the path so, when the pup unexpectedly tugged the lead from her hand, she'd taken a tumble. She winced at the tenderness in her hip, wishing she'd never agreed to walk her daughter's new dog. The pup would be filthy. It had been raining all night, and the ground off the path was muddy.

She soon lost sight of Charlie but could still hear Ginny's barking, more and more frenzied; a high-pitched yelp then ... nothing, not a sound.

She hobbled as best she could through the trees, emerging out into scrubland. There, a few feet in front of her, hanging from a makeshift wire fence, a battered wooden sign;

DANGER KEEP OUT scrawled in peeling blue paint.

There was a dull ringing in her ears, as if she'd slipped under the bathwater.

'No ... ,' her voice strangled. 'Charlie ... Charlie; where are you?'

A faint echo from behind and a tug on her sleeve.

'Nan ... it's okay, Nan ... I'm here ... I'm here.' Ginny's gone. She ran through that wire and was just gone ... like magic.'

Wiping tears away with the back of her hand, she turned, peering into his face; needing to know he was real. 'Charlie, oh thank God.'

Charlie's bottom lip quivered as he pointed to where short, rotten posts once holding taut barbed wire, lay scattered, like kindling; Ginny's collar tangled in it, lead still attached; caught as she'd raced through and wriggled free.

Meg knew what lay beyond. Cornwall was littered with disused mine shafts; hundreds of feet deep, and her daughter's dog had gone down one.

Charlie's face crumpled. 'We've got to find her, Nan, we've got to!'

Meg felt a sharp twinge as she bent to his level. 'I'm sorry my lover but we can't go after her.'

'But I want to go see; she might be hurt, she'll need me.'

Grabbing him tightly, Meg reached across and tugged Ginny's collar from the wire;

'Charlie,' she said firmly, 'we can't go after her, it's too dangerous. Now promise me, if I let you go; you won't run back here.'

He nodded. Meg could feel the rise and fall of every stifled sob through his Cornish Pirates t-shirt, damp with sweat from his tense little body. He took hold of the dog's collar. The silver tag etched with Ginny's name, glinting as he ran it through his fingers.

Then, as they walked away, as if out of the aether; a bark, distant, echoing, but unmistakably Ginny's.

Wriggling from her, Charlie turned. Meg grabbed him.

Pulling her mobile from her pocket she dialled 999

***

When Meg spotted three firemen walking up the lane towards her, she was both relieved and embarrassed. Ginny hadn't barked again, and she worried the dog was dead and this was all a dreadful waste of public resources.

Another thought crossed her mind; was there a charge for this? On a tight budget, if she had to pay, she'd be eating egg and chips for a month.

She took one of the men aside. 'I'm so sorry to ask, but will this cost me anything? You hear about old ladies calling you out to rescue cats. I feel so daft about all this. I'm not even sure she's alive,' she whispered, trying to avoid Charlie hearing. 'We heard a yelp about half an hour ago, but nothing since.'

'About once a year someone's garden collapses into one of these; it's good for us to keep our hand in. Let's call it an exercise,' he smiled kindly, then, dropping his voice; 'but the shafts are full of rubbish people chuck down - old bikes, lawnmowers, all sorts. This one is not so deep according to the plans we've got, but the chances of her not hitting something sharp when she fell are slim.'

Meg's stomach roiled.

'You'd better take the boy back to the car. The engine is following us up with the winch. I suggest you go now before we start. If she's dead, shall we say we couldn't find her?'

'No, bring her up. I think that's best, otherwise, there won't be any end to this, no closure, as they say.'

'Okay, I'll come and fetch you when we're done.'

They arrived back at the car as the fire engine headed up the lane.

She passed Charlie her mobile as a distraction. 'Why don't you find a game or something while we wait?'

She retrieved a blanket from the back seat. She would ask one of the firemen to wrap the puppy in it and put it in the boot for her. She'd need to comfort Charlie, and in any case, she knew she wasn't up to the task. It would be bad enough ringing Sally to tell her the awful news.

As she closed the door, two police cars, lights flashing, screeched into the car park.

'Are they going to help rescue Ginny?' asked Charlie, ready to jump out of the car again at the slightest provocation.

'I don't know. You wait in the car, there's a good boy, I'd better go and see what's going on.'

Meg felt the tension welling as she walked back up the pathway. It was at times like this she felt every bit of her sixty-five years. As she got within sight of the shaft, a young officer came forward, arms outstretched.

'I'm afraid you can't come through, madam.'

'But they're here for Ginny ... my daughter's dog.'

'There's been a development.'

What on earth did she mean; why were the police even here?

'Bring it up ... slowly ... slowly now,' she heard someone shout.

Meg braced herself; heart vaulting, waiting for the dog's limp body to come into view but instead caught a glimpse of a bundle, way too big to be Ginny.

As the harness swung above ground level, the fireman's body twisted sideways, and Meg saw long red silk flowing over his back. Then, as the hoist rocked and his feet settled on solid ground, she realised with horror, the red wasn't material at all. It was hair, long shiny red hair.

She watched with disbelief as a milky white arm slipped from the bundle and hung lifelessly from what was clearly the body of a young woman.

'It's the girl, it's Carly Taylor, and she's alive!' she heard someone shout; 'she's in a bad way, but she's alive.

FIVE

It was taken on the nod Carly's fall was an accident. After all, it was hardly an isolated incident. Whole houses had collapsed down disused mine shafts before now, not to mention livestock. Only the year before, a hiker walking the coastal path from Cape Cornwall to Land's End had fallen down a shaft and been trapped for two days, wedged tightly between the rocks by his backpack.

The local paper latched onto the outcry against the council for not capping them properly, until three weeks later when the police revealed Carly had been bound when they found her. A reporter blind-sided Ross while leaving court after giving evidence in another case.

'Can you comment, Detective Inspector, on the Carly Taylor case; the motive for the crime? Is this about the girl's learning difficulties? Can you reassure the public all known sex offenders known to prey on vulnerable teenagers have been questioned?'

'Carly Taylor does not have learning difficulties. She doesn't talk, that's all, and *whoever* wrapped her in a tarpaulin and left her to die down there will pay for what they did.'

'But was the girl assaulted; *sexually*?'

'No, she was not,' Ross snapped. 'You people should concentrate on getting anyone who has information to come forward. Whether intentional or a vicious prank that went wrong, this could have ended in a girl's death. She only survived because she landed on a ledge and by pure luck was found before it was too late.'

'A prank, you mean, because of her disability?'

'No, I ... I've got nothing more to say.'

The Taylors were horrified by the headline in the local paper the next day;

PRETTY MUTE FALLS PREY TO PRANKSTERS

The article ranted on about the need for a public sex offender list and the ineffectiveness of ASBOs in the face of chronic antisocial behaviour and hate crimes targeting the disabled. John shuddered. He hated the freighted meaning; the constant quest for lurid headlines at his daughter's expense. It was grubby and voyeuristic and wouldn't stop.

When Ross called to apologise, he bore the brunt of his frustration.

'I know it's not what you want to hear. I know you're going to be disappointed we can't find and punish who did this, but with Carly not remembering anything and no DNA found on her or the tarpaulin, there's just no evidence. Forensics have been all over the site, but there's only so much they can do within the limitations of health and safety and the Council is eager to cap the shaft after the bad publicity,' Ross tried to explain.

John could feel Alice's eyes glued to his back as he paced.

'What you're saying is, cos she was found no harm has been done, it's all okay,'

'That's not fair, John; you know we've spent hundreds of police hours on this. I'm under pressure to close it down. The file stays open, but we have to face it, as time goes on, the less likely it is anyone will come forward with anything new,' Ross replied defensively.

'Bollocks! Why the hell did you have to tell the press this was some sort of prank; some teenage bullying shit, when we all know who did this?' John seethed, fists clenched, as he reeled to face his friend. 'It might have only been days she was gone, but it'll take a lifetime for us to get over this. She's not the same girl; we're not the same people we were.'

'I know, I'm so sorry. I was caught on the hop.'

John could tell Ross was shame-faced. He knew he'd let him and Alice down.

'Just get out ... leave us alone.'

John knew Carly's survival meant her case was unlikely to benefit from over-stretched resources in a county whose population quadrupled in the summertime, driving the budget to breaking point.

He overheard Alice apologise as she showed Ross to the door.

'I'm sorry, Ross. John is so angry ... mostly with himself. He feels he should have protected Carly better, and he's scared it's not over.'

She was right. He was scared.

As the door closed, he hoped Carly hadn't heard the shouting . The last thing he wanted was to scare her too.

SIX

Carly

Before the pit, the voice in my head lapped softly, like the echo from a seashell held to my ear, but now, it thunders like winter surf.

If the boy's dog hadn't chased a rabbit, I wouldn't have been found. That's what the paper said, in the piece they ran with the photo of the spaniel with its bandaged paw.

It's a good story, but it's not the whole truth.

I heard its bark; distant one minute, above me the next, but my voice as always, died in my throat as if trapped by a pebble. Only this time, I coughed and gulped to dislodge it; to spit it free, and when I opened my mouth and my silent scream grew to a high-pitched ring, like a tuning fork against a wire, the dog came to me.

I braced myself as it crashed through the planks, somersaulting towards me; legs pedalling air, reaching for invisible ground. Yelping its surprise, it landed on me with a thud, its body slouched across mine, tongue lolling from one side of its dribbling mouth as its hot, sour breath hit my face, and it sluggishly shook the confusion from its head to let out one last whimper.

Mine's a better story, but not for telling yet. For now, I must keep the secret, the way you keep secrets from children, for their own good.

Since leaving the hospital, I sit glued to the TV in my bedroom. Crime dramas and psychological thrillers are banned by Mum. I'm not fussed. I'm not watching. I have other things to think about.

I look down at the thick colouring pad full of intricate patterns and the pack of felt tip pens. It was kind of Karenza to drop them in, but I don't see the world in paint-box colours anymore.

Earlier I heard Uncle Ross leave after arguing with Dad. I know the argument was about me; it always is. The doorbell rings, Ross, I expect, coming back to make up.

Raised voices again.

Pushing the pens aside, I slip off the bed and tip-toe to the door; feel for the handle and peer with one eye through the narrow opening.

The man has his back to me. He's carrying a bouquet. Not Uncle Ross.

'You've got some nerve showing your face around here,' says Dad.

'I don't know what you're on about, I was passing and thought I'd drop in to congratulate you on finding your girl.'

'That's rich coming from you.' Dad shouts, lunging forward.

'No John, please no,' Mum says.

'You should listen to your wife, Taylor,' the man says. 'You ought to watch that mouth of yours; you're a little too quick with your accusations. I'm prepared to let it go because you've had a shock, but I won't be so generous next time. I came here to let you know my offer to buy you out stands. You know you're better off not having to worry about this place. You had a lucky escape, but luck has a habit of running out.'

I tense as I recognise the voice of the man who ridiculed my silence, the man who had his men bind me.

'I'm calling the police,' cries Mum.

'No love, put the phone down,' Dad shouts over the man's shoulder, 'it's fine he's leaving now. You go into the kitchen; I'll be there soon ... go on. it's fine.'

Pausing at the door, the man turns.

'Each week, the price goes down; do you understand? I'll have this place off you, with or without your permission. Leave now, and I'll make it worth your while. Do yourself a favour, Taylor, for once in your miserable fucking life.'

He places the bouquet on the hall table. 'You'd better put them in water before they die. I hate to see beautiful things die,' he smirks.

I listen to Mum's wail as Dad slams the door after the unwelcome guest.

'I don't want his bloody flowers. Throw them in the bin, John, I mean it, throw them away, I can't bear it, I can't.'

Later, when Mum and Dad go to bed, I creep into the kitchen and lift the bin lid. Lilies; stems bent double. The sickly-sweet scent fills my nostrils as I retrieve the screwed-up florist's card.

To the Future.

Jem Fielding.

I take the card. I need to remember his name.

Before turning off the lights, I reach for a knife from the block on the kitchen counter.

Bolting the bathroom door, I slide to the floor and pull up my nightdress. Splaying my thighs, I flinch as I trace the criss-cross of tiny cuts mapping my skin. I find comfort in making them; the same way I found comfort in the pit, clawing with my broken nails.

I scratch out the letters;

J E M.

With pain comes the promise of deliverance.

SEVEN

After the meeting with Fielding, John knew two things; Jem had taken Carly, and his family was still in danger. The certainty of both gnawed away night and day, sapping his confidence and fraying his resolve.

Every punter who came into the pub wanted to talk about Carly, and when he told them 'to mind their own bloody business,' they didn't come back.

Week on week, the takings were down; week on week, things got worse until he called the agents and told them to put the pub on the market. They did exactly what he knew they would the minute he put down the phone; called Fielding, who paid cash.

In a matter of weeks, he'd sold his birth right and lost the battle.

With the proceeds, he and Alice moved to St. Ives. Karenza lived there and knew of a small gallery coming up for sale with a flat above they hoped would be a new start.

Initially, it was. They filled the place with the landscapes and wildlife paintings Carly had done before she'd been taken, and they sold well, but they weren't replaced. Carly had stopped leaving the house to paint. She had discarded the tubes of Cerulean Blue and Indian Yellow and instead, now locked herself in the studio at the back of the gallery laying down a new sombre palette; scratching and splattering, thick daubs of black and grey across huge canvasses. She worked well into the night, falling into bed, her clothes filthy; broken nails grouted with paint. The monumental results of her nocturnal endeavours spoke of desolation and despair.

Alice hung the largest canvas in the gallery, and it became a cause celebre amongst the arty types who frequented Tate St.

Ives. They pontificated about the unknown artist; the masterful handling of space and form; the purity of line and the angst in the paint.

It was all too much for her, and one day when one particular critic deduced the artist was wrestling with hidden demons, she finally snapped.

'I just couldn't listen. I took the painting off the wall and chucked them out; the whole bloody lot of them.'

'Good for you!' John whooped trying to be supportive.

'You should have heard them, 'picking over the bones of our child, dissecting her as if she were a thing to be gawked at just to make them look clever. I'd had enough.'

Carly's paintings stayed in her studio after that.

They brought in stock from other local artists and seemed to turn a corner business-wise. They were both glad to be working more sociable hours and felt they were finally moving on. Then Carly began to wander.

It began with her taking the bus to Penzance; something she'd never done on her own before. She'd walk the streets ending up at the pub. She never actually gained access because now it was a lap dancing club it was closed during the day.

One of their old neighbours usually called him or Alice to come and pick her up, until the day she wouldn't come home.

EIGHT

One of Jem's girls had let Carly in. It wasn't the first time she'd turned up. Usually, she banged on the door for a bit but gave up after a while and went away. Today she'd kept banging, and they weren't sure she could hear them when they told her to push off.

Once inside, she was no trouble. When Jem walked in, he didn't even notice her sitting at the bar nursing an orange juice. It was only when she took off her hoodie and without warning, made her way towards the stage, he looked up and recognised her.

He'd heard she kept coming back. At first, it worried him, but he'd got the nod from his source at the station - the girl remembered nothing. He suspected she was *not quite the full shilling.* Perhaps she didn't realise she didn't live there anymore?

She'd been blindfolded when the boys brought her round before dumping her. She'd been gagged too until he'd told the daft sods there was no need for it because the sad little cow couldn't speak. Looking at her now, he couldn't see any sign of the doolally dumb girl he'd seen the night he'd taken her.

She loosened the belt holding her dress and let it drop to the floor.

He wondered what the hell she was doing. Then it came to him; she wanted to dance, and he'd always had a soft spot for dancers.

Semi-naked, she eased herself up onto one of the poles.

As Jem watched, a warming sense of contentment welled; the feeling he always got when in control. This was turning out better than he could have imagined. Taking her had forced her stubborn father to cave in and sell him this place, and now here *she* was.

This glorious creature had come to him, and he couldn't afford to lose her. She could make him money. Big money. He'd been around beautiful women for most of his adult life, and one way or another, he'd paid for the privilege, but he'd never seen anything like her. She was reeling him in. Spellbound, he longed to be tangled in those copper tresses; to touch her milky soft skin. She snaked her sinuous form back and forth; her movements fluid and effortless to the pulse of the tinny sound system. It was mesmerising, as if with every ripple of her undulating body, she promised some primal secret.

Out of the corner of his eye, he could see the other girls, arms folded, rocking on their stilettos. Their eyes, too, were fixed on the strange, pale girl as she pulled her lean torso upwards, wrapping her legs around the pole, leaning backwards, so her hair swept the floor.

Jem knew men would come again and again to watch a woman who made them feel like this; a woman to help them lose themselves and forget about the shitty job and the mortgage.

He'd been angry with his boys for not doing their job properly and leaving loose ends that might incriminate him in the girl's disappearance. But now he was glad of their ineptitude; glad she hadn't died. It was crystal clear to him why she was there. Carly Taylor was meant to be his. She'd survived for a reason.

NINE

A blonde in a skimpy lurex bikini answered the door to John. Normally he might have noticed the overstuffed breasts poking out like missiles above a tiny waist. When he didn't bat an eyelid, the woman's provocative pout slid from her face.

'Where's my daughter; where's Carly?' he demanded, nudging her out of the way.

'Well, don't mind me,' she shouted after him.

John rushed through to the main bar seconds after Carly finished dressing. The very sight of her in the same room as Fielding made his blood boil. He hated everything about the man; his smug face, his shiny shoes and even shinier shark-white grin.

'Mr. Taylor ... and what can we do for you today? Have you come for a private dance? We're not open yet, but if you come back later I'm sure one of these lovely ladies will oblige.'

John ignored him, striding purposefully to where Carly stood with the other girls. Grabbing her arm, he turned to walk out the way he'd come, but to his surprise Carly pulled away, rooting her feet to the ground like a tantrummy toddler.

'Come on, Carly, your mother's waiting. She's worried sick.'

Carly slipped from him and ran behind the bar.

'What are you playing at; I told you before, we don't live here anymore? We don't belong here; you must stay away. This place is bad, do you understand me, bad.'

Carly didn't move.

'Seems she's not so sure about that, or you for that matter,' mocked Jem, playing to the room.

'This is nothing to do with you, Fielding. I don't want any trouble. I'm here to take my daughter home, that's all.'

John moved towards Carly, but this time his progress was stopped by the tattooed knuckles of one of Jem's minders, who grabbed his wrist. John noticed the other girls in the room had begun to look at him warily as if they thought Carly might have a good reason for not wanting to go with him. He suddenly felt uncomfortable; his head swimming.

'Carly please,' he pleaded, 'enough now.'

Fielding lounged casually by the bar watching with obvious glee as John's desperation grew.

'Leave the girl alone; you're frightening her to death, poor thing. Is he frightening you, darling? Never mind, I'll look after you,' he sniggered.

John couldn't stop himself. He sprang at Jem, grabbing him by his shirt.

'You leave my family alone ... you leave them alone, or I swear to God, I'll kill you.'

It was as if he'd been hit by a sledgehammer as the force of the flunky's punch to his lower back sent John crashing to his knees.

Carly moved towards him, but John signalled her to stay where she was. Clinging to the leg of the nearest stool, he slowly pulled himself to his feet, resting against the bar for support as his deadened legs inched back to life.

'I've called the police; they'll be here in a few minutes,' the bikini-clad woman shouted to Jem.

'Good idea, we can't be expected to put up with louts like this, can we? It's a pity though, I was gonna offer him a drink. Then again, it looks like he's had a few too many already. What do you think girls, do you think he's pissed. He's certainly acting like he's pissed? Needed a bit of Dutch courage, did you, Taylor?'

'Come on, love, let's go through to the back,' piped up the leggy blonde; her arm around Carly.

'Carly ...' John shouted after her.

Carly paused to look at her father before following the woman out of the room just as to John's relief, the police arrived.

'You need to arrest him. He's got my daughter,' he shouted, pointing at Jem, who in answer held his hands up in a comic-book gesture of surrender.

'Don't look at me. I haven't got a clue what he's on about. If you ask me, he's been on the sauce. Look at him. He can barely stand up straight. He came in here looking for his daughter, grabbing her, trying to force her to go home with him, and when she wouldn't leave, he kicked off. Something funny going on if you ask me,' he said, giving a knowing nod.

'You lying shit,' shouted John.

'See what I mean? There's no reasoning with the man,' complained Jem, beginning to look as if he was enjoying himself.

John made a move towards him. He was immediately restrained by a young police officer.

'Woah ...' shouted Jem, backing away. 'That's right, you hold onto him. He looks dangerous; who knows what he's capable of?'

'Now, sir, you must calm down,' said the officer holding onto John.

'But it's him, don't you see? He took my daughter, left her for dead and now he's taken her again ... it's him, not me, you need to arrest.'

'Now, I'm not having that,' Jem chipped in, 'I've had enough of this clown's unfounded slurs on my character. The man's clearly off his head. I want him off my property. I've got young women here. I'm afraid for their safety with this nutter hanging around.'

'Okay, sir, can we all just take a step back here,' assuaged the officer. 'I want you to sit quietly with my fellow officer over there, Mr. Taylor, while I talk to your daughter and try and resolve this. Is that okay?'

'Yeh ... okay,' mumbled John, drained and needing to sit. 'Can I use my phone to call my wife? She'll be worried for Carly?'

'Yes, of course,' she replied gently and then turning to Jem said, 'and if you could wait here Mr. Fielding.'

John rang Alice to tell her the police had arrived. He resisted the urge to hold back the truth.

'I'm so sorry, love. I've let you down. It's Carly, she came here to Fielding's club this afternoon and now she won't leave.'

'What do you mean, she won't leave?'

'She won't come home.'

There was a long pause at the end of the line, and for one terrible moment, he thought Alice had put the phone down on him.

'I'll ring Ross then call you back.'

Five minutes later, she was back on the phone.

'He says to stay put; not to worry; he'll sort it.'

John tried to unravel the winding knot of things he should have done. He wished he could believe Ross could help his troubled child; the child who had changed beyond recognition since her abduction. He'd never needed speech to know his daughter's thoughts, but these days she was distant; secretive even. Carly was avoiding him at the very time they needed each other most. This going back to the pub made no sense either; it had to stop. What on earth was she looking for? He'd tried to reassure her they'd brought everything with them; that whatever it was she couldn't find was probably stored away, and once they'd settled in they'd get the boxes from the storage units and sort through everything. It had made no difference.

***

By the time Ross walked through the door, the constable had

spoken to Carly who had made it very clear she wanted to stay put.

'Can I see her?' asked Ross.

'As long as Mr. Taylor keeps his distance. Any sign of distress from the girl, I want him out of there. She's in the back room. I'll stay here,' she glanced at Fielding, raising an eyebrow.

Ross got her meaning.

Carly sat wedged between two young women in dressing gowns, each holding a hand.

'Ladies, can I have a word with Carly alone please?'

'She's very upset what with her dad coming in and grabbing her. That policewoman has already asked if she'll go, and she shook her head, poor thing.'

Ross bit his tongue at the barely disguised accusation levied at his best friend. He smiled politely, although the irritation in his tone was harder to conceal. 'I am a friend of the family as well as a police officer, so if that's okay with _you_ I just want to make sure I understand what's going on here?'

Muttering as they left, the women moved to the far end of the room.

Ross knelt beside Carly, gently taking her hands in his. 'I think you should come with me and your dad. This isn't a good place to be. Your mum's worried; we all are.'

Peeling her hands away, Carly rose from the chair and walked to where the other girls were standing. There was quiet defiance in her action and a rebellious look in her eyes he had never seen there before, and he knew there was nothing he could do.

Back in the bar, John looked grey; his face set. Eyes fixed on the lime-washed wall opposite Fielding. To Ross, it looked for all the world as if he was searching for something to crawl from the cracks and save him. Ross had lived by the sea all his life but knew well enough you didn't need water to drown. He and his friend were fully submerged now, with the rest of the room watching them go under.

Ross finally spoke.

'Look, I'll take him home and make sure he doesn't come back. Can't we just let this one go?'

'I would love to, but Mr. Fielding isn't happy. He's made a formal complaint, and I've had to call it in. Look, we can settle for a caution back at the station, but that's the best we can do.'

'No ... no ... no. Carly ... Carly!' John wailed.

Jem looked across at them.

'Get him out of here, this is bad for business.'

'Okay ... okay,' Ross shouted.

Ross smarted at every word Jem uttered but he couldn't help. No one could.

TEN
Carly

I've come looking before but today was different; today they let me in.

As I dance, I see the soft shadow of desire cross my abductor's face, and I wonder if the promise of ecstasy alone can stop a man's heart? I watch the sickness take hold; the plague of want and longing I'm destined to spread and know it's time to be a woman and make this man want me; show him what it's like to be the captive.

My parents' new life is not enough. I can't stay there. If I do, I'll have to remain a child. It's what they've always wanted; how they thought they'd keep me safe. It didn't work before and it won't work now. That fish has been gutted and found crawling with worms. How does the Bible verse go, *when I was a child I spoke like a child ... but now I am a man ...* Funny, it doesn't mention what happens when we girls grow up. I know the answer.

I have clawed my way out of the pit, and I'm never going back.

ELEVEN
Sister Two
Karenza

Karenza looked out across St. Ives harbour; postcard-perfect in the glinting morning sunshine. Once, there would have been more boats tied up having delivered their catch to Newlyn fish market for sale. In her grandfather's time, you could have hopped from deck to deck and never got your feet wet, according to the old trawler-men who complained in the pub. Her father, Gil Martin, reminded them what a risky, thankless life it had been, but even he had to admit if things carried on the way they were going, give it another five years, and they'd all be decommissioned and the men who worked them history just like the tin miners before them. Now it was all about the tourists.

'Renna!' he shouted, 'Can you come down and sign the chitty for the brewery? I'm in the middle of cleaning the cellar pipes.'

'Alright, Dad, I'll be down in a sec.'

Straightening the curtains, she took one last look around the bedroom, now spick and span, ready for the weekend's bed and breakfasters.

'You look like crap,' she muttered, catching a glimpse of herself in the dressing table mirror.

It was to be expected. She hadn't slept much last night.

She made her way downstairs to sign for the delivery, poking her head around the cellar door as she passed. Her father was at the far end, tapping a new barrel.

'Okay with you if I get off once I've booked the guests in? I want to tidy up next door and have a shower before I pick up Treeve from Penzance this afternoon.'

Her father's silence marked his reticence on the subject of her partner, Treeve.

'We might pop in for a drink later. I'm cooking a bit of a welcome home supper, so probably we'll be over after that.'

'Mmm.'

Karenza guessed that was probably the most she was going to get.

Treeve was getting out of prison after serving a year of a two-year sentence, primarily for catching protected fish with low stocks or 'black fish' but also for assaulting a police officer who happened to be Karenza's ex-husband, Ross. Treeve had received a suspended sentence and a large fine he couldn't pay, but which her dad settled. That would have been the end of it had Ross not, on finding him celebrating in the pub afterwards, told him he ought to curb his drinking habit until he paid back the money he owed.

Treeve thumped Ross, shattering his cheekbone and breaking his nose. The attack was witnessed, and Ross was on duty, so the matter was taken out of his hands. The judge lost patience, and Treeve was sent down. Another one who'd lost patience with him was her father, who'd never been a big fan in the first place. He thought of him as a lumbering muscle-bound pretty boy punching above his weight, who wasn't a patch on his former son-in-law.

'When you gonna learn, girl?' he'd ask Karenza. 'You keep the decent fish and throw the others back.'

At first, she'd visited him in Exeter prison, but things were strained. She was angry with him for ballsing up the second chance he'd been given, and he'd seemed puffed up and swaggering inside that place. She didn't like what she saw, and a year into his sentence, she had started to question whether she wanted him back. She liked her independence and the tranquillity of the house without the constant friction between him and her two teenage children, but something in her couldn't bear to be proved wrong. She had picked Treeve. It was the only real choice she'd made without interference after her divorce. Every other decision was foisted upon her by family or well-meaning friends.

Treeve's train was due in at three-thirty. After she'd finished signing in the guests, she slipped next door to the adjoining cottage she shared with him, her eighteen-year-old son Piran and fifteen-year-old daughter Livvy.

She was feeling inexplicably nervous. Life had gone on for her and the family, but she appreciated that for Treeve, time would have stood still. She began to wonder whether the show of bravado she'd witnessed when she'd visited him wasn't just that, his way of creating barriers and putting on a brave face. Perhaps the alternative to playing the hard man could have resulted in a beating from his fellow inmates, and if that was the case, who could blame him for acting a knob?

She showered and put on some skinny jeans and the lilac silk blouse Treeve had bought her for her birthday the year before. She looked around, pleased that the place looked homely and welcoming. It had taken her time to settle there after her split from Ross.

After her mum died, it had been her dad who'd suggested he could easily move next door above the pub.

'You might as well have the house,' he'd said. 'I don't need the room, and you'll never be able to afford much with what you got from the divorce, especially here in St. Ives with the second homeowners pushing up the prices.'

He'd been right, of course, and in the end, had convinced her it made sense. She was glad to be close to work and her father, knowing how lonely he'd be without her mum, his wife of over forty years.

It made sense. The decision to allow Treeve to move in

wasn't taken well by Gil, but he'd eventually come around. Ross had moved on; had a new young family, and it was time for her to do the same. The problem was, two years on, Ross and Trudy, his second wife, had split, and Karenza could see her dad's mind ticking over every time his former son-in-law came to see the kids. The disturbing thing was, her mind, despite every effort to keep it in check, was ticking too.

It hadn't been easy to store away and replace her parents' things without feeling guilty or disrespectful of her mother's memory, but looking around the bright, airy room with its views of the harbour, she felt as if it was finally hers.

***

She arrived late at the station. Treeve was waiting by the exit, and she flashed her lights. He'd always been easy on the eye but looked better than ever, having taken advantage of the prison gym. He smiled; the same wide, slightly crooked smile which hooked her in the first place, and her stomach flipped as he opened the car door. Shuffling in beside her, he filled the space in the little Fiat. Cramped and uncomfortable, they clashed heads as he leaned in for a kiss. She started up the car in the hope of breaking the palpable tension between them.

'You got away okay then?'

What a ridiculous thing to ask.

'I'm sorry. I meant there were no delays; they processed you quickly?'

'Yeah, no problems.'

'And it was a good journey down?'

'Yeah, yeah fine, thanks.'

Oh God, this is painful. She racked her brain for something - anything - she could say to cover the cringing discomfort of the silence. They were a full ten minutes into the drive home before either spoke.

'Renna, you know I've agreed to work for your dad until I've managed to pay him back and have saved enough to get the boat up and running again. Well, something else has come up ... it'll pay better money, and I'll be able to get sorted that much quicker ... and anyway, we both know I'm not your dad's favourite person, and there's bound to be friction if we're under each other's feet.'

She couldn't mask her impatience.

'If there's a problem, Treeve, for god's sake, spit it out?'

'Not a problem exactly; it's just I met someone inside who's managed to get me a job working for Jem Fielding.'

Her fingers tightened around the steering wheel.

'It's some driving and a bit of security work at his clubs, you know bouncing and what not and it pays well ... and there's a bonus available based on performance.'

She'd stopped listening with the mention of Fielding's name. She knew things about Jem Fielding; shocking, terrifying things Ross had told her that she could repeat to no one, especially Treeve.

She remembered the day Alice rang, desperate because Carly had gone to Fielding's club and wouldn't come home and Ross and John coming back from the station empty-handed two fraught hours later.

Ross had offered to walk her home, and once they were alone, the inquisition had begun.

'What the hell's going on; did you see the look on John's face?' she'd screamed. 'Alice and John are our friends; they're broken, completely broken. Why didn't the police force Carly to come home?'

'She's a grown woman. We can't *force* her to do anything. She's not done anything illegal. She's fully compos mentis. She can't speak, but that doesn't mean she's not capable of knowing her mind and making herself understood, and she made it perfectly clear she wanted to stay where she was.'

'But they know about Fielding; what he did.'

'They know nothing of the sort. The allegations were investigated, and we found no evidence, you know that; just bad blood between John and Jem and even that doesn't stand scrutiny, after all, what exactly did Jem do? Offer John a shed load of money for a pretty crappy pub. Hardly extortion.'

'But ...'

'But nothing. We did all we could with what we had, but the fact Carly couldn't help, and there were no witnesses, made the investigation a non-starter and with today's antics, Jem's well and truly out of the frame. After all, if he was the one who took her, why the hell would she want to be anywhere near him?'

Deep down, she'd known he was right. She believed her friends about Fielding, but John had been the one left on the wrong side of the law. She had seen her friend's life torn apart by Fielding, and now the man who shared her life was planning to work for him.

The rest of the journey was spent in silence, and by the time they arrived home and settled down to eat, the tension was palpable.

Piran gobbled down his food in a matter of minutes.

'I'm off.'

'But I've made rhubarb crumble,' Karenza protested.

'Sorry can't; I've got band practice tonight.'

Before Karenza could say anything more, Livvy followed suit.

'I've got loads of homework; I think I'll make a start.'

'But you've hardly eaten anything. Surely, you'll have some crumble, it's your favourite.'

'Do you want me to pass my exams or what? Anyway, I'm dieting.' The look on Livvy's sullen *I'm a teenager, take me on if you dare* face let Karenza know there was no point arguing. She watched her stroppy daughter stomp off upstairs; in no doubt, she would be texting her friends to tell them what a loser her mother was for hooking back up with a jailbird.

Once they were alone, she decided to broach the subject gnawing at her since Treeve dropped the bombshell in the car.

'So, who's this bloke hell-bent on getting you hooked up with Fielding?'

Treeve examined his plate, avoiding her hostile gaze. 'Mike ... his name's Mike. He's the one I shared a cell with; showed me the ropes. Look, whatever you think about Jem, he pays decent wages. Mike got out a couple of months ago. He got in trouble, mostly cos of drugs.'

'An ex-con and a drug addict, this just gets better and better.'

'For your information, he's moved to Cornwall to get away from his old connections. That's what they recommend you do if you're serious about getting clean. He was given Jem's name as an employer who might be willing to take on someone who had a record and started working for him as a bouncer when he got out. He mentioned me to him because he knew I'd be in the same boat, that's all.'

Karenza bit her tongue, not saying what she really thought; *decent people don't take lifestyle tips from junkies.*

Treeve, assuming her silence indicated a softening in attitude, took his chance. 'You've got to remember; I was in for fraud and GBH. People aren't going to be queuing up to employ me, and with the boat in the state she's in, there's no chance of earning a living from fishing. I probably won't even get a licence, and I'll have to fit her out to take tourists. It'll take money to get her up to standard for health and safety, and where's that sort of cash going to come from, eh? So, if you could show a bit of support, I'd be grateful.'

'I *do* support you! This is *my* house, the roof over your head is *me* supporting you. My dad paying the fine you got from getting involved in dodging the fish quotas *was supporting you*! I do little else but support you through all the crap and all the embarrassment you bring through the door. I even supported you when you beat up my children's father!'

She knew as soon as she'd said the words, she'd gone too far and jumped as he banged both fists down on the table, making the plates shake and the cutlery bounce and clatter.

'Shut up, Karenza; shut the fuck up. You're so bloody perfect ... you and your father and precious bloody Ross. Some of us live in the real world; some of us are human. Not all of us can claim the moral high ground all the bloody time ... to always be right. I don't even know why you bother to have anything to do with me.'

Karenza sat dumbfounded as he ranted.

'You treat me like some charity case, someone to steer towards the straight and narrow. What if I don't want to be steered? What if I want to find my own way ... what if I'm happy being me, and I don't want to be Ross bloody Trenear or Gil Martin. What if I like being Treeve Penhaligon? Have you ever thought of that, have you?'

He pulled his jacket from the peg and left, slamming the door behind him, leaving her nursing the remains of their second bottle of wine.

She was feeling light-headed but even in her less than sober state knew enough to only whisper her reply to his parting question.

'No, I never for one moment imagined you enjoyed being Treeve Penhaligon.'

Treeve came from a dysfunctional family. The years of being teased and ridiculed by the other children for his shabby clothes and even shabbier mother had taken their toll, leaving him with a chip on his shoulder the size of Cheddar Gorge and something to prove. She had to admit he was right, she was always trying to better him, but it was because he needed it. So many of the stepping stones of development had been missed; gaping holes that needed filling. She was beginning to understand why she found their relationship so hard; she was trying to be too many things to him; lover, teacher, social worker and often surrogate mother, and it was exhausting.

TWELVE

Treeve hadn't come home. As she pulled her dressing gown around her and made her way downstairs for a cup of tea and a couple of paracetamols, she wasn't sure whether to be worried or relieved.

She had about an hour before she needed to be at the pub for the morning deliveries. Her tongue felt thick, and her brain fuzzy. She brushed her teeth to get rid of the metallic sourness, and left, hoping a walk would clear her head.

Leaving the quay, she made her way up the empty narrow street to the island. It wasn't really an island. As a child, she'd always wondered why it was called one. She'd learnt at school that an island was a body of land surrounded by water. This island was only surrounded by water on three sides. It was a piece of high rocky ground rising from the beach, on top of which perched a coastguard lookout. The lack of geographical correctness hadn't dulled its impact as a place to play. She and her sure-footed friends had raced across its precarious slopes, oblivious to the dangers of tumbling off the edge onto the rocks below. Why was it with every passing year you grew more nervous about life? It was as if from the moment you left the womb you began the spiralling decline towards self-doubt and anxiety; fear of strangers, fear of change, fear of what others might think; fear of tumbling off a cliff.

Hit by the impact of her early morning exertion and lack of breakfast, she sat on one of the wooden benches dotted around the island dedicated to the dead from all over the country who wished to be remembered in the place where they'd spent happy family holidays. Karenza knew the inscription on this one off by heart.

In Loving Memory of Ron Williams 1936- 2008. Always with us.

She wondered who Ron had been. Whenever she sat on one of these benches, she felt morbid curiosity about the person who'd died and their family's need for a relic, some tangible reminder their loved one had existed. She wondered if, without it, they'd forget them and whether her children would invest in a bench when she died and sit on her, reliving the past? Her dad wanted to be added to her mother's memorial high above the town, in the cemetery overlooking the sea next to the Tate gallery. It always made her smile that her mum had managed to get two of the best views in the country, one whilst alive and an even better one when dead. How did the estate agent's mantra go? Location, location, location!

She wondered what her mother would say about the mess she was in if she were alive. She'd always been the one to guide her through her domestic squabbles. If she was honest; this wasn't only about Treeve or the fact he'd decided to work for Jem; it was about her and Ross. With Treeve inside, he'd started to do more with the kids, then *her* and the kids, and it felt the most natural thing in the world. Now everything would change, and she hated the thought of it.

She rose from Ron's bench and headed down the slipway to the beach. The tide was on the turn, the sand pristine having been washed clean. She stood for a while letting it run through her toes, watching with envy the early morning surfers; paddling ahead of the breakers, rising knees bent, arms semi-stretched like broken wings. She remembered the feeling of rooting your feet to the board, the roar of the water pounding beneath, holding you there; the wave and you in perfect sync. When had all that become not enough; when had life become so complicated?

***

Treeve was in the kitchen nursing a cup of coffee when she got home, looking as rough as she felt. She guessed he'd had an all-nighter with his mates. He looked up, sleep-deprived eyes full of remorse.

'About last night; I'm sorry I lost it. It was getting out, not knowing what to expect from everyone. I won't take the job if you don't want me to. I'll go and tell Jem I've changed my mind. You can let your dad know; I'll start for him as planned.'

'No, it's okay, I've been thinking; maybe you're right. Maybe it's best if you aren't working here on the doorstep. I understand you want a bit of independence. Who knows, maybe it'll be fine, and you'll be able to settle the debt quicker, like you say. Dad's job isn't going anywhere. If things don't work out, I'm sure he'll have you back.'

She was lying. Her father would never give Treeve a second chance once he knew he'd turned down a job with him to go and work for Jem. She knew she had an ulterior motive in pushing Treeve away. If he was working for her father it would be another obstacle to overcome should they split up. This way, it would be less messy. He wouldn't have so much invested in her and her family.

Her feelings for Treeve had changed and his getting out of prison confirmed it. The Jack-the-lad thing he'd had going for him when they first met; the bad boy charm, the antithesis of Ross's sensible steadiness, had worn thin. She couldn't spend the rest of her life with a man who thought sophistication meant having your tattoos spelt correctly. For all his handsome swagger, he felt flawed, and the fact he'd even consider working for a tinpot thug like Fielding was proof of it. She wanted to be rid of him before he dragged her and her kids down with him and this was the first step towards escape. She knew it was cowardly but hated the idea of kicking him when he was down.

Treeve was right about his prospects.

The other fishermen wouldn't want him on board their vessels. It could draw unwanted attention from those who doled out the fishing licences and monitored the quotas, and he'd made a lot of enemies when he'd punched Ross. It would mean turning him out and admitting she'd been wrong all along. At least this way, when she ditched him, he'd have a job and a roof over his head, even if it was with Jem.

Her father always said water found its level. She felt in her heart Treeve was about to find his, and the tidemark would be particularly low.

She arranged to see him later, once he'd been across to Penzance to sort out his schedule with his new employer. What that schedule would be, God only knew.

Livvy would get herself up and out in time for school without her help, but just in case she forgot to eat, she put a box of cereal and a pint of milk on the table before changing and heading next door for work.

***

The dazzle of the quay gave way to the hollow darkness of her father's pub, and her eyes watered a little at the whiff of bleach rising from the newly mopped flagstones.

Gil Martin was already hard at work. Though in his late sixties, he had a full head of wavy hair and the strong, wiry frame of a much younger man. Karenza found it impossible to imagine him old.

'You alright, maid?' he asked, lifting the first of the upturned chairs from the tabletop back to the wet slate floor.

'Fine thanks,' she lied. She was dreading telling him about Treeve and his job with Fielding, knowing he'd hit the roof.

'How's me laddo then; happy to be home from Alcatraz?'

'Ha bloody ha.'

'I heard he was painting the town red last night,' he said, continuing to move around each table, lifting down the chairs, not meeting her eye.

Her father knew everything that went on in St. Ives and further afield for that matter. She'd long since stopped trying to get anything past him. If he'd heard Treeve was out with his mates, rather than home with her on his first night of freedom, he probably knew about the row and the job already/ She decided to save herself the humiliation of allowing him to toy with her further.

'If you know that much, I expect you know the rest?'

'About Fielding, you mean?'

She knew it! She was a tadpole in a jam-jar in this town, swimming back and forth for local entertainment. Scooped up, swilled around and gawped at until there was no fun left in it and they tipped her and the muddy slop back into the communal pond.

'Heaven forbid anyone minds their own business in this place.'

Slamming down the chair he was holding, hard on the floor, Gil met her eye for the first time. Karenza knew the look. He wasn't a man who bawled, red-faced and foaming. His weapon of choice was a withering stare that dared you to defy him. He was the gentlest man she knew, but when he gave you that stare, it was like an ice-pick through your forehead.

'Calm down,' he growled. 'I can't help it if that daft sod decided to go out last night shouting the odds, telling the whole town he's got this *great opportunity* to make some *real money* working for Jem Fielding.'

A tingling heat swept up her neck.

'I know ... I know it's his fault and I'm sorry, okay? I know you offered him a job, and he was grateful, really he was, but he thinks he'll be able to make more money working for Jem and then be able to pay you back sooner. He wants to get the 'Aunty Lou' sorted so he can get back to fishing, but it'll take cash he hasn't got and is unlikely to get from a few shifts working here.'

'Look, it's none of my business what he does, none whatsoever. Truth be told, I didn't expect to see that money back anytime soon, but if you pair think any good will come of working for that piece of filth, then you're both out of your tiny minds. Jem's no bloody good; everything he touches turns bad. No one in my family will be beholden to that slimy bastard if I have anything to do with it, and if that man of yours is going that way, I suggest you give him his marching orders pretty damn sharpish, girl.'

Her father was verbalising everything she felt, and it annoyed her the more for that; reluctant to admit he'd been right about Treeve all along. Thankfully, saving her from having to fight her rickety corner, Lowdy Solomon walked in, armed with her bucket of cleaning materials.

They'd been at school together, and she'd been witness to many arguments between her and her father over the years. She knew them both well enough to take them with a pinch of salt.

Lowdy had a successful housekeeping business, employing people to clean the local pubs and clubs along with many of the holiday homes in the town. She was single and, much to the dismay of the local males, not interested in men. She had a steady stream of adoring female partners. She was not the type to settle down, but any one of her exes would take her back, given half a chance. Karenza envied her independence and her long legs, tanned and toned, flexing in her denim shorts. A huge grin played across her cheerful face.

'Listen, you two, you've got all day to fall out, but I'm on a tight schedule. I have, however, got time for a quick cup of coffee while I have a well-earned break, and you're ruining my peace.'

She cast her eyes sideways towards the front door and the tables on the other side of it in a *meet you outside* gesture to Karenza.

Five minutes later, they were sitting in the sun. Lowdy, legs stretched out in front of her, leaning back in her seat, hands folded on her stomach like some old boy snoozing after his Sunday lunch.

Karenza's mother always said Lowdy was lucky from birth, her proper name Loveday, reserved for girls born on a feast day when traditionally, any old rivalries or animosity in the town was put aside for a day of drunken revelry; a 'Love Day'. Karenza thought it was more to do with the fact she was a male-free zone.

'So, what's this I hear about Treevey Boy crossing to the dark side?' Lowdy teased, stretching her arms above her head to reveal what the magazines termed continental armpits, Lowdy could get away with it, but Karenza knew she could never pull it off.

'Not you as well. What the hell was he doing last night? Did he get himself a megaphone and parade through the town shouting out our business for all to hear?'

'Do you mean telling everyone he had a row with you and wasn't going to work for your dad, who hates him apparently? Or do you mean telling everyone he was gonna earn a fortune working for Jem Fielding?'

Karenza hadn't smoked for years, but Treeve's antics suddenly rekindled her craving.

'Both; now, give me one of those cigarettes.'

'No way, lady, there are too many trying to corrupt you already without me contributing my two penneth. Talking of which; I suppose you'll have to kick Treeve out now, so the lovely Ross can shimmy back under the old marital sheets?'

The thought of Ross shimmying anywhere made Karenza giggle.

'Shush ... shut up ... you fool, Dad will hear.'

'Come on,' Lowdy laughed. 'Gil would be lighting fireworks and popping open the bubbly if he thought that was on the cards!'

'Tell me about it,' sighed Karenza; not yet willing to confide in her friend, she'd be doing a fair bit of celebrating too if that particular promise came good.

'Well girl, you're not doing badly; two blokes on the go at your age.'

'Hey, cheeky bitch! I'm only thirty-six, and you're only a year behind me. Anyway, they're nothing but trouble the lot of them; *men* I mean.'

'You're not thinking of joining my lot, are you?' Lowdy squealed. 'Don't look at me. I'm taken.'

Lowdy checked herself, but it was too late. Karenza had spotted the slip.

'Oh yes, who's the lucky lady then. It *is* a lady, I assume?'

Lowdy glanced up, sheepishly.

'Of course.'

'Well ... spill the beans, or is it a secret? Is she some bored second homeowner you're having a fling with on weekdays while her husband's away in the city?' Karenza sniggered, glad the attention had shifted away from her.

Lowdy didn't laugh back.

'No way ... you're not. No, really ... what are you like?'

Lowdy leaned forward on the table to get close to Karenza and whispered, 'It's closer to home.'

'Who?'

Lowdy hesitated, chin trembling.

'Josie Fielding.'

Karenza stopped her giggling and looked at her friend's lovely, honest face as it searched her own for signs of reassurance.

'Josie Fielding! What the hell. Jem will bloody kill you if he finds out you've been having an affair with his wife.'

'I know, I know,' Lowdy quivered.

For the first time in all her years of knowing her, Karenza thought Lowdy looked worried; biting her lip in between long nervous drags of her cigarette.

'It would be bad enough if you were a man but a woman! That macho prick will do his nut. He'll take it as a slight on his manhood, and he'll be right.'

'She hates him. He's a real bastard to her. They've been married for fifteen years, and he treats her like shit. She wants to leave; she wants to be with me.'

Karenza thought Lowdy was about to cry. Another first.

'Loveday, listen to me.' She hoped by using her proper name, she might impart the seriousness of what she was about to say. 'He'll never let her go; never! The best, the very best you can hope for, is it's beyond his wildest imaginings she'd ever been with another woman, and he never gives it a thought. Then you two can carry on as you are. You cannot tell him and you cannot allow her to think of leaving him! I'm serious he'll kill you both.'

She thought of Alice and what Jem had done to Carly.

'I love her. For the first time, I'm in love, and I can't let her stay with him. He hits her; not all the time. Most of the time he's too busy shagging one or other of the girls in the club; but now and then he gives her a smack, just to keep her in her place, to remind her who's the boss.'

'Look, promise me you'll tread carefully. It's not only him; he's part of something bigger. He has eyes everywhere. You'd never be able to escape once he's onto you. He'll find you wherever you go. Please, for both of your sakes.'

'Okay,' said Lowdy stubbing out her cigarette with her shaking hand. 'I get it.'

Karenza wasn't sure if she got it at all.

THIRTEEN
Sister Three
Josie

Josie Fielding woke with a smile on her face; her first thoughts of Loveday.

She looked at the empty place in the bed next to her; no Jem. During their fifteen years of marriage, he'd often not made it home for one reason or another; usually, because he was warming some other woman's sheets. When had she ceased caring; after the second, third ... tenth time, she couldn't remember, it had been hard to take at first, realising for him she was just one rather than *the one*; humiliating, but in the end, she'd lost interest. There were no two ways about it; he was a nasty excuse for a man, and his infidelity was the least of his sins.

Had he been there, she'd have hidden her unsolicited smile. Otherwise, he'd have asked what she had to smile about. The usual round of accusations would follow, ending with him smacking the smile off her face. He was tediously predictable. Time and a strong sense of self-preservation had taught her how to read the signs. She spent hours in front of the bathroom mirror perfecting the appropriate responses to Jem's paranoia-fuelled mood swings.

It worked most of the time, but not always. Often, she'd see in his eyes, there was no placating him, and a beating was inevitable. On those occasions, when someone had rubbed him up the wrong way, or a deal had fallen through, or his latest girlfriend hadn't done the business, she'd know and want to get it over and done with. She didn't fight him; it only made it worse.

She knew her role; posh totty to be paraded at cocktail parties and charity balls where he bid high on all the crappy items in the auction and made toe-curling comments like; 'My wife Josie gets tickets to Badminton every year.'

Whenever he was on one of these social mountaineering exercises, she felt like shouting; 'and I can duck and weave like Tyson Fury if you're interested,' just to see the look on his stupid face.

Friends always said she must have known what he was like. Maybe, they were right?

She'd been brought up in middle-class drabness, the eldest of two sisters. Her parents had scrimped and saved to provide them with a pony and a private education. On Sunday afternoons, Verity painstakingly plonked out a tune on the piano while she pirouetted around the room as they proudly looked on, satisfied they'd got their money's worth.

They never swore, never argued and never went anywhere, and she couldn't ditch their dull respectability fast enough. Looking back, she was destined to hook up with Jem or someone just like him. Had she not, she'd have spent the rest of her life hankering for a walk on the wild side.

The ballet lessons had been her way out, and she'd swerved university and got herself a job working as a dancer in the West End. It was easy work.

Jem relentlessly pursued her, sending her bottles of Moet, flowers and expensive jewellery. He'd been charming and handsome in a rather obvious, overdone way, in his Savile Row suits and Oliver Sweeney shoes. He was way shorter than her; at five foot seven. She was six feet in her stocking feet, but she didn't mind. He had a certain terrier charm, and he said she reminded him of one of those eighties' supermodels. He was right. She was slightly out of touch with her own time. Her job required her to be glamorous twenty-four seven and over the years, she'd lost the knack of being casual. She felt at home with the latest trends for 'more is more'. Pencilled eyebrows, bronzer and lip liner were her best friends.

Only since Loveday had she started cutting down on the slap; peeling it back, layer by layer.

It had started when they'd gone away together on holiday for a week. Loveday had held her bare face in her hands and told her she was beautiful. Josie had learnt, via one of his loose-lipped bar staff, Jem was planning a week in Vegas with his latest fuck-buddy. She'd seen the tickets in his desk drawer. She'd asked if she could go in his absence to their villa in Marbella.

He'd asked who she was thinking of going with and when she'd said Loveday, he'd fallen about laughing.

'I know you're too posh for housework, but taking the cleaner to tidy up after you takes the bloody biscuit.'

'No, I mean it, Jem. She's had a hard time lately with her sister dying. We get on well, and you like her, so I thought it might be okay just this once. The place could do with a bit of an airing.'

She could see Jem's brain ticking, thinking this might play to his advantage. He didn't know she knew about his trip. It was true Loveday's sister had died earlier in the year. She'd battled with breast cancer but had eventually lost the fight.

'You know your trouble, you're too bloody soft. You're a sucker for a fucking sob story.'

She held her breath as he poured himself a whisky.

'All right then, but take Mike with you. He'll drive you and stay the week. He can take you out on the boat when you're there. Give you both a treat.'

She was delighted, fit to burst, but knew enough not to show it. That would arouse his suspicion.

'If you're sure you can spare him, that would be great.'

She turned to leave, hardly able to believe it had been so easy.

'Watch yourself, mind, you know she's a dyke that one. Make

sure you keep your tits under wraps; wouldn't want her to get all excited, would we.'

He gave a little girlish wriggle as he said the word 'excited' as if someone was tickling him. God, how she hated him

The week in Marbella was one of the happiest of her life. She and Loveday managed to persuade Mike, who was new to Jem's team, to do his own thing, and so the two of them found themselves without supervision on several hot afternoons.

It never crossed Mike's mind anything was going on between them, and when they told him they were taking the boat out and wouldn't need him, he jumped at the chance to have a day sunning himself by the pool with some girl he'd met in Puerto Banus the evening before.

Loveday's lean, sensuous body melted with hers as their sunburnt limbs tangled beneath cool cotton sheets. She watched her lover sitting on the deck, her legs pulled up beneath her, sucking at the flesh of a piece of lemon scooped from her drink and thought; *that's what she does to me.* She'd never felt anything like it, the way Loveday gave her pleasure. It was selfless, uncompromising and glorious, the mixture of passion and kindness she'd longed for, but never found with men.

The holiday had been transforming.

She no longer gave a damn what Jem thought or what he did, for that matter? She was free of him in her mind, and one way or another, whether it took months or years or a lifetime; she'd be physically free of him too one day.

She'd do anything to be with Loveday.

***

The smell of bacon wafting from downstairs confirmed Jem was home, and sure enough, he was tucking into a full English as she entered the kitchen. He wiped the last piece of toast around his plate, picking up the smear of the egg yolk as he chewed.

'Get your glad rags on, we're off out.'

Her heart sank. He never asked her to go with him on weekends. Saturday was his busiest day. On the rare occasion he wasn't working, he was off playing golf with one of his cronies. She'd arranged to meet Loveday.

'I've just had a shower. I haven't even dried my hair,' she protested, 'do you really need me to go with you?'

'Yeah, I do. So, stop buggering about and do what you've got to do. You've got ten minutes to get your ass back down here. I'll get the Aston out of the garage. I said we'd be there by eleven.'

'Where are we going?'

'Theo Morgan's down. He needs to talk over a bit of business with me. He rang last night to say he was getting a plane down to Land's End Airport and has rented a house in Sennen Cove.'

'What's he want to talk about?' asked Josie.

Jem ignored the question.

She was not usually remotely interested in her husband's dodgy dealings, but the name Theo Morgan jolted her out of her apathy. She and Theo had been an item before she got with Jem, but it was going nowhere. He was married with a couple of kids and in his mid-thirties. She was young, just starting out, but Theo was a player. He was easy company, and their relationship had only ended because she wanted to be something more than someone's bit on the side.

Jem liked the fact Theo approved of her. Theo was higher up the ladder than him and known for his good taste in cars and women. It didn't matter to Jem he was getting sloppy seconds, as long as it was still fine dining.

She'd not seen Theo since. Soon after, they were sent to Cornwall and Theo was re-located to Cardiff to take over there. She knew from the few conversations she'd had with Jem about business, he'd turned the operation in Wales around and had risen through the ranks. For him to be coming down to their part of the world meant something big was going down.

Josie's mind was racing. What if Theo was here to tell them they were being moved on? Her thoughts returned to Loveday. She couldn't leave, not now she was finally happy.

'Come on girl, get yourself upstairs and smarten yourself up. Aren't you excited to be seeing your old flame? You wouldn't want him to think you've lost your touch,' Jem goaded, desperate to get a rise out of her. She was determined not to bite.

Although good for her age, she wasn't the leggy young blonde Theo had fallen for, and Jem knew it. The comment was meant to sting. He'd probably known the meeting was going to happen weeks ago but hadn't told her. He wanted her not to have had time to get her roots done and look her best. He was in his element; full of himself, with her on the back foot. No wonder he was cheerful. There was no escape, and anyway, she needed to know what was going on.

She walked back upstairs, scraping her damp hair back into a ponytail as she went.

Only a few months before she'd have been completely thrown by the order to get ready in ten minutes, but now, she simply threw on some tinted moisturiser and a swipe of lip-gloss and she was done. She was getting used to this new barefaced woman and recognised something about her she liked and had once had in barrel loads before it was beaten out of her. She pulled on a pair of white jeans and a black t-shirt, then texted Loveday:

Sorry, Jem's got plans; make it up to you, I promise. J xx

FOURTEEN

Karenza's mobile rang.

'What you up to today?' asked Loveday.

'You mean other than worrying about you?'

'Yeah, I'm sorry about that. I just had to tell someone, but I'm a big girl. I can look after myself.'

'Okay, if you say so.'

'I do ... so, have you got plans?'

'Nothing much. My shift's not til this evening. Treeve's working on the boat. I promised to take Livvy into Penzance to do some shopping with her friends, but she's made it blatantly clear I'm not to tag along, so I've got a free day; why?'

'Fancy visiting Carly?'

'What?'

'I'm at Jem's place now cleaning the rooms upstairs. It's only me here. The decorators are in, so the place is shut for the week. I've sent my team to other jobs. Carly's here though, in her old room.'

'Shall I call Alice?'

'No, that's not a good idea after what happened with John, is it?'

Karenza knew she was right.

'But you could check on her and then reassure Alice she's okay.'

'And is she?'

'Seems to be. She seems more ... grown up, I suppose, less drippy.'

'Lowdy,' Karenza chided, but she knew what her friend meant. Despite her beauty, Carly could come across as listless and lacklustre, especially to someone as in your face as Loveday.'

'Well, are you up for it?'

'I don't know. She might react badly to me; think I'm spying on her for her mum and dad?'

'Well, you are, but there's nothing wrong in that given the circumstances and what's the worst that can happen. She's hardly gonna scream the place down.'

'Lowdy!'

'Alright ... alright,' Lowdy giggled, 'yes or no?'

Karenza knew only too well how difficult teenagers could be. She had a fifteen-year-old daughter of her own, and it was no picnic. It was a fact of life perfectly good kids turned their backs on their parents and became nightmares every day of the week, was it her business to interfere? Then again, what if it had been Livvy who'd gone to work for Jem after being abducted, wouldn't she have wanted her friends to intervene on her behalf? Ross had failed, but maybe Carly needed a woman's touch; not her mum, but someone she knew and trusted.

'Yeah ... okay. Livvy's meeting her mates at midday. Is that too late?'

'No, that's fine. I'll meet you by the door in the alley.'

FIFTEEN

Jem was waiting in the Aston Martin, roof down, immaculate white leather seats shining.

Josie hated the car. It was ostentatious; in your face. Most of the locals were on low wages, eking out a living as best they could on zero-hours contracts through seasonal work. The car stuck out like a sore thumb. It screamed; *look at me, you sad mugs.* Every minute in the damn thing with everyone staring felt like torture. She wouldn't have blamed the seagulls if they crapped on them.

Jem was buoyed up, almost jolly, although Josie detected a slight nervousness and wondered what was going on. She knew better than to ask. If it was good news and Theo was here to pat him on the back, he'd spill the beans soon enough.

True to form, after ten minutes of fiddling with the radio dial to find some cheesy eighties tunes, he obliged.

'I knew they'd see the sense in bringing me in on this one; after all, no one's better placed than me to control the situation down here,' he boasted. 'As I said to Theo, it's all very well you planning things from that end, but you've got to know what makes the dozy locals tick; how to smooth the way,' he said, turning the radio down. 'It takes years of oiling palms. You can't just walk in and expect to be able to control all the bases. Now I've got this new bloke, Treeve, it'll be a piece of cake. Smooth as a Brazilian tart's pussy.'

Josie winced; her husband had a lively turn of phrase and used it often to embarrass her. Today though, he was like an excitable child at show-and-tell; his face flushed and animated.

'This will show those fuckers who've had their snouts in the trough for the last few years; all them ass-lickers. I've bided my time, waiting for the right deal, and this is it. With this one, I'm made ... back in the game.' He reached across and squeezed her knee.

Josie still had no idea what he was talking about or why his latest flunky was going to play such an important part in whatever it was.

Loveday had told her Treeve was the partner of her friend Karenza, although the relationship was going through a bad patch. He'd been to prison; something to do with fishing quotas and for beating up Karenza's ex who happened to be a policeman. He seemed just the sort of bloke Jem would warm to.

'What's this Treeve going to do then?' she asked, genuinely interested.

'It's more what he's got.'

'And what's he got?'

'A fishing boat.'

Josie knew to quit while she was ahead.

They drove out of Penzance along the coast towards Sennen. It had been a while since she'd driven with Jem in the car. She wondered what she'd find if she opened the glovebox, some woman's knickers; who knew. Who cared?'

The Cornish road with its high hedges and hairpin bends meant Josie had to look straight ahead if she wanted to keep the contents of her stomach. Jem's driving didn't help. He alternated between stints of high speed and heavy braking, occasionally swerving to avoid oncoming traffic in the narrow lanes. Josie knew from experience if she gave him the slightest hint of her discomfort, he'd find it hilarious, becoming even more reckless.

Jem sang along to the music, tapping a rhythm on the steering wheel. She glanced across at his hands. Immaculate and manicured, they were one of his best features. You'd never guess to look at those sensitive well-tended hands, how adept they were at causing harm. How quick with a slap; swift with a punch. How often they'd held her by the throat against the bathroom wall.

His attacks were never frenzied. His viciousness, a tempered blade, not a bludgeon. He never marked her face. It might attract attention. People would notice her walking around in sunglasses attempting to hide successive shiners. That was not the type of publicity he cultivated. Jem wanted people to think he was someone. She knew better. At best, he had an instinctive knack for making money and none of the moral restraint that held others back.

Emerging from the mottled shade into the vivid light, she closed her eyes for a second opening them again, only on feeling the sharp right-hand bend out of Sennen village and the steep descent to the Cove. Gulping in the reviving sea air, she was glad the white-knuckle ride was over. The place was busy with summer tourists out early to get the best spots on the beach and guaranteed space in the car park. The tide was coming in, and the prospect of a decent clean swell had the surfers pressed against the railings of the promenade, debating when it would be best to enter the water. The fanatics had been out early and were now loading their boards back into their vans and going off to work their shifts in the bars and hotels; counting the hours before they'd be back. Embarrassment rose again as they drove at snail's pace through the village, and people turned to look at the car. Jem sat up in his seat. Josie felt like crawling under hers. At the end of the narrow road, bordered on one side by the sea and the other by the pub and a few seaside shops and cafes, they turned up a sharp incline onto a long gravel driveway and parked behind an Audi estate Josie guessed belonged to Theo. Jem looked at it and gave a self-satisfied grunt.

SIXTEEN

The single-storey stone property stood like a full stop at the end of the village where the road ended and the coastal path to Land's End took over. It sat amidst yellow gorse and pink thrift sloping down to the rocks with nothing but Cape Cornwall in the distance and the Atlantic beyond.

Theo stood on a raised deck at the front of the building taking in the magnificent view.

'Good to see you took my advice and kept it low key,' he said, taking a sip of his espresso and giving a disapproving nod in the Aston's direction.

Jem shuffled from foot to foot.

Placing his mug on the table, he stepped forward, hands outstretched.

'Looking good, Josie,' he smiled pulling her in to plant a kiss on both cheeks.

She knew better than to say 'you too,' but her hesitation betrayed her.

His voice was deep and lyrical, with the hint of a Welsh accent. It was one of the things she'd always loved about him. It was the voice of an educated man and could soothe or terrify. When angry, its booming ferocity shook the room and kept his men in check, but in the throes of lovemaking, it trickled like warm honey.

He looked good, athletically lean. His hair, cut very short, sported a dusting of silver, which added a certain gravitas to the fine-boned features inherited from his Barbadian mother. Cool and elegant, in a crisp white shirt and tan shorts, he made Jem look squat and conspicuously overdressed in his navy golf club blazer as he squirmed like a sweaty, red-faced page boy at a summer wedding. From the expression on Theo's face, it was causing him amusement too.

'For Christ's sake, Jem, sit down, and take that bloody jacket off before you faint with heatstroke.'

Josie, determined not to let Jem see her smile at his discomfort, walked to the end of the deck. The sea was mesmerising here. Dark and ominous one minute, full of reflected light the next. The waves hit a cluster of rocks just offshore, sending high-flying sprays of white spume across their inky surface. The air smelt of salt and freedom and she was certain on stormy days you'd feel the spray on your face standing there. The views from their house in Marazion of St. Michael's Mount were tamer, more Mediterranean. She liked this better.

'You've rented this place?' she asked.

'Yeah, just for a couple of months. Feel free to have a look around. Oh, but before you go could you bring us the bottle of wine chilling in the fridge, darling.'

She could feel the anger crackle off Jem like static.

'No problem; anything else?'

'No, that'll be fine and make sure you bring three glasses.'

Josie did as he asked.

She guessed he'd brought the bottles of Corton Charlemagne stacked in the fridge with him. She doubted the Costcutter at the top of the hill stocked it. She opened the wine before she took it out to the men, who by now were hunched over a map spread flat on the table.

Theo paused to pour the wine before handing her a glass, his long fingers lingering a little too long. She blushed, then felt foolish for doing so, hoping Jem, still engrossed, hadn't noticed.

'Mind if I take a look around? she asked.

'Help yourself, *Mi casa es tu casa*,' Theo grinned, closing the patio door to the deck behind her.

The place had the look of a holiday rental, neutral colours, prints of the ocean, insipid scatter cushions designed to appeal to all tastes; nothing too personal to raise an uncomfortable feeling of squatting in someone else's home, nothing too precious it couldn't be replaced. It was clear none of the rooms had been slept in, and the bathrooms were free of the usual male paraphernalia; shaving foam, razor, toothbrush. She'd thought the property was all on one level, but as she wandered, sipping the delicious wine, through the huge lounge, then the kitchen and into the hall, she could see there was a staircase she assumed led to a bedroom.

She guessed Theo slept there.

She knew it was rude, and if she was caught, he'd think she'd been snooping. Nevertheless, she found herself climbing the staircase and opening the door to reveal a large bright room with a vaulted apex ceiling, furnished with a double bed, two small cabinets and little else. Through an open door at the end, she could see a small bathroom.

The wall facing the sea was entirely glass, and double doors in the centre opened onto another balcony. The view was even more magnificent than from the deck below, where the men sat. She couldn't resist the temptation to lay down on the bed, to experience the view from there.

She lowered herself onto the unmade duvet cover, leaned back against the headboard and stared out past the tumbling cauldron of water to the horizon. She imagined what it would be like to wake up to this every day. She twisted to plump up one of the crisp white pillows behind her and, for a second, smelt something familiar; a blast from the past that sent a small but definite pulse between her thighs. She got up quickly, not wanting to go there. Not now she had Loveday. Instead, she wandered onto the balcony. She could hear the men talking below.

'So, you're sure of this what's his name?'

'Treeve, yeah, he's a good boy. None too bright but solid enough. He's a fisherman but landed up inside for dodging quotas and for punching a copper.'

'Not a hot-head, I hope?'

'No, there was history; his girlfriend's ex. He needs the money to do up his boat and get back to fishing.'

'Does he know what we're moving?'

'He knows. He was a bit iffy at first but didn't take much persuading once he could see the fringe benefits, and of course, I've told him it's only the once. It is only the once, isn't it?'

'We'll see. If you don't cock it up, we might use this route again. The bastards are down on us like a ton of bricks now, shutting down all the routes. It's these reckless sods transporting people across the channel; they're fucking it up for all of us. There are patrols out there looking for Syrians, and God knows who else, and it's making it impossible to move product.'

Josie knew *product* meant drugs. Cocaine, cannabis, or both.

She stepped back into the bedroom. She needed to hear this without risk of them looking up and seeing her.

'The Spanish boys will meet your lad ... about here.'

Josie assumed Theo was pointing to the map.

'My lads will bring the stuff ashore and drive it to the warehouse in Newlyn. That's when your lot re-pack it into the polystyrene freezer boxes stacked with fish bought from the market the previous day.'

Josie could tell the planning of this little venture had been underway for some time and was amazed Jem hadn't let something slip.

'I understand these boxes are full of ice?' Theo continued. 'It's important the packaging is watertight. They should be okay if the Spaniards have done their job properly, but you'll need to check. No one's going to buy gear stinking of fish.'

'No problem. I've had the fishmonger's vans going back and

forth with fish for a couple of months now. I'm thinking of keeping it going after. I've got a few connections with some restaurants willing to pay for lobster and fresh crab, and I do a bit of monkfish, and the markup's good. It's proved a nice little earner.'

'Alright, Captain Birdseye, just make sure the vans are there with the fish on ice so we can move it as quickly as possible the following morning!'

'Yeah, yeah ... sorry,' mumbled Jem.

'There's a slipway down by the beach here. My boys have hired two ribs. They've been out already for a reccy along the coast to make sure the drop is safe.'

'And Treeve knows the place like the back of his hand, so I don't see any problems from my end.'

'Has this Treeve got family? Does he know the risk he runs if things don't go to plan or he decides to bale?'

'I haven't been too heavy but he knows not to cross me. He knows if he's caught and goes down because of his cock-up, we've got people in there watching cause it's where we recruited him.'

'I assume you've had the good sense not to mention me or the details of the rest of it?'

'Course not. He knows nothing about the fish or the bigger deal.'

'Good. Now, where's that lovely wife of yours?'

Josie started, she moved quickly and quietly to the rear of the bedroom and down the stairs, emerging from one of the bathrooms as Theo came around the corner.

'Lovely,' she said 'really spacious and nicely decorated. How many does it sleep?'

'Ten I think.'

'But there are only four bedrooms, is there a pull-out sofa in the lounge then?'

'No, my bedroom is upstairs, you're welcome to come up and see it sometime,' he smiled, 'I'm here for the next few weeks if you're interested in a trip down memory lane.'

The corridor was narrow, and he was blocking her way.

What she'd heard had set her thinking maybe, just maybe, she could see a way forward for her and Loveday; a way to get rid of Jem once and for all?

'You never can tell. I just might be,' she whispered in his ear as she squeezed past.

SEVENTEEN

Karenza pulled in behind a van delivering veg to one of the restaurants in the main street.

'What time shall I pick you up?'

'No need, I'm sleeping over at Lucy's tonight. Her mum said she'll give me a lift home in the morning,' said Livvy

'You didn't tell me that.'

'I did. I told you last week; it's been planned for ages.'

'I'm sure I'd have remembered if you had?'

'What do you think this is for?' Livvy said, poking the backpack on her lap.

'I don't know ... you said you were going shopping?'

'Why would you remember anyway? All you're interested in is Treeve.

'That's nonsense, Livvy, and you know it. All I'm saying is if I'd known, I would have rung Lucy's mum to check it was okay first.'

'Ruin my day, why don't you ... are you saying I can't go?'

'I didn't say that. Are you meeting Lucy now?'

'Yeah, why?'

'Well, I could come with you and get her mum's number.'

'Why are you being so nuts about this?'

'I'm not. It's just I don't know Lucy or her mum, and you don't seem to meet up with any of your old friends anymore; not since Lucy came on the scene.'

'Like who?'

'Well, you and Lilly used to be inseparable, but her mum came into the pub last Wednesday and said they haven't seen you for ages.'

'Lilly is so lame. All she talks about is horses and Harry

Potter.'

'Well, you used to like horses and Harry Potter too.'

'Yeah, but I grew up. So, can I go or what?'

'Yes, I suppose so, but make sure you ring me later and put Lucy's mum on the phone.'

'Okay, I will, promise, and Mum, can I have some money for lunch?'

'I've only got a fiver on me. What about your wages for helping grandad collect the empties?

He gave you thirty quid. You haven't spent that in the last week, surely?'

'Forget it. I'll borrow some off Lucy.'

'I never said ... '

The man in the car behind beeped his horn. She wound down her window, gesturing for him to go around. She heard the passenger door clunk shut, and Livvy was gone. The idiot beeped again, then swerved past, wheels spinning, middle finger raised.

She waited for him to reach the end of the junction and turn left before indicating and pulling out. She was annoyed with herself for rowing with Livvy yet again. She couldn't seem to open her mouth without annoying her these days. Piran had never been like this, but girls were different; everyone said so.

Her head was pounding. It was too hot. She could feel the pressure in the air like a weight on her head and reckoned there would be a storm before the day was over.

She parked in a side street around the corner from Jem's club, taking the cut through to the side alley where she'd arranged to meet Lowdy.

She shivered in the shade. Even on a day like today, no sunlight reached there. She'd always parked there when John and Alice had the pub; taken the rickety Edwardian fire escape up to the living quarters above to save going through the bar. The fire escape was gone now. She could see a piece of the twisted metal poking out of the overflowing skip parked at the far end of the alley. Its replacement; a fancy stainless-steel affair which looked at odds with the old granite wall.

Loveday was waiting by the cellar door.

'Here, put these on. If someone asks why you're here, you can say I'm short-staffed and you're helping me out,' she said, handing her a plastic apron and a pair of pink rubber gloves.

'Whose gonna ask?'

'No one; like I said it's only the decorators, but if one of the girls should pop in, we've got a story.'

Karenza saw the sense in what she said, even though she questioned whether all this was such a good idea after all.

Following Lowdy inside, she caught the unmistakable whiff of sweat, stale booze and another even less pleasant odour emanating from the open door of the gents.

'Just as long as you don't expect me to clean,' she said.

Lowdy smiled back at her.

She could hear banter above a radio playing in the bar, and the occasional scrape of ladders across the floor as the decorators worked.

They hung a left before they reached them, climbing the narrow stairs to the first floor.

Though the bones remained the same, the rest had changed. Wood floors had been replaced with a velvety navy carpet; magnolia walls covered with striped wallpaper. The door to the old living room was shut; **Private Keep Out**.

'Jem's office.' Lowdy said.

A shout came from the bottom of the stairs, followed by the sound of heavy boots.

'Okay if we use the sink to clean some brushes?'

'I'd better go, or he'll trail paint all over the carpets. Carly's at the end of the corridor, in her old room.'

'But ...'

'Coming ... ' Lowdy shouted, leaving Karenza alone and uncomfortable as she crept along the corridor like a burglar casing the joint. *Why the hell had she agreed to this?*

Carly's room was straight ahead. The door was ajar and she could hear music playing softly.

'Carly?'

There was no reply, and she crept closer. She peered into the open room, noticing the ditsy daisy wallpaper she'd helped Alice pick for Carly had gone, the walls now painted the same dark blue as the stripes in the corridor. She was about to knock when she caught a glimpse of Carly's reflection in the wardrobe mirror facing her. She was dancing, and Karenza instinctively stepped back, not wanting to intrude.

The girl's body rippled, arms outstretched as she twisted and reached as if fighting an invisible force trying to pin her to the ground. It was unsettling to watch, but it was not the dance riveting Karenza to the spot or the fact the girl was in her underwear but the look on Carly's face; the huge wide smile lighting her up.

She turned tail, retracing her steps back downstairs and out the way she'd come. She'd ring Lowdy later; say she'd had a call and had to leave. She could never tell anyone about Carly, not Lowdy and certainly not Alice. How would it feel for her to know the daughter she'd lost seemed so happy without her?

EIGHTEEN
Carly

Stretching forward, I twist my fingers around the invisible umbilical cord joining me to my reflection; an exaggerated mime of the struggle to haul my other self in, hand over hand, a tug of love. I like this other me; the way she flexes her muscles and arches her body; this pirouetting doppelganger, with the wind at her heels.

Though the same, we are different. Yin and Yang. I have known she was there all along. I've felt her fingers down my throat trying to spill from my mouth. I've never been brave enough to let her win because I know once the words scatter, they'll linger like Christmas glitter in the pile of the carpet. There can be no return to silence once the words are out and Jem desires the silent me, not the Carly with a voice; that Carly is dangerous. She could shout his guilt from the rooftops for all to hear.

As long as I can dance, I can keep the words inside. The liberty to fly is the price of my buttoned lip. My silence is my greatest accomplishment, and I'll not discard it lightly. Not until this is over. It's okay, I can bear it because I can call the other me any time I like. I've known it since the day in the pit.

NINETEEN

By the time they hit the road, Josie's mind was made up. She'd make it her business to find out exactly what was planned and, in some way, use it to her advantage. This could be her only chance to free herself and start a new life with Loveday. Their relationship couldn't be kept a secret forever. She'd lived with Jem's violence, but she'd not stand for him harming Loveday.

He'd been different over the last couple of months, and now she knew why. An important job had been entrusted to him, although he'd been less effervescent walking back to the car. Something was niggling him. She didn't have to wait for long to find out what.

'That Morgan's a right prick if you ask me. Talking to me as if I don't know my ass from my elbow when I've been in this game as long as he has.'

'I'm sure he didn't mean anything. He seemed pleased to see us.'

He shot her a viperous glance. 'Pleased to see *you* that's for fucking sure. I saw the way he looked at you when he handed you that glass.'

She had to stop this before it got out of hand. 'You've got nothing to worry about in that direction,' she said, placing a reassuring hand on his arm. 'I chose you, remember.'

Jem loosened his grip on the steering wheel, a sign he was calming down to her well-trained eye. She touched his knee, 'You looked so smart today. I like that colour on you.'

He swelled with the compliment, and she carried on; 'I thought Theo looked old, with his hair grey, and I was surprised he didn't have a better car. He seemed quite envious of yours.'

A smile crept across Jem's face.

'We can stop for a drink as we're out,' Jem said. 'It seems a shame to rush home, and I could do with a real drink, not that muck that scruffy bastard served us. He could have run to some fizz, the tight bastard. There's a pub a little way from here in a place called Zennor, I've been meaning to give it a visit.'

Josie had no idea why he seemed so keen to visit some country pub. He never strayed into pubs unless he owned them, or was thinking about buying them, but it suited her not to question him. The village was tiny; a few houses, a pub, a church and little more. They parked in the car park behind the beer garden. It was teeming with visitors decked out in walking boots and carrying rucksacks as if they were going mountaineering rather than walking the well-trodden coastal path. The pub looked like it had been there for centuries.

Jem lingered at the bar reading a dog-eared info-poster before bringing their drinks across to the table and downing his pint in one. He was itching to leave.

'Drink up, girl. I want to go visit the church.'

Josie spluttered, choking on her G&T. Jem in a church?

He raced ahead, across the road, taking the granite steps to St. Senora's two at a time. The door was open, tourists milling about inside and around the ancient graveyard. The air in the vestibule was heavy with the scent of the white chrysanthemums left over from a wedding the previous week. She never liked the smell. They reminded Josie of her parent's postage stamp garden with the border flowers arranged like soldiers. The handstitched pew cushions were cheerful though and gave the place a welcoming, homely feel, not the way she remembered church growing up with its *Hail Marys full of guilt*.

She joined Jem. He was engrossed, admiring a small, high-sided pew big enough for one person to sit. The chair was old; handcrafted out of dark wood. Etched primitively on the side facing them was a mermaid holding up a mirror in one hand, her face indistinct. Josie traced the ancient scales of the faceless woman's fishy tail and shuddered.

'Brilliant ... bloody brilliant,' he said, snapping more photos.

What was he so excited about? Yes, it was interesting, but hardly a masterpiece.

'What's the interest in the chair?'

'It's not the chair I'm interested in. It's the mermaid thing; read that,' he said, pointing to a plaque nailed above the chair.

She read over his shoulder. Legend had it, the Mermaid Morveran, in the guise of a beautiful woman, visited St. Senora church. She spoke to no one, always sitting in the same seat, and disappearing after the service. She came to hear local fisherman Matthew Trewella sing and one day lured him back to the sea with her, to be her husband. He was never seen again. The chair was carved to commemorate the event.

It was a quaint little Cornish tale like many she'd heard before. She had no idea why Jem was so interested. He wasn't the Jackanory type. When he took out his phone and photographed the plaque, she was even more bemused.

'It's for the show,' he explained

'Show?'

'For the club.'

'A bit Disney, don't you think, for a lap dancing club?'

'No, not like that, the proper kind, like the one in the church. The ones that trap men.'

'Oh, I see,' she said, not seeing at all.

She'd seen Jem's routines and found them dated and sad. Despite using every hip thrust and splayed squat in their repertoire, the girls look bored. The drunken lads who watched had seen it all before. It was a bit of a laugh to them. For Jem to be thinking about upping his game came as a surprise.

'How do you fancy coming down the club and putting a few routines together for the girls?'

'Of course, if you'd like me to, but are you going to have time, with the stuff you're doing with Theo?' she asked, picking her words carefully, not wanting him to cotton on she knew more than she should.

'That'll be done and dusted in a few weeks. If things go to plan, it might lead to other things, but the club's my baby and no one else's business. I'm thinking this could be big. It might lead to other things when I build the casino; a theme like ... to link it all together.'

'Yeah ... but you've got to be realistic. It's hardly Vegas, is it?'

His face darkened, and she thought she'd blown it.

'I know, I know, but what with all those talent shows on the telly; maybe we could get other acts in, comedians and singers and what have you.'

She wondered at what point he'd begun to think he was Simon Cowell.

'What's brought this on?'

'Carly Taylor,' he said

'Carly Taylor, isn't she the girl they found down a mine shaft?'

Josie had read about the girl in the papers; how she was the victim of a terrible prank that had gone wrong.

'She's going to be working in the club; she's my headline act.'

'But isn't she deaf or something? How can she be a dancer if she can't hear the music?' asked Josie, more confused every minute.

'No, she can hear okay, she just doesn't speak, but she can dance alright and what with that red hair, she's a perfect fit. She's my very own mermaid.

Josie had no idea the girl was one of Jem's dancers. She guessed he'd approached her not only because she looked the part but also because the press was bound to give the new show a bit of free publicity on the back of the girl's story. It still seemed odd, though; a girl who'd been through what she had. It made her feel uneasy, and she hoped there wasn't more to it than Jem was letting on. Things were never quite what they seemed with him, but *whatever* this was, the new Jem was a vast improvement on the old, and if she could get regular access to the club, she was more likely to get to know when the job with Theo was going down.

'I'd love to help,' she said. 'It'll be like old times.'

TWENTY

Karenza couldn't shift the image of Carly from behind her eyes as she lay awake listening to Treeve's snoring. Perched as far away from him as the bed would allow, the gap was still nothing compared to the emotional chasm between them.

Eventually, she fell asleep only to be awoken by the rumble of her phone on the bedside table. She reached for it, willing her dry, sore eyes to open. She registered it was Ross, but had no idea why he was calling in the middle of the night.

Heaving herself out of bed, she staggered zombie-like onto the landing, closing the bedroom door behind her, so as not to wake Treeve. She glanced at the time; two-thirty, she'd been asleep hardly any time at all.

'Ross?' she croaked; groggy anxiety gathering.

'Renna, I want you to stay calm. It's Livvy.'

Shocked back into the room with the mention of her daughter's name, her tiredness fell away. 'Livvy? What ... what about Livvy, what's happened?' she demanded, deafening alarm bells ringing.

'She's in hospital.'

'What?'

'Stay calm,' Ross soothed, 'she's okay.'

'I don't understand? She's at Lucy's for a sleepover. What's she doing in hospital?'

'Can you drive, or do you need me to pick you up?'

'No, I mean ... yes. Yes, I can drive, but what's happened; talk to me?'

His unwillingness to give any details made her all the more agitated. 'I'll explain when you get here, and Karenza, if you are going to drive, don't drive like an idiot.'

'Yes, yes, which hospital?'

'Penzance.'

That was something, at least. It was only a short drive.

'I'll be there.'

She ended the call; hands shaking.

Back in the bedroom, she turned on the light, no longer giving a damn about waking Treeve. Not bothering to change the baggy t-shirt she'd worn to bed, she slipped on her jeans. Treeve stirred for one second as she opened the wardrobe door to find a pair of trainers but then turned over and went back to sleep. Grabbing her car keys from the dressing table, she turned off the light and left.

Once on the road, she tried to call Ross back, but his mobile went straight to answerphone. It was a fifteen-minute drive to West Cornwall Hospital, but the road stretching out in the darkness seemed infinite as her mind raced with scenarios of what could have happened to her daughter. *An accident*, she thought, some kind of accident at her friend's house, but why hadn't Lucy's mum called her instead of Ross? She'd been awake and was sure she hadn't missed her call.

'Please let her be alright,' she moaned, ignoring Ross's advice and flooring the accelerator.

Hot tears blurred her vision. There was little other traffic at that time of the morning, nevertheless, she was relieved when the delivery van ahead turned off before she reached it, avoiding the need to overtake on the narrow, unlit road.

She switched on the air-con to clear the misty windscreen, but its whirring drove her mad, and she turned it off again; wiping the condensation away with the back of her hand. She slowed as she reached the hospital entrance and, ignoring the pay and display sign, abandoned the car as close to the entrance as she could; racing up the ramp, through the swing doors marked;

24 HOUR EMERGENCY.

Ross was waiting for her. He moved forward and, grabbing her sleeve, manoeuvred her to a seat.

'Where is she? I want to see her,' she sobbed trying to slip his grasp.

'We'll go and see her in a minute. She's fine, I promise. Just sit for a minute and get your breath before we go in.'

Ross spoke quietly, in the police voice Karenza guessed he reserved for times like this. She was annoyed he was using it on her. Nevertheless, the tightness in her chest subsided a little.

'Livvy has taken something,' he said.

'Taken something, what do you mean taken something?'

Fear gripped again.

'Drugs, Karenza. I mean, drugs.' He looked up at her, eyes glassy and red-rimmed.

Karenza's stomach lurched. 'But ... she went to Lucy's for a sleepover.'

'That was the story. Lucy told her mother she was at yours and the pair of them went to a festival near St Just, intending to camp overnight. Livvy took drugs and landed up here.'

Karenza jumped to her feet. 'I'll kill her ... stupid, stupid ...'

'Calm down and listen for a second. She came in here unconscious. Lucy didn't have a clue what she'd taken and wasn't making much sense because she was off her head too. She was discharged, and her mother took her home. Luckily the paramedics knew what it was. They've seen a lot of it this summer; MDMA, an amphetamine the kids call *Mandy*. According to Lucy, Livvy was fine at first, dancing like a mad thing and then suddenly she fell backwards and began to shake. The paramedics say she's had a seizure.'

'Oh my God, where is she? I want to see her; I need to see her now.'

'This way,' sighed Ross.

Karenza followed him down the corridor, her feet sticking to the knobbly rubber flooring; legs like lead.

Livvy lay alone in the room. The light in the corner cast a blue glow across the bedsheets. She looked so small, much younger than her fifteen years; her ashen face smeared with the remnants of festival glitter. Karenza choked back a gasp as she reached to push away a stray hair from her daughter's sweaty forehead.

Livvy opened her eyes and on seeing her began to cry.

'I'm sorry, Mum, I'm so sorry.'

'Shush, never mind that now. How do you feel?'

'I've got a terrible headache, and I'm so tired. I don't remember much.'

'That's okay, love, you get back to sleep. We'll talk about this later.'

Ross glared at them from the opposite side of the bed, his mouth a grim gash.

Livvy's eyes closed. Karenza let go of her hand and walked towards her ex-husband.

'Ross, don't be angry with her, it's ...' He didn't let her finish.

'I'm not angry with *her*,' he spat in a whisper so as not to wake his daughter. 'I'm angry with the bastards that gave her the stuff and myself for letting it happen.'

'I don't understand where she got the money to go and buy this *Mandy* or whatever you call it?' she said.

Ross took her arm and led her out into the corridor. 'She didn't have to buy it,' he whispered, 'there were blokes at the festival giving the stuff away to the kids.'

'Why would they do that?'

'To get them hooked. Every junkie starts somewhere. It's a ploy used by dealers, and it works.'

The idea Livvy was cynically targeted made her want to scream.

'Did they get the ones who gave it to her?'

'No, we were called because the organisers phoned concerned something was going on. They've got medics on-site and they'd had loads of kids in the tent this evening; way more than usual. When Livvy collapsed, they called an ambulance and pulled the plug on the festival. One of our officers questioned the kids recovering in the tent. None of them were making sense, but one told him the drugs were being given away. Whoever they were, they were long gone by the time we got there.'

'What now?'

'They're getting fluid into her, that's what the drip is for. They'll check she can pee properly to make sure she hasn't damaged her kidneys.'

Karenza groaned.

'It's standard,' he reassured her. 'Once that's done, she can leave. You go home; you look done in. I'll stay here with her until she's discharged tomorrow morning and bring her home. It'll be okay ... she'll be okay, I promise.'

'What the hell is happening, Ross?' sighed Karenza, trying to stifle a yawn, as the panic subsided and hollowing fatigue began to creep through her limbs.

Ross pulled her into him and kissed the top of her head. Although she wanted to stay, she could barely keep her eyes open, and she reluctantly took him up on the offer.

Driving home, she couldn't help feel things were drifting away from her. First Carly and now this. Livvy knew the dangers of taking drugs. She'd always taught her to be sensible and honest, but she'd lied to her and risked her own life on the pretext of having a good time.

She had been with Ross most of the night, tethered by bindings of parental anxiety, but had not broached the subject of Treeve and, more importantly, his link to Jem Fielding. Deep down she knew why. He'd blame her for Livvy. After all, she was living with a man working for a drug dealer. How could she tell Ross and expect him to allow his daughter to live under the same roof?

Once home, she took herself off to Livvy's room to sleep. She needed to feel close to her and didn't fancy an interrogation from Treeve. The room smelt of peach shampoo and chewing gum and, as usual, looked as if it had been ransacked; clothes and school books strewn across the bed. She folded a Jack Wills hoody and gathered the wet wipes and grubby balls of cotton wool. Plonking them in the bin under the dressing table, she noticed the photo wedged in the corner of the mirror of herself and ten-year-old Livvy, heads together grinning for the camera and wondered where her little girl had gone.

The rain had finally stopped. She walked to the window, lifted her face to the watery moon, and made a promise. She wouldn't let this happen. Not to her family, not to her home. Jem and his kind couldn't have this little corner of the world. It was hers and she wouldn't let them have it.

TWENTY-ONE

Josie arrived at the club the next morning just in time to see the workmen making the final adjustments to the new signage. She wondered whether the banner boasting a topless woman with a fishtail and reading 'Mermaids' would encourage those on the hunt for fish and chips. Maybe that was Jem's plan. Perhaps confusion was his USP.

An unfamiliar handsome face opened the door for her; not one of the thick-necked gorillas Jem usually employed.

'Thanks.'

'No worries.'

A local from the accent. Her mind wandered back to the conversation she'd overheard between Theo and Jem. *Treeve*, she thought; *so, this is Treeve.*

She was hit with the smell of fresh paint as she entered the bar. The decorators had finally finished, but their handiwork was barely dry. Jem had refurbished the pub when he bought it, originally going for an ancient Greek theme, complete with pillars and faux marble. The wood floor had been ripped up and the ancient panelling used in the upstairs office. He'd completed the look by installing a couple of plaster statues of Aphrodite he'd bought from a reclamation yard in Walthamstow.

The decor had needed to change again with Jem's plans for his Mermaid. He'd kept most of the marble, but the stage now boasted a full-width mural of an underwater scene complete with jellyfish, giant clams and sunken wreck. He'd also invested in turquoise fishing nets, which he'd hung from the ceiling.

The look he'd finally achieved was Pirates of the Caribbean meets Zorba the Greek. Any allure was strictly nocturnal; without the girls and the twinkling lights, despite the money he'd sunk into it, the place looked tawdry and cheap. She walked through to the back room, half expecting to find Jem in a compromising position with one or more of the girls. Not that she cared if he was. The way she saw it, the worse he behaved, the easier it was to turn the tables and betray him.

Surprisingly the women in the room were fully clothed.

Lorraine, Jem's manager, who'd been with him for years, pulled a long silver sequined skirt from a cardboard box and held it up against herself. The skirt rested on her hips and tapered the length of her legs to her ankles, splaying out in elaborate frills at the bottom

'I just don't see it working. The punters want to see the girls' legs, a lot of them have a leg thing. How are they gonna see their legs in these?'

'Well, try it on, before you kick off,' said Jem, annoyed.

Lorraine was right; there was no way the girls could move in those things. The costumes were designed for sitting, not gyrating. Josie knew she had to try to diffuse the situation before it turned nasty. 'How about we send this lot back, and I get Mary, you know the woman who did the curtains for the house, to run something up? Maybe, something floaty and sheer that'll give the impression of a tail, but will move with the girls and will fall back to show their legs.'

Jem's face lit up at the thought of her buying into his vision.

'Good idea. Yeah, I can see where you're coming from; That would give the whole routine a bit of class.'

It was only then she remembered the other girl in the room, the pretty delicate featured redhead who had moved away from the box when she entered. She sat motionless on the velvet-covered chaise longue to the side of them.

Looking at her more closely, she could see she was stunning in a fragile, delicate way. She wasn't the usual type picked for the club; that was for certain. She had no bust to speak of and had not suffered the tango tan treatment Jem usually insisted on. She was pale, except for the lightest spattering of amber freckles across her cheeks.

Josie had met girls like her before, not as lovely, but the same body type, back when she aspired to be a real dancer before puberty kicked in and her body exploded into curvy C-cup womanhood. This must be Carly.

Her silence was unnerving. It had rendered her invisible whilst they were distracted with the skirt, and Josie felt uncomfortable about excluding her from the conversation.

'Hello, I'm Josie, Jem's wife.'

The girl looking up at her with beautiful pooling green eyes gently squeezed her hand. It felt like an affirmation of something, but Josie couldn't imagine what.

'Right then, I'll leave the costumes and stuff to you, Josie,' said Jem. 'The girls are in the dressing room waiting. You can start your rehearsals straight away if you're ready? Just tell Mike what music you want, and he'll get it set up for you. I've got work to do. Treeve can drive me.'

As he walked past, he kissed Josie on the cheek. He also kissed Lorraine, slightly closer to her lips and Josie wondered if there might still be something going on there. She, like most of the women he employed, had at one time been in a relationship with her boss, but now as far as Josie knew it was purely business. Nevertheless, she made a mental note to be careful what she said around Lorraine. Then just as he was about to leave, Jem did the strangest thing; he leant down and kissed Carly on her head, as you would a child. The kiss was so gentle, so full of tenderness, it brought a lump to Josie's throat.

TWENTY-TWO
Carly

I like Josie. She is an observer, like me; a reader of people's moods and motives like today, when she moved to keep the peace. Instead of my wall of silence, she has a fake face she hides behind, but she can't hide from me.

I've watched her come and go for weeks; watched her mask slip as she smiles at Loveday; a secret smile reserved for secret lovers. It's returned less covertly than she'd like. Loveday's open, devil-may-care love has no place around Jem.

I can keep them safe. I knew I could from the moment Jem kissed me. So gentle, so chaste; so possessive. He doesn't get he's the one possessed, not me.

Yeah, I like Josie. We're alike, her and me. We're both freedom fighters.

TWENTY-THREE

Over the next week, Josie worked for hours with the girls on their routines. She'd barely had a minute to herself, but today everything had finally clicked, and she'd felt confident enough to let them knock off early. She'd arranged to meet Loveday. They needed to talk, not in the club but somewhere private. Keeping her plans to herself was driving her mad. The more she thought about it, the less clear it became, the only constant being if she was going to get a handle on Jem's deal, she needed to meet up with Theo.

Her marriage had been riddled with lies and petty deceptions, and she didn't intend to make the same mistake again. She was going to be straight with Loveday; explain she may need to give Theo a bit of encouragement to part with information. Given their history, that could mean some intimacy, but it would be worth it to buy a Jem-free future.

Rehearsals had gone well on the whole. Carly mastered the choreography easily, and the other girls upped their game. She was proud of them and herself and felt more relaxed about the whole thing. Tickets had sold well for the first show tomorrow night. The hoarding at the front of the club promising a free round of drinks to parties over six and a free private dance for the groom and best man leading every stag party had done the trick. She knew there would probably be elements in the audience who came only to satisfy their morbid curiosity about the girl, who not long before had been the subject of local press reports about her kidnapping. Her mute, strange beauty added to the voyeuristic intrigue. She hoped the first show would change all that, and they'd see past the tragedy and appreciate her talent.

Her lover was waiting at the pub around the corner.

'How did you get on?'

'Good, really good.'

'What about Lorraine; she okay with you being in charge?'

'To be honest, I think she's as bored as the rest with the same old routines. She seems genuinely interested in what I'm trying to do.'

'What about Carly?'

'Her level of musicality is truly extraordinary. No formal training, but we can fix that; she's a natural.'

'Maybe, but who cares? It's not the Royal Ballet. They're not queuing up to see Darcey Bussell. They're there to ogle the girls' tits.'

Josie felt a flush of indignation. She'd listened to this sort of crap from so-called feminists since she'd started in the clubs all those years before. It was no more convincing now than it was then. Being a lesbian didn't give Loveday the right to judge other women and find them wanting; belittle what they chose to do for a living because it didn't fit her mould.

'Those girls have worked bloody hard all week. So what if the punters don't know their arabesque from their elbow? Maybe it's not about them. Every one of those girls wants to be a dancer; probably had lessons since they were toddlers. They read books about Margot Fonteyn; wanted to be Sylvie Guillem, but they can't all be. Most of them can't even make it past the chorus of some second-rate panto, but they don't need people telling them all they are a pair of tits, especially not other women.'

Loveday's chin dipped; her ears under her dark curls turning pink.

'I just hope John Taylor's as impressed.'

'Who?'

'Carly's father. This whole thing has pushed him over the edge, according to Karenza. First her disappearance, then the mine shaft and now, her leaving home and working in the club. It's not exactly what you'd want for your only child, is it?'

'No, I suppose not,' said Josie, remembering the terrible events around the girl's disappearance and the rows she'd had with her parents when she'd told them she wouldn't be going to university and instead was going to work as a dancer.

'He hangs around, you know, trying to see Carly, but Jem won't let him.'

'What do you mean; Jem won't let him?'

'He's not rough with him or anything. He sends one of the boys to tell him Carly doesn't want to see him and to sling his hook.'

'How does he know she doesn't want to see him?' Josie asked, unease rising. Perhaps Carly's silence was a sign of something else; other problems which, despite her being over eighteen, meant it would be inappropriate to have her dance at the club.

'Her father's tried to take her home before, but she fought it, and the poor man was arrested. He's barred now but still comes back now and then to check with the girls she's alright. I'm pretty sure he'll be back when he knows she's going to be dancing.'

'Why does he think she's here, if not to dance? She can't communicate, so working in the bar would be a challenge. Does he think she works in the kitchen or something?'

'I don't think he realises she works at all. He thinks she's come to the club because it was her home for so long.'

Josie looked blankly at Loveday who, seeing her expression took a deep, *once upon a time* breath and continued.

'The pub has been in the Taylor family for years. Jem bought it from John shortly after Carly was found down the shaft. The girl sleeps in her old room above the bar. Didn't you know?'

'No ... no, I didn't.'

Jem was always buying or selling something and not just in

Cornwall; all over the place. She didn't keep tabs and hadn't really thought about how he'd acquired the club.

The dots were not difficult to join. Carly's appearance at the club was not some fluke. Jem had been behind the girl's disappearance. It was a practised trick; the worst type of intimidation. You concentrated on your enemy's weakness; those he loved, threatened them and waited to see how long the opposition held out. Generally, not long. He'd terrified the Taylors into selling their business. She expected he hadn't bargained on the girl being found, let alone coming home.

Perhaps what he felt for this girl wasn't lust or greed but guilt?

She forgot about her plan to tell Loveday about Theo. All she could think about was Jem and what he'd done to the girl and her family.

TWENTY-FOUR
Carly

We finished rehearsals early today, so I went to the library. I'm a regular there. The librarian lets me stay for hours flipping through the glossy reference books you're not allowed to take out. I know she enjoys my silent company. I shut the lid of the toilet, sit down and open the book I've borrowed, feeling its weight on my knees as I turn the pages.

The book is full of pictures. Sails billowing in breezes blown from the puffed-out cheeks of the gods; prowling Minotaurs and Medusa's snaking head, turning the over-curious to stone and the Siren, of course; on the page I've marked with a paperclip. I need it to copy the pattern from the mermaid's tail onto my legs for the show. I've practiced laying down the blue background with acrylic paint, then drawing the scales, shading and highlighting, so they mirror those in the picture. I've struggled with the back of my thighs and I've settled for brushing a little silver where I can't reach. The results are not as realistic as I'd like, although I've covered the cuts on my inner thighs easily enough. I could, I suppose, have my legs tattooed? Holding them out in front of me, I imagine the pulse of the tattooist needle.

Laying the open book on the toilet seat, I move over to the sink and wonder what it must be like to tattoo your whole body; to escape your old skin. I've worn my mermaid costume in rehearsals and will soon be wearing it every night for the show, but what would it be like to really become something new and powerful, feared and longed for at the same time?

Mum let me watch the old Hollywood film one Sunday

afternoon about Odysseus because we'd been studying the Greeks at school. Aboard ship, surrounded by his crew, their ears plugged with candle wax, only he was brave enough to listen to the Siren's voice, knowing he couldn't follow because he was shackled to the mast. I wondered at the time whether the Siren's voice was like the one in my head; the voice I tell no one about.

I lift my toothbrush from the stand and imagine my teeth shifting to make way for rows of tiny sharp replacements; their needle points scoring my tongue as they break through my gums. I'd only be able to eat liquidised food until my human teeth were discarded. I wouldn't mind that. I like smoothies. I squeeze out the toothpaste and begin to brush, imagining sticky squid ink coating my tongue; its silky blackness leaving my lips stained and salty.

Pulling my hair into a ponytail, I feel behind my left ear. Tracing my fingers along the pulse I imagine a slit forming, fluttering like a butterfly. I raise my hand to the other side, wondering what it would be like to watch your ears shrink away altogether. I cup my hands over mine. Up until now, they have been the most important part of me, but now my voice is coming. It rises from inside me, strange and imperfect, and the words follow.

I clear my throat, pick up the book and try to read aloud from its pages, but tears blur my eyes, and I jump, startled by banging on the bathroom door.

I close the book, pack up my washbag and leave, passing Lorraine on the landing.

The woman has a curious look on her face, and I worry I've forgotten myself and spoken too loudly. I need to be careful. There can be no forewarning.

Just like I called the dog, just as the Siren called Odysseus, I'll call Jem. Only there must be no lifeline for him, no mast to strap himself to.

TWENTY-FIVE

Josie took her time getting ready. The last time she'd seen Theo, she'd been dragged to Sennen at short notice. This time she had a job to do. She began the regime she'd all but abandoned since meeting Loveday. It felt strangely comforting, like pulling on an old jumper. She'd relied on the methodical paint by numbers way she applied her make-up for most of her adult life as a prop to steady herself.

When she'd been a dancer, it had been a distraction to calm her nerves before going on stage. Later it had been something to do with her hands as Jem paced behind her incensed at some petty insult or wrong word. She'd calm herself by concentrating on putting on her slap.

The blusher, the powder, the eyeshadow and mascara. The familiar ritual would stop her hand shaking and suppress the urge to run. She felt the same sense of security now.

Once finished, she wore an extremely well-applied mask; one a young make-up blogger on YouTube would be proud of. It was just as well, she needed it to conceal her motives from Theo and to hide her shame from Loveday. She had to drop off some bits and pieces for the girls at the club on her way and knew she'd be there until about eleven and was bound to see her.

She'd texted Theo the previous evening.

Hi, wondered if you fancied meeting for a catch-up? J.

She'd wondered whether to put an x, but then had thought to hell with it, in for a penny, in for a pound and typed xx

He had replied almost immediately.

Couldn't think of anything I'd like more. Haven't been able to stop thinking about you since we met! Can you get away tomorrow?

It was the opening night of Carly's show, and she should be at the club putting the girls through their final paces, but she knew Jem was tied up in a meeting in Bristol all day preparing for a planning appeal. He wouldn't be home until early evening. She might not have another opportunity to spend so much time with Theo.

I'm free during the day.

Lunch at my place 1.00?

Okay ... she deleted, needing to sound more enthusiastic.

Excited, can't wait.

Me too! T xx

Loveday was pouring over her list of jobs with the bar manager, Ray, when Josie arrived at the club. She took a deep breath as she approached. She needed to keep it brief and breezy.

'Just a few costume repairs Mary dropped over,' she smiled, dropping the cardboard box full of glittery slips on the bar.

'Where are you off to looking so glam?' asked Ray.

She could feel Loveday's eyes pouring over her.

She'd chosen to wear a deep green dress speckled with small, yellow-eyed daisies held up with spaghetti straps crossing her shoulder blades. The dress skimmed her hips, flaring to a full skirt resting just above the knee. She had dancer's legs, long and lean and the kitten-heels she'd chosen, meant they looked even longer.

Loveday said nothing, but Josie could see she was waiting for her answer.

'Oh, one of those ladies' lunches, talking handbags and shoes; nothing in common apart from our husbands playing golf together. Sorry, but I've got to fly, or I'll be late.'

As she turned to head for the door Lorraine emerged from the back room, heading her off.

'Can I have a word before you go?'

'Yes ... sure, as long as it's quick.'

'In the back, if that's okay?'

'Yes, fine, if you like?'

Josie wondered what was so important and why she couldn't say it in front of Ray and Loveday? Perhaps Lorraine wanted one of those talks about how she and Jem were in love and how she, the old ball and chain, was standing in the way of their happiness by not letting him go. She'd had many such talks with many delusional young women, but she'd thought Lorraine was beyond all that.

The woman closed the door behind them.

'It's about Carly.'

'Carly; what about her? Jem's not been doing anything to worry about?'

'No ... no nothing like that, he's the perfect gentleman as far as she's concerned. It's not about Jem, it's about her.'

'What do you mean?'

'You know she doesn't speak; doesn't make any sound at all, really?'

'Yes.'

'Well, the night before last, it had been a heavy evening, and I decided to stay here in the spare room rather than go home. I do that sometimes.'

Josie tried to remember whether Jem had come home that night.

'Carly sleeps in the bedroom next to the bathroom. I was knackered so thought I'd just have a quick shower and go to bed. I was on my way to the bathroom with my towel when I noticed Carly slipping in before me. She was in her nightie, so I assumed she was on her way to bed, so I waited outside for her to finish. Then, I heard the voice.'

'Whose voice?'

'A voice, a strange, garbled, sort of voice.'

'Talking to Carly; you mean there was someone else in the bathroom with her?'

'That's what I thought, so I listened at the door. I couldn't hear what was being said. It sounded like a woman ... high-pitched. Someone talking though, not tinny like a radio or a phone.'

'Did you wait to see who came out?'

'Yeh, I waited because I was worried. I banged on the door, and she came out carrying a wash bag and a book under her arm.'

'Who was with her?'

'That's the odd thing; no one. I went into the bathroom and looked everywhere, the shower, in the airing cupboard. I even tried the window in case someone had climbed out onto the roof, but there was no one.'

'Are you saying it was her, talking to herself?'

'Yes ... I mean, it must have been. I don't know, but it was really strange and gave me the creeps.'

'Maybe you should just ask her outright if she can speak? Quietly I mean, so not to embarrass her in front of the other girls. Take her to one side, just in case she's got some kind of speech impediment that might get her teased.'

'Look, I'd prefer not to get involved. I'd rather you and Jem saw to it. I don't know what it is, but something about her freaks me out. I've told Jem I won't be staying over anymore, and I've cleared my stuff from the spare room. I don't want the responsibility, and I don't want to be here on my own with her. I'm just letting you know.'

Lorraine looked physically shaken, and Josie knew there was no point trying to change her mind. She was generally hard as nails, and nothing much fazed her, but she was clearly scared half to death and no amount of persuading could shake her out of it.

'Okay, leave it to me.'

She touched the woman's hand and saw real gratitude expressed in her eyes.

Back in the bar, Loveday had gone, and Josie noticed Carly, sitting at one of the tables drawing. As she brushed past, the girl looked up.

Maybe she could speak after a fashion but had chosen not to because it sounded strange when she did. It wasn't what Loveday had told her, but she might have been wrong. In any case, she had more important things to think about than the antics of Jem's pet teenager and his easily spooked ex-mistress.

TWENTY-SIX

As she parked, her stomach began to squirm at the thought of playing the seductress. Not banking on actually getting any lunch, she'd made the mistake of eating a chocolate bar on the drive over and was regretting it. She imagined Theo ushering her inside for sex with the minimum of foreplay. She took a deep breath, and one last look in the mirror to check her make-up wasn't smudged. The door opened before she reached it. Theo came out, grabbed her handbag, threw it inside the hallway and pulled the door shut behind him.

'You won't be needing that,' he said, 'I've got a table booked for one o'clock, and I don't know about you, but I'm starving.'

'I thought we'd be eating here?' she said, bemused at the speed he was turning her around.

'No, I've got something special planned. You look lovely by the way,' he said, lifting his sunglasses to his head to take a proper look at her.

He was dressed as before, in a t-shirt, shorts and soft leather loafers, and she felt ungainly in her heels as he held out his arm as if she were his elderly aunt to help her negotiate the steep cobbled pathway from the drive down to the main street. At the bottom, he slipped free and ran on ahead to the tiny general store, leaving her on the pavement to contemplate a pile of depressing dried starfish displayed in a tatty wicker basket marked; **Lucky Starfish-£1**.

Not that lucky, Josie thought.

When Theo re-emerged, he was carrying a pair of pink flip-flops and a white plastic bag. He lifted the flip-flops to his lips and bit through the thin knot of elastic holding them together.

'There!' he said, pleased his teeth had stood the test, 'they only had pink in your size. You're a seven, that's right, isn't it?'

She was stunned he'd remembered after all these years.

'Put them on and give me those.' He pointed to her kitten-heels.

She slipped them off and slid the flip-flops between her toes.

'Good, now we can get on,' he said, dropping her shoes into the plastic bag and dragging her by the hand as she tried to master the sandals, which, slightly too big, slapped the ground.

She took a sneaky sideways glance. His face had filled out, losing some of the bony sharpness of youth, and it suited him. A brisk sea breeze whipped along the promenade above the beach, parachuting up her dress, so she had to use her free hand to push it down or risk the tourists catching an eyeful. Theo, on the other hand, didn't seem to care who saw them.

By the time they reached the restaurant at the end of the beach car park, her hair had blown across her face and stuck to her lip gloss. At one stage, it had caught on a false eyelash, and she was sure her mascara had run.

'Table for two, in the name of Jenkins,' Theo said to a technicolour board-shorted waiter who'd come to meet and greet.

This felt like familiar territory; the false names and clandestine meetings that had marked their affair. She pulled her hand away and, catching her reflection in the large glass window, tidied her hair. A perky jean-clad waitress led them to a table at the end of the long deck overlooking the beach. The restaurant was full of twenty-somethings dipping rustic chips in aioli and nibbling on focaccia; a perfectly contrived picture of casual dining.

A bottle of white wine cooled in a bucket to the side and as soon as they sat, the waitress poured them a glass before adjusting the triangular awning, secured like a sail over their heads.

'Thanks, just leave it there, we'll help ourselves,' Theo said, flashing a smile that coloured the young woman's sun-freckled face.

'I've pre-ordered a seafood platter to share,' he said, reaching forward to clink a toast. 'To old lovers.'

'Hey, enough of the old,' she flirted.

The platter arrived to gasps from the surrounding tables; piled high with lobster claws, rubbery rings of peppered squid and whiskery beady-eyed prawns in all their crimson glory.

Theo looked pleased with his choice.

'Go on, tuck in.'

Josie tentatively helped herself to some shelled prawns and nibbled on some artisan bread, unnerved by the prospect of claw cracking and crab picking.

Theo was an expert, shattering shells with tools laid out like instruments of torture, he talked rapidly, paused only to dip his fingertips in a finger bowl full of tepid lemony water growing murky with grease.

'So are we going to pussy foot around each other all afternoon or get to the thing playing on both our minds? When are we gonna put right what we fucked up so spectacularly before?' he asked.

Josie dropped her bread and reached for her wine, taking a long cool mouthful, letting it travel slowly down her throat. She felt as if she'd been hijacked.

He dipped his fingers again and wiped them on his napkin.

'I'm being straight with you, Josie. It's a genuine question.' His face was deadly serious as he met her eyes, reaching across the table to touch the tips of her fingers. 'We've wasted too much time already. What's keeping you here anyway? It's a pretty neck of the woods, I grant you, but we both know there are pretty places all over the world, made prettier by the fact Jem's not there.'

He was right, and if they'd had this conversation a few months ago, before Loveday, she'd have packed her bags before he had a chance to dig into another lobster claw.

'I have a good life here. Jem doesn't bother me much anymore.'

'That's not what it looked like the other day. He was like a hawk, watching your every move.'

She scrambled for clarity, unable to make up her mind whether Theo's proposition was a good or bad thing. How was she going to play this? She'd expected sex, not this show of commitment. His unwillingness to commit had led to her leave him for Jem. A lot of water had passed under the bridge since then, and people changed, but she'd never in her wildest imaginings thought Theo would be looking for a full-blown relationship.

'I don't know, how can we ... I mean, what about your wife and kids?'

'I've been divorced for ten years, and my kids are all grown up. They've got their own lives. I see them occasionally, when they need money or want to get into some club or other and ring to ask me to fix it, but they don't *need* me. I want to be needed, and the only time I ever felt needed was when I was with you.'

'Then why didn't you come for me before? Come to think of it, why didn't you fight for me in the first place?' she asked, genuinely interested in his answer.

'Because I had nothing to offer you and no way out for us. Now, it's different. I want us to be together, properly free, free of the job as well as Jem.'

'How?' disbelief creeping onto her voice, despite trying to control it.

The waitress returned to retrieve the dishes and tell them their main course would be arriving shortly.

'But we haven't ordered anything,' said Josie.

'It's all pre-ordered; both courses.' she replied, smiling at Theo, who grinned back.

Josie watched his amber eyes glint following the young woman's rear as she walked away.

'I've ordered you a steak, medium rare with fries, onion rings and a pepper sauce, just as you like it.'

She didn't have the heart to tell him she hadn't touched red meat for over five years.

'Just going to wash up,' he smiled, wriggling his fingers.

She watched him saunter back into the restaurant, sidle up to the waitress, a broad grin crossing his face as she pointed in the direction of the loos.

'Oh, Mr. Morgan, I've got your measure,' Josie whispered under her breath.

He needed her now because he was running slowly out of options. There were only so many young waitresses left to impress before they wouldn't give him a second glance. He knew she'd take care of him, and he'd take care of her too in his way. He wouldn't be violent or spiteful like Jem, she knew him well enough to know life with him would be a picnic compared to the one she'd led with her husband, but he'd still be controlling and self-centred, and she'd be expected to tow the line; put her aspirations on the back burner, and she had no intention of doing that anymore. She wanted to be free of the Jems and Theos of the world. The kind of clipped winged independence men like Theo preached wasn't worth having. To get it, there was always a price to pay.

By the time Theo got back, she'd devised her strategy.

'What you were saying before, are you telling me you're retiring; properly retiring?'

'After this job, if all goes well,' he replied.

'And if it doesn't, what then?'

'You mean if Jem cocks up? Well then, that's me and him

done for. You either deliver, or you're dispensed with. That's why it can't be allowed to go wrong.'

'So why involve Jem?'

'I've no choice. Believe me, if I did, I wouldn't pick him, but he knows the area. We need this coastline and his local knowledge. He's been told exactly what to do, so it should be simple enough, even for him.'

'I see,' she said, deliberately sounding puzzled.

Throughout the rest of the meal, Theo talked about his divorce; the money it had cost him and how he now lived in a Penthouse apartment in Cardiff Bay. He had three bedrooms so his two kids could visit, but they rarely did. He divided his time between Spain and South Wales dealing with 'business'. He'd made enough money to change his life for good, and several years ago had bought a plot of land in Barbados. An architect had drawn up plans, and he intended to spend the rest of his life there when the house he'd designed was complete. They'd already levelled the little wooden shack that sat on the acre site. Theo had relatives there, and it had always been his dream to go and live on the island where he'd spent happy holidays as a child with his mother's family. Josie noticed how his eyes glazed with nostalgia as he spoke.

She pushed her steak around her plate, claiming she wasn't hungry after the huge starter. She managed a few chips, but the greasy, blood-tinged juices seeping from the hunk of meat turned her stomach.

They talked well into the afternoon until he looked at her and, reaching for her hand, said,

'Come on time to go, we'll skip the dessert.'

She returned his gaze, and an understanding passed between them. Telepathy they'd shared years before.

By the time they left the restaurant, the place was practically empty. The car park cleared of holidaymakers needing to get back to their hotels to change for their evening meal. The tide was fully in, leaving only a thin strip of sand at the top of the beach, and the day, though still warm, had lost its fiery heat.

Theo had left the patio doors to the deck wide open, and the breeze had kept the place free of the stuffiness she'd felt the last time she'd visited.

'You go on up,' he said, planting a fleeting kiss full on her mouth.

'Where is it again?' she asked brightly, not wanting him to guess she'd been there before.

'Through the kitchen, up the staircase, then straight ahead.'

She picked up her handbag, taking the staircase she knew led to the vaulted bedroom with the glorious sea views.

She kicked off her flip-flops and opened the patio doors.

The sea reflected the amethyst hues of late afternoon; the rocks just offshore rendered invisible now by the incoming tide.

'Beautiful,' Theo whispered, following her gaze as he wrapped his arms around her waist. She felt her body respond to his warm palms in a way she hadn't expected.

'Yes, it is.'

'You too,' he whispered, moving her hair to one side and kissing the nape of her neck; his sensitive fingers tracing the contours of her back, as he slid down her dress strap and turned her towards him. Josie touched his face, and the years fell away, a dizzy, familiar passion grabbing her.

He felt lean and muscular as he lifted and carried her to the bed. She tried to think of Loveday; her smile; the softness of her skin, but her face remained elusive. Theo joined her and as their sun-warmed bodies touched, she smelt his desire, carnal and fierce.

Her emotions were looping, telling her to bolt one moment and give in the next as he undid the tiny white daisy buttons running the length of her dress, plotting reverential kisses along the way. She knew she was being treated to a demonstration of lovemaking finely tuned over many years of conquests but it made no difference. Try as she might, she couldn't control the raw longing toppling her as her body slowly uncoiled, inch by trembling inch. She arched her back as his lips brushed her inner thigh, overwhelmed by a yearning she thought long forgotten. She'd thought so many times of making love with him; closed her eyes when having sex with Jem, trying to imagine this moment; Theo wearing her like a second skin, limbs merged in a tangle of melting flesh; climaxing, before falling away from each other, scorched and exhausted, their lax, spent bodies entwined.

Suddenly she was conscious she was not in her twenties anymore and that closer scrutiny of her might reveal the inevitable changes that came with gravity and middle-age. She caught herself thinking these ridiculous self-deprecating thoughts and wondered why the hell she cared. All those fantasies may be coming together; only they didn't belong to her anymore. They belonged to someone else; the young her; her before Loveday. She thought of the woman she loved; her smile; the softness of her skin.

'Stop ... stop. I can't; it's too soon. Theo, stop.'
She felt him tense as he rolled away, rose from the bed.
'I don't get it. Is this about Jem?'
'What do you think?'
'I think I could do with a drink.'
She felt herself flush like a teenage girl, half expecting him to turn on her; label her a prick-teaser and throw her out.
'I'll be back in a minute, don't go anywhere,' he said, grabbing his robe from the back of the door before heading back downstairs.

As soon as he'd gone, Josie grabbed her dress and rushed to the bathroom, bolting the door behind her. Her hands trembled as she struggled to do up the ridiculously fiddly buttons. Looking down at her rumpled dress, she felt ashamed. She hardly recognised the woman staring back at her from the mirror; her face full of guilt. What the hell was she thinking?

She had no idea how she was going to gather the nerve to walk out there and face Theo.

She ran her wrists under the cold tap, trying to quell the heat coursing through her like lava, then reached for a sheet of toilet paper to rub away the black smudges from beneath her bottom lashes. For good measure, she took another sheet and removed the last smears of lipstick from her kissed bruised mouth and splashed her face. Taking a deep breath, she smoothed her hair behind her ears, unbolted the door and walked back into the room.

Theo was standing by the patio filling two glasses with champagne, one of which he held out to her, and she nervously took.

She was in unfamiliar territory.

'I was being deadly serious before when I said I wanted us to be together.'

She took a gulp; feeling the acidic sting of bubbles on her silent tongue.

'So, what's the problem? You must see nothing's changed between us, other than for the better,' Theo said, tilting the bottle to top up her glass.

'Better?'

'We've grown up.'

'I suppose we have,' she agreed, wondering where all this was leading.

'We know what's important, that we love each other, the sex will come in time.'

He dropped his eyes, considering his glass as if embarrassed by his confession.

'You don't even know me, not anymore.'

She was surprised how hurt he looked at her fly-away comment.

'I do, I've always known you, and I've always known if I ever got another chance that no matter what, I wouldn't blow it, so I'm not going to press you now. I can wait for you, Josie.'

Wasn't this why she'd come; to win his trust; charm him into confiding in her about his scheme? She'd been willing to spread her legs to get information if necessary but, faced with his declarations of undying love, was feeling more uncomfortable by the minute. She'd been here before, seen the way he looked at that waitress; so, what the hell was wrong with her? She'd got him where she wanted him without the sex. Now all she had to do was reel him in, extract what information she could and get the hell out of there.

'Look, even if I thought what you were proposing were possible, you're asking me to rely on someone I haven't seen or had contact with for years and who won't even tell me what he's really doing here. Maybe I'm just a convenience while you're in Cornwall? You want to share your life with me but don't trust me enough to tell me what your plans are? That makes you no different to Jem.'

'You know the rules.'

'Fine, but if you think I'm going into another relationship full of secrets, you're mistaken. I'm done with all that shit.'

She could tell from the look on his face he was beginning to panic; thought she was going to leave.

'Where's the bag with my shoes in?'

'Look, don't go like this, trust me, this deal will make everything possible for us.'

'How will it, Theo? Unless you're prepared to tell me, then I'm out. I trusted you before and look how well that turned out.'

'Okay, okay, sit down, please just sit down.'

She paused, counting to ten before turning around.

'Pour me another glass of champagne and tell me everything, and I mean everything.

TWENTY-SEVEN

Karenza made sure Piran and Livvy were both at home for dinner. Treeve had already left. It was Mermaids opening night. Since he had come out of prison, meals together had been far and few between. Livvy tended to eat early and Piran managed to come up with a variety of excuses, including when working a shift at the pub, that he'd had dinner there with his grandad. She wanted them to be together, just the three of them, that way she could pretend everything was hunky-dory; not the shit-storm it was.

Piran arrived dressed for a night out. She knew her father had given him the evening off.

'This looks good, Mum, I'm starving.'

Her son was always starving, clearing his plate no matter what she put in front of him, but it was nice to receive a compliment.

'So, what have you two been up to lately? It seems I see less and less of you these days; ships in the night.'

'Oh, you know big boys things,' her son smiled at her across the table.

He looked so like Ross at that age, sometimes she had to pinch herself.

Livvy was growing at a pace too. Her skinny jumbled limbs had settled into a rhythm and filled out as her body became her own. She had gradually cast off her shyness like the braces on her teeth to reveal a confident young woman. Whilst recent events may have dented that confidence, Karenza had every faith she'd bounce back. Everyone made mistakes. She hadn't exactly been an angel herself; drinking underage and smoking the occasional spliff in the dunes, but she wouldn't let that get in the way. Her job was to be the fun police just as her mum had been with her and she was up for it. She was up for anything that ensured her daughter never took another recreational drug for the rest of her life. One day Livvy could be mean to her children. It was a perk of the job. As far as Karenza was concerned, if your teenage daughter didn't say *I hate you* at least once a month, you were doing something wrong.

She'd read her the riot act, grounded her for a month and confiscated her phone for a week. The latter being the equivalent to a sentence of hard labour in the colonies for the average fifteen-year-old girl. She seemed mortified by the whole experience, wanting to put it behind her. Livvy swore she'd never taken anything before and had done all the experimenting she was ever likely to do. It didn't make Karenza any less angry with the suppliers of the filthy stuff.

All in all, she was proud of her children. They'd taken the divorce hard and found her relationship with Treeve difficult, but in the end, in their way, they'd supported her. They'd made themselves scarce, avoided conflict, and got on with their lives.

'What are you doing this weekend then?'

'Going surfing at Fistral on Saturday and tonight is Jack's stag night, and we're all going into Penzance to see Carly dance.'

'What?' Karenza couldn't believe her ears.

'Come on, Mum, you can't expect us local lads to be different just because we know her.'

'But you've known her all your life. She's almost like a sister to you.'

'Don't compare me to her; taking her clothes off for money,' chipped in Livvy, screwing up her face in disgust.

'Anyway, she's not like a sister. Yeh, I grew up with her, but I grew up with all the girls around here. If everyone avoided everyone they'd grown up with living in a place like this, we'd have died out years ago.'

'Yeah, you grew up with Dad, didn't you?' said Livvy.

'That's different.'

'You think of Carly as different because she can't talk. For us who grew up with her, she's not that different at all. She was every bit as strong as any of us; stronger than many,' snapped Piran.

'But after all that's been done to her ...'

'Mum, you were like this about her before she was taken, all of you were; her mum and dad, everyone. You all treated her like a baby who never answered back.'

'That's not fair, no one can go through what she has without there being some effect, and it's so ...'

'So what, Mum, tragic; terrible? Yeh, it is, but it's not Carly who's having trouble getting over what's happened to her, it's your lot, all the so-called adults.'

She'd heard from Loveday the club was fully booked and likely to be packed every night with men coming from far and wide to see Carly dance; coach trips from across the county on the back of the publicity gathering speed on social media.

There had been protests in the press from women's groups, and the local church got involved. It changed nothing.

'She's weird anyway,' Livvy piped up, 'she was weird before all this. I remember once she was in charge of all of us small ones down the beach. We were at the water's edge at low tide, mucking around and she had a knife, you know a bait knife like Granddad uses. She ran it through the sand like you do when your sand-eeling, and one came up, and she ate it.'

'What are you talking about, you idiot?' blurted Piran, choking on a piece of chicken.

'She did; she ate it, there and then in front of us. Washed it off in a rockpool, lifted her head back and swallowed it. Then she opened her mouth wide to show all of us it had gone, like this.' Livvy wriggled her tongue about by way of demonstration.

Karenza had been sand-eeling with her father many times as a child; run a blade through the sand in a letter S to reveal the silvery skinned fish the size of your finger. To think of someone eating one alive, made her want to gag.

'Oh my God,' snorted Piran as both he and Livvy collapsed into fits of giggles and Karenza found herself joining in.

'To be fair,' he said, 'she was always pulling stunts when we were kids. It was probably a trick. I expect she did the thing with the eel to shock you into behaving yourselves.'

'Well, she did that alright. We were scared stiff of her after that.'

'I remember once when we were jumping off the cliffs into the water off the island ...'

'Tombstoning? I told you never to do that,' said Karenza.

'I know, but reality-check, Mum; we did it anyway.' Piran carried on. 'Anyhow, we'd all had a couple of goes, including Carly, then she jumped again. Her dive was good and she entered the water fine, but then didn't come up. Minutes went by, and me and the rest jumped in, diving down trying to find her, but there was no sign. Then suddenly, we spotted her sitting on the pontoon way out. None of us to this day can think how she got there. She didn't break the surface, and it's a hell of a way out. To tell you the truth, when she first went missing, I half thought she'd pulled another stunt like that.'

'See. Weird,' said Livvy, tucking into her cheesecake.

'She's a grown woman, Mum, who knows her mind. If she didn't want to dance, she wouldn't, trust me.'

Maybe he's right, Karenza thought. Perhaps he sees Carly's strength rather than her weakness and knows she doesn't need protecting anymore? Like Carly, Piran was all grown up, and she should come to terms with letting go. But not quite yet, not until Treeve was out of the picture and she could relax knowing her children were safe out of the reach of worms like Fielding.

TWENTY-EIGHT

By the time Josie got back in the car it was seven-thirty. Over the past couple of hours, Theo had divulged the nuts and bolts of the plan. Some of it she already knew, but she'd learnt the size of the shipment and the product was cocaine, arriving from Spain.

'The Spanish boat will meet Jem's boy just off a place called the Gurnard's Head not far from here. The exact time and location will only be given on the morning of the drop-off. He'll take the stuff inshore and dump it overboard. It's packed in waterproof holdalls linked together with buoys to make it easy to pick up. My lads will bring it back here to be checked before driving it to Jem's warehouse in Newlyn to be packed in fish boxes and moved out of the county by road. If successful, the route could be used again.'

'When you say Jem's boy, do you mean just one man; isn't that a bit risky?'

'It's some new bloke. It's his trawler, and apparently, he's a big strong lad. It's best to involve as few locals as possible; those unfamiliar with the chain of command. As far as he's concerned, this is Jem's deal.'

'And when exactly is this happening?'

'Soon babe, soon,' he'd said, kissing the back of her neck.

'When exactly; I've got to prepare to leave, especially if I'm doing it behind Jem's back. I can't just up sticks?'

His look had been quizzical, and for a second, she'd thought he might be suspicious until he kissed her and grinned from ear to ear.

'So, you're coming with me?'

'Yes. But until then, we take no more risks; no more

afternoon delight. There'll be plenty of time together when we're away from this place.'

She hadn't pressed him further. He'd divulged all he was going to; for now, anyway. She plugged in her mobile. It had been off all afternoon. She'd only driven a short distance before it began to ping with messages. She glanced at the screen; Loveday. She pulled over. Five missed calls, three from Loveday, two from Jem. Loveday hadn't left a voicemail, she knew better, just in case Jem picked up her phone and got inquisitive. Jem had left two; she played back. The first was fairly innocuous.

"Hi Josie, where are you? I'm back now and getting ready for the big show! Looking forward to it, babe! Money!" The second, made an hour later, wasn't so friendly. "Where the bloody hell are you? You know how important this is to me. Get your ass here now, if you know what's good for you."

She hadn't stopped to think how she'd bluff her way through her absence if Jem came home early. She rang him back, just to be able to show she had, letting the phone ring only a few times before hanging up, willing Jem not to answer. She didn't have time to go home and shower and decided to go straight to the club. She'd tell him she'd gone there to watch the final rehearsal. She'd say her phone was switched off because she didn't want to be interrupted, or better still, say she'd left it in the car. She wasn't sure he'd fall for it but didn't have a lot of choice.

***

She arrived at the club at eight, parked and made her way to the rear exit hoping it would be open and she'd be able to slip in unnoticed. As she walked down the poorly lit alley, she spotted Mike leaning against the door, smoking.

'Left my phone in the car!' she smiled, waving it in front of his gullible face.

'Right,' he said, quickly dropping what was left of his spliff to the ground like an errant teenager. 'I'm just off to fetch Mr. Fielding.'

Relieved Jem wasn't there yet, she walked through the basement room, up the narrow back staircase to the main bar. It was empty other than for Ray, filling the shelves with mixers. She headed past him towards the dressing room where the girls were putting the final touches to their make-up. Lorraine was in the middle of brushing shimmery-blue shadow onto one of the girl's eyelids. She looked up, an expression of relief crossing her face.

'Hiya, you wouldn't mind doing Carly, would you? I ... I need to make sure the other girls have got everything they need,' she smiled nervously.

'No problem,' Josie replied, as Lorraine handed her a tiny pot of silvery glitter and a brush. Clearly she was still not keen to have contact with the girl.

Carly sat across the room in front of the mirror.

'Hi Carly, are you excited?'

Carly nodded.

Josie, tilting the girl's chin upwards, brushed a slick of glitter across her cheekbones. Her face was so perfectly sculpted, the delicate bones so precisely put together, it seemed almost a sin to gild the lily. There was something special about her; something precious that needed to be protected. She took a deep breath.

'Carly, you don't have to do this if you don't want to. You can go home to your family; I'll take you if you like? One of the other girls can stand in, I'll tell Jem. It'll be okay, I promise.' She wanted the girl to know she could leave. She knew she'd pay for it if Carly took her at her word but couldn't bear the thought of this beautiful silent girl being coerced into all this.

Carly met her eye in the mirror and slowly, so there could be no mistake, shook her head in a definitive *no*. Then, reaching up, pulled the loaded brush back towards her face in a gesture for Josie to continue. Josie didn't push it; she had more than enough on her plate to be going on with. She'd offered and was glad she had, but the girl had turned her down, and she couldn't deny she was relieved. Even more so when she heard Jem's voice.

'All right, my lovelies, are we all ready?' he shouted, bursting through the door, stopping in his tracks, on seeing Josie.

'You're *here*.'

'Yeah, I've been here, getting everything ready. Just putting the final touches to Carly's make-up,' she said, lifting the pot and brush as evidence of the fact.

'I've been trying to get hold of you all bloody afternoon,' he said, an almost indiscernible twitch drawing one side of his mouth into a reluctant smirk.

'I left my phone in the car, I just went out and got it and saw you'd left a couple of messages ... Sorry.'

Her stomach spasmed as she struggled to think of something else to say to fill the uncomfortable pause.

Then, to her utter surprise, Lorraine saved her from the drop.

'Josie's been brilliant. I don't know what we'd have done without her this afternoon. Thanks for lending her to us.'

Jem's face relaxed. 'I see ... good, good ... well done Josie ... brilliant, then I'll leave you to it. I'll get some drinks brought in to you lot before the show begins.'

Once he'd gone, Josie turned to Lorraine and mouthed, 'Thank you.' She was sorry she'd misjudged Lorraine, who clearly understood the need to stay on the right side of Jem and had gone out on a limb for her. She wouldn't forget the kindness.

She left the dressing room in time to see the first of a succession of men entering the club, some solitary and nervous, others in hunting pairs or larger groups full of swagger, shouting the odds. The staff were under strict orders to push the expensive cocktails as the warm-up dancers spun on their shiny chrome poles. Girls paraded the floor, showing off boob jobs and Brazilian butts paid for by Jem, singling out candidates for private dances downstairs. Bouncers stood at either side of the stage warning off punters who got a little too feely-touchy with the merchandise. It all looked very familiar to Josie.

Carly was due on at eleven. By quarter to, all of the tables in the club were taken, and the bar was two deep, everyone desperate to get their orders in before the main event.

Josie returned backstage to check everyone was ready.

Whilst the other girls wandered around flexing their calves and adjusting their costumes, Carly sat motionless, her glittery face expressionless. Copper waves hung in silky drifts over her small breasts reaching well past her navel. She wore a long, pale blue chiffon skirt, split into four panels so she could stretch her long legs around the pole. Like the other girls, beneath the skirt she wore a tiny silver thong and nothing else.

'You ready, Carly?' Josie asked, placing a reassuring hand on her shoulder.

Carly nodded and rose from her seat.

'Everything okay, Lorraine?'

'Yep, good to go.'

'Good, then I'll catch up later,' smiled Josie, remembering how she'd saved her earlier.

Back in the bar, she felt the fizz of testosterone. She overheard loud voices discussing the logistics of screwing a Mermaid and whether you'd have to be, "careful not to catch crabs".'

Josie wasn't surprised but found the freak show dynamic, deeply unsettling.

It was almost eleven. She gave the lighting guy the thumbs up and the stage was plunged into darkness as Jeff Buckley's

'Everybody here wants you' drifted into the room. The soulful, soaring voice trickled from the sound system like honey as the spotlight flared to life and shone on Carly. She stood motionless, her back to the crowd; light playing on her silvered body, flame-red hair licking her back. At first, the chatter continued unabated much as before, the drunken predictable taunts and lads talk, ringing out in effervescent bursts, but then slowly, the talking fell away. Those queuing at the bar turned to face the stage and gradually wound down, like sluggish old clocks. The lax, spellbound men swayed with the rhythm of the room; the heat rising from their bodies in suffocating pheromone waves, the stifling thickness of the still air making Josie's head spin as she tried to fathom what was wrong, why they weren't cheering? She knew only too well what the room was supposed to sound like and this wasn't it; but for the music, the place was as quiet as a church. Jem would be furious, and he'd be blaming her. She glanced in his direction. He was heading through the swing doors into the foyer. She saw the glint of gaudy red walls as the black double door swung open with the force of his push as two bouncers followed him out.

Two minutes later, they were frogmarching a middle-aged man into the club. The men escorted their charge to the table Jem reserved for his guests and sat either side of him. He looked completely out of sync, glancing around as if searching for someone to rescue him, but no one other than Josie seemed to notice. Jem sat directly behind and now and then leaned forward and whispered something in his ear.

Unlike every other man in the room, he tried to look away. The men on either side held his chin, so he had to watch. He struggled, managing to break free. Shielding his eyes, he lunged towards the podium, staggering around grabbing at the air like a blind thief, while Jem and his mates laughed hysterically. Josie looked around; *was no one else seeing this?*

Eventually, Jem's heavies wrestled him back down into his seat, wedging him between them, one gripping his head like a vice from behind. She scrutinised the scene for clues as if watching a silent film, trying to piece the action together without sub-titles. She followed the man's agonised gaze to Carly, noticing the girl had discarded the sheer blue skirt to reveal legs painted blue and green as if tattooed with fish scales. She didn't remember seeing the paint earlier in the dressing room, but now the scales were visible and meticulously executed. Looking closer, she could see the silver thong had gone; Carly was completely naked. The girls weren't allowed to be naked; it was a breach of their licence; they weren't a strip club.

Jem remained seated, watching Carly, oblivious it seemed to the fact she was starkers. There was none of the heckling Josie would have expected with a full strip, and the audience remained eerily silent as the lights died. It wasn't until they went up again and new dancers took the stage that they began to chant.

'Carly ... Carly ... Carly.'

She leaned over the bar to speak to Ray.

'Who was the man, sitting over there with Jem, the one the men were holding?'

'John Taylor, Carly's dad.'

She looked back at Jem, working the tables; chatting to his customers, a huge grin playing across his impish face. She knew he was unlikely to come home that night. He'd invited several of his cronies to the show, and they'd be drinking into the early hours. He'd sleep at the club with or without company, depending on how pissed he was. He sickened her, and she wasn't going to spend another minute in the same room as him. She needed air and, grabbing her bag, made her way through the crowd to the back exit.

Emerging into the alley, she felt nauseous; the tell-tale sign of an impending migraine beginning to play out a zig-zaggidy light show in the corner of her left eye. The smell of spicy food seeping from the kitchen of the takeaway next door didn't help. She knew she had to get home before the psychedelia turned to thumping pain, and she couldn't see to drive.

Rummaging through her bag, she retrieved her keys and a battered box of Migrelieve and made her way to the car park. It was only when she looked up, she saw Loveday leaning against her car.

Her heart sank. The last thing she needed was a barrage of questions about what she'd been up to. She'd dodged a bullet once already that evening.

'Hi, what are you doing here?' she smiled, trying to sound nonchalant.

'I thought I might catch you *eventually*. I've not had much luck phoning you.'

Loveday folded her arms across her body like a bullet-proof vest. Josie could tell she was seriously pissed off.

'I'm sorry, I've been rushing around all day and left my phone in the car. What with rehearsals and the show, I haven't had a minute to myself.'

'So, can you spare me a minute of your precious time now?'

'Yeah, of course, where's your car?' Josie asked.

'Around the corner.'

Josie threw her keys to Loveday and walked around to the passenger side of the mini. 'Drive mine, I've got a filthy headache coming on.'

As they pulled away, Josie popped a pink tablet in her mouth and took a swig of water from a bottle retrieved from the glove compartment. She closed her eyes, hoping to quell the rising nausea; glad of the respite Loveday's silent treatment gave.

Josie opened her eyes as they drove along the coast road to Newlyn. The neon lights peppering the quayside warehouses suggested they were already coming to life and she wondered which one Jem had set aside for the job. She was amazed he'd managed to keep all this from her, especially the part about the little fishmonger's business he'd grown on the side. Skirting the harbour, they'd only just ascended the steep winding hill out of the village when Loveday swerved sharply into a lay-by.

'So, what's going on?' she demanded, hands twisting on the steering wheel.

After the day she'd had, Josie was too tired to tell her about her plans and certainly too tired for a lover's tiff.

'What do you mean? I told you, I've been run off my feet all day, that's all,' she countered unconvincingly.

'It's not just that, I know you. Something is going on. You always answer your phone. Then this morning, when you came into the club, dressed up to the nines, I knew something was up. I'm not stupid! So, tell me now, have you got someone else?'

Josie had spent years perfecting her poker face under the scrutiny of her husband but somehow couldn't bring herself to use the trick on Loveday. She turned away, knowing the minute she did, she'd betrayed herself.

The tension in the car felt as thick and stifling as the atmosphere in the club, and Josie was relieved when Loveday started the engine, swung the car around, and headed at speed back the way they'd come. When they reached the narrow street around the corner from where she'd parked her car, she pulled up sharply, got out, and, leaving the engine running, walked away.

To Josie's amazement, her headache had disappeared.

TWENTY-NINE

By the time he arrived at the club, Piran was already having second thoughts. He had dismissed his mother's protests earlier that evening because he was fed up with the hysteria in the town about Carly, but he loved and respected his mum and understood why she objected so much. It was difficult for her generation; brought up on a diet of old school woman's lib. She was always on about men objectifying women; about how generations of them hadn't fought for equality just so girls like Livvy could spend their time pouting into their iPhones. She didn't buy into the whole 'this is my body and if I want to show it off, it's my right' bit.

She'd read a book recently that had debated why throughout history, whenever women gathered strength, men tried to put them back in their place. How after WW2, women were forced to swap boiler suits for pencil skirts, and in the fifties, nylon aprons confined them to the kitchen. In the sixties, apparently, even greater sins were committed; women were tagged dolly-birds and encouraged to wear skirts so short no one took them seriously. According to her, now girls were outperforming boys in school, they were once again being redefined; required to have bigger tits, bigger lips, bigger bums just so long as it detracted from their bigger brains. She ranted on about it all the time, and it pissed him off.

He'd never objectified anyone, but it didn't stop her lumping him in with every man who ever had. As a result, he'd had no intention of climbing down when she'd told him he shouldn't be going to watch Carly, even though he didn't want to. He'd gone along with it because Jack was his best friend and he hadn't wanted to let his mate down.

The rest of the boys were well on their way to oblivion by the time they got there. He, as usual, had paced himself. He didn't know why he found it so difficult to let himself go. He didn't like the feeling of being out of control, and not for the first time he was the only one sober as they queued to enter Mermaids.

Once inside, they made their way to the bar and ordered a round of shots. Ten minutes later, the lights dimmed, and Carly took to the stage.

She posed in the spotlight; head tilted back; eyes following the contour of her outstretched arm towards the canopy of starry lights in the ceiling above her.

Then slowly, she curved her body around the pole; swinging herself high, then sliding back down. He wasn't the novice his mother thought. He'd been to places like this before, but Carly's moves were unfamiliar. He looked around at the vacant expressions of his friends. The contents of Jack's tilted glass had dribbled down the front of his shirt. Save for the lilting music, the place was eerily quiet. He alone, among them, was not a participant in the trance. He could see how mesmerising Carly was; how seductive and provocative, but he'd remained an observer.

He touched Jack's shoulder and got no response. He was like a waxwork dummy, a facsimile of himself; as if the real Jack, the rampant stag of an hour before, had left the building.

He weaved his way around the scene of frozen rapture towards the loos. He didn't want to see any more. Out of the corner of his eye, he noticed Treeve and his mate Mike, the bloke he'd met in prison who'd got him the job with Jem. Thick-set, in a cheap black suit, Treeve looked well at home. His mum deserved better.

It was then he'd noticed John Taylor sitting between them.

'Come down ... come down off the stage,' he yelled.

Fuck, he thought, those animals are making him watch.

He ran out then, found the loos and sat in a cubicle until he heard the music stop.

Carly was leaving the stage as he re-entered the room.

He didn't know why, but he shouted out to her above the deafening applause, and she turned to look at him, her lips parting in a broad warm smile.

He stretched to help her off the stage.

He imagined any minute one of the bouncers would come and chuck him out, but they were still fussing at the other end of the room. He could see Jem and Treeve, but Mike and Carly's dad had gone.

He expected Carly to let go once she'd stepped down, but she didn't. Instead, she pulled him past four scantily clad girls up the narrow staircase to the first floor.

He followed the magnetic sway of her hips, blue and silver. On the landing, she turned left, opening a door into a small, dimly lit bedroom. Once inside, she let go of his hand, shut the door and gestured him to sit. He'd looked around and, finding no chair, pitched awkwardly on the edge of the bed.

He suddenly felt embarrassed. This, unlike the club, felt intimate. Here, he was the lone voyeur. Carly had seemed to sense his unease and unhooked a turquoise silk robe from the back of the door.

He studied his fists, clenched tightly in his lap. He'd felt himself harden as he walked behind her up the stairs and was desperate to conceal the tell-tale sign of arousal.

Kneeling in front of him, she'd gently peeled his hands away, placing his palms flat on the bed, either side of him, her fingers deliciously cold. He ached for her. She kissed him gently; inching her tongue between his teeth. Releasing him for one agonising moment, she'd pulled his t-shirt over his head before letting her robe slip to the floor and pushing him back onto the bed.

Straddling him, she'd let her silky hair fall about his head onto the pillow like a veil, so he could see nothing but her. Her small breasts skimmed his chest as her knees clamped his sides so he could barely move. He'd tried to lift her away for just a second, to free himself from the rest of his clothes, but she wouldn't release him, pinning his thighs together as she guided him. Her pale skin seemed to glow with soft, paper-lantern light, and as her hair fell away from her lovely face, her eyes flashed the colour of sea glass.

Pulling himself up to meet her, they clung to each other, rippling like waves. He felt a rush, like electricity, chase through him as his hips lifted from the bed.

As the tension subsided, he'd felt at risk of melting away; disintegrating like a sandcastle consumed by the tide, until nothing was left of him. Carly had laid on top of him; head resting on his chest for several minutes before peeling away, retrieving her robe and leaving.

As the minutes passed, he'd guessed she wasn't coming back and left to re-join his friends. On the way out, he had looked for her, but she was nowhere to be seen.

He crept home in the early hours, making as little noise as possible so as not to wake his mother and run the risk of an inquisition.

THIRTY

John felt the thumping music through the skin of the building as he steadied himself against the wall and retched.

'Do yourself a favour, mate, and fuck off; the show's over,' the thick-necked bouncer standing guard outside shouted across at him, disgust spidering his face.

John wiped away the trickle of yellow bile with his sleeve and shivered.

He knew every inch of this street. He could walk in any direction, knock on any door, and know the occupant's first name when they answered, but he felt like a stranger; an imposter who they'd have every right to turn away.

He lifted a hand to his shoulder. It was tender where he'd been grabbed. He felt old and wasted, a dry sob heaving its way into his chest.

Should he cry, would it make him feel better to let the pain escape? Alice would say so if she were here. He hadn't cried for years, not since those days after Carly was born before they knew she was okay. Perhaps he couldn't cry anymore. Perhaps the years of holding it in, of being strong for Alice and Carly, had left him dry and brittle as an autumn leaf, all the green had gone; all the youth and all the fight.

Jem had seen it. He had smelt defeat on him when he held him and made him watch Carly.

He'd tried desperately not to but had been forced to watch his daughter, writhing and swaying, while men leered on. *Oh, God ... Oh, God.* He balled his fists to his eyes, trying to gouge the image away, but it wouldn't budge.

He remembered Jem's voice rasping in his ear as the men held his arms.

'She's lovely, isn't she. Look at her ... go on, look at her. Have you ever seen anything so bleeding lovely in your life? Look around the room; all those men with their tongues hanging out. Like the song said *everybody wants her*. They'd do it to her right here and now if I let them ... Oh, don't worry, I won't. Unlike you, I know how to protect her; she's safe with me. I give nothing away; leastways, nothing that belongs to me. Of course, she knows that. It's why she's here. How does it feel to know she'd rather be here with me than with you? I'd be furious if it were my daughter up there, flaunting herself. I'd do something about it, but not you, you pussy. You're all mouth.'

The man was right. He was no use to anyone. All he'd ever wanted to be was a husband and father. As long as he could provide for Alice and Carly, it was enough for him, but Jem had taken everything; his business, his daughter; his pride. He could barely look Alice in the eye anymore. She deserved better.

The wind sent his jacket billowing like a sail as he staggered back to his car. He grabbed at it, pulling it tight around him, clinging onto himself in case he blew away too. *Would it matter so very much if he did?*

Later, he slipped silently into bed beside Alice. He lay awake watching the reflection of the harbour lights twinkle on the bedroom ceiling, the image of Carly's naked body returning, again and again, coiling around his thoughts like a snake.

THIRTY-ONE

Jem glanced down at his Rolex as he climbed the stairs to his office; three-thirty.

The show had been a success; better than he could have imagined. Lorraine had counted the cash and given him the good news. All he had to do was enter the figures in the ledgers and put them in the safe for banking tomorrow.

He half expected to see Lorraine upstairs but then remembered the conversation they'd had where she'd told him she wouldn't be staying at the club anymore; that she'd made different arrangements. He wondered if she had a new boyfriend. He didn't much care and certainly wasn't going to fall out with her about it. Mistresses were two-a-penny, but good managers were harder to find. He wandered through to his office and poured himself a drink.

He'd looked for Josie downstairs but couldn't find her and guessed she'd gone home, knowing he'd stay at the club tonight. The boys had seen the last of the punters off the premises and gone home. There was only him and Carly there now.

She'd been incredible but would have been even better had her dick of a father not tried to ruin it, he thought. What a loser Taylor was. Some people never knew when they were beaten; when to lie down. He'd told him a few home truths and made him sit and watch Carly dance and what had he done, run off like a scalded cat. Now, hopefully, he'd have the sense to keep away. He didn't want the man's antics upsetting the girl. It wasn't just about the performance; he didn't want Carly being constantly reminded of her old life.

He heard her bedroom door open. Jumping up, he walked quickly to catch her as she made her way to the bathroom.

'Carly,' he said, trying to sound matter of fact, despite the ridiculous thumping in his chest, as she turned to face him. 'I just wanted to say you were wonderful tonight; brilliant.'

She nodded and smiled, turning away again to continue her walk along the corridor.

He reached out his hand to pull her back, retracting it quickly, thinking better of it.

'Would you like to join me in a drink to celebrate? Just a small one, a nightcap.'

He expected her to shake her head, but she swerved left, leading the way into his office, taking a seat at his desk.

He grabbed another glass from the cabinet and, lifting the decanter, poured her a small brandy, topping himself up at the same time.

To his surprise, he was suddenly lost for words. It was a sensation he was completely unfamiliar with. He'd always had the gift of the gab, but staring at her lovely face, still sparkling with silver glitter, he felt like a tongue-tied schoolboy. He knew he could wait forever for her to say something and felt awkward. His mind flashed back to John Taylor.

'I'm sorry about all that stuff with your dad. I hope you understand, I only did what I did to make sure the show went smoothly and nobody, especially you, got hurt.'

He noticed a small frown knot Carly's brow and parried quickly, worried he'd taken the conversation down the wrong track.

'I just had a quiet word to reassure him you were perfectly happy and not to worry,' he lied.

She reached across the desk and gently touched his arm in a gesture he took to be understanding. He tingled with pleasure. He was having difficulty coming to terms with his feelings for this girl. Beautiful as she was, the not speaking bit would have usually freaked him out. He gifted a good whack to charity; it was good for business, but he turned down the invites to the open days. Josie always did her bit, though he told her in no uncertain terms she could go if she wanted, but those people creeped him out.

Carly was different. Her silence made her more attractive. He could talk to her, confide in her, divulge his deepest fears and greatest hopes and she wouldn't interrupt, criticise or repeat any of it. He didn't have any real friends he could talk to. He had to keep his own counsel; watch what he said; never show weakness, but he could relax with her. She was like a brief or a priest, but without the price tag or religious bullshit.

'I've got such plans for us,' he continued. 'That prick Theo Morgan thinks he's god's gift, but I'm the one who is gonna pull this deal off, not that I trust him to admit it. He thinks he's smart, but I'll make sure everyone knows it was me who made this work. They'll see they don't need him, and it's me who runs the show and controls the dozy locals; no offence.'

Satisfied his backtracking had done the trick, he continued.

'It's a blank canvas see ... this place. All those kids desperate for a bit of fun stuck down here with sod all to do. If I'd been born in the sticks, I'd have started on the smack when I was still in my pram.'

Raucous laughter exploded from his mouth; a rasping fit of coughing leaving him red-faced and reaching for the Jameson's.

Once he'd recovered and checked he still had her attention, he continued. 'It's ripe for the picking, whereas in the cities, London and Manchester, you've got Ukrainians and Armenians peddling the stuff; carrying it around on scooters chucking acid in people's faces ... it's bloody barbaric. No bugger's in control anymore. It's a free-for-all, not like the old days.'

He noticed tears puddling in Carly's beautiful eyes. Reaching across to touch her arm he whispered, 'Oh no, no, you mustn't worry, we won't have any of that down here. Don't you fret.'

He pulled a neatly folded hanky from his pocket, pausing for a second to admire the monogram before handing it to her.

'As long as people are happy to pay for the shit and spend money in the club and the casino when it's built, why come over all heavy. It's bad for business, I realise that now. No, we want as many people hooked as possible without any of the wrong kind of attention.'

He smiled broadly, patting her hand again.

'It's gonna be a classy operation and, you, darling,' he raised her fingers to his lips, 'will be by my side all the way.'

He surveyed the piles of money on the desk.

'That lot's down to *you*.' he said.

He knew Lorraine had taken care of everything money-wise when the girl moved in. He knew she had free board and got her wages with the rest of the girls but had no idea how much they were? Whatever it was, it wasn't enough. He grabbed a pile of notes and pushed them across the desk to her.

'That's for you, for doing such a great job. Go buy yourself something nice, a dress or some jewellery, whatever you want.'

Carly pushed the money back towards him, shaking her head.

'No ... no, that's for YOU,' he insisted, unsure if she understood him.

Carly finished her drink and, leaving the money where it was, walked out of the room, consigning Jem to stunned silence.

She was the only woman who had ever turned down his money, including his mother. She'd been more than happy for him to stray on the wrong side of the law, so long as she got a share of the spoils. He thought of her with her peroxide hair and bottle of London Gin tucked in her stocking top and shuddered, *bloodsucking bitch*, he thought. He'd got away from her as soon as he could. He hadn't known his father and hadn't wanted to either. He knew he was one of his mother's Johns, *some desperate prick stupid enough to pay money to get into her skanky knickers,* he thought pouring himself another drink.

Josie wasn't much better with her hand always out; wasting money on clothes she already had in her wardrobe. Same with Lorraine and all the others like her who got more than their fair share too. None of them were like Carly, she didn't want his money, and if she didn't want his money, maybe there was something else she wanted; him? He hardly dared to hope it. There was a stirring deep inside his gut he'd never felt before, not for anyone. All he wanted was to make her happy.

He finished his drink and walked to the landing. Pausing, he searched for light coming from under Carly's bedroom door. There was none. *She was probably tired,* he thought, *after all the excitement and had gone to bed.* He turned to walk away, then paused.

Overwhelmed by the urge to enter, he gently turned the handle and peered into the darkness. He could just make out the line of her body under the sheets. In the light shining from the landing, he saw her red hair spread in waves across her pillow, and his heart leapt. She looked so peaceful, so still. He wanted to touch her but dare not; not yet.

Taking care not to wake her, he backed out of the room and closed the door.

He felt a tightness in his throat he barely recognised and generally only experienced when watching *Rocky* on TV at Christmas.

Sitting back at his desk, he began to write the details of the takings out in duplicate. One set for the tax man, one set for him. The figures looked blurry, and he blinked. Raising his hand to rub his eyes, he felt the wetness of tears.

Bloody hell, Jem, get a grip, he moaned, as he carried the money to the safe.

THIRTY-TWO
Carly

What shallow creatures men are; driven by the thing that hangs between their legs; casting their scent around the club like tomcats. I smelt the same perfume on Josie tonight as she stroked my face with streaks of silver and blue. Not Jem, or the honey-dew sweetness of her pretty lover, but the heavy civet of an alpha male. At that moment, I knew Josie had been with the man called Theo, the one Jem hates, whose tawny skin, warm and spicy as cinnamon, I'd smelt as he brushed past me a week ago at the club.

I wonder if he needs Josie, or she needs him?

People confuse need with love, but they are not the same. Love is about want. Need is about ownership.

I saw Piran and his friends come into the club from behind the stage curtain. I know them all; went to school with most of them but was surprised Piran came. I knew once I saw him I was dancing just for him, and the other men would have to wait; knew it was time for my needs to be satisfied, my time to fall in love. It's why I didn't notice my father; had to hear about him from Jem. In a way, I'm glad. If I'd seen him, the urge to leave the stage and embrace him, make him feel needed, would have overwhelmed me but would have ruined everything.

His mulish persistence achieves nothing. He'll always lose against men like Jem; he's not built for battle. He thinks my silence makes me weak, makes me vulnerable to men. He worries that without his protection, I won't survive.

I hear Jem creep into my room and feign sleep. I'm not afraid of him. I'm in control. I don't need his pathetic handouts; I want much more than that. I've made him need me, and now he's mine for the taking. It's my guess Josie has made Theo need her too.

THIRTY-THREE

As morning's marmalade glow lit the room John had an idea. It was his turn to do the weekend shop at the supermarket in Penzance. *It was obvious; why hadn't he thought of it sooner?*

'I thought I might call in on my mother on the way, so I'll probably be a bit late home. Can you manage without me?'

'Yes, I'll be fine. It looks like it's going to be a scorcher. The tourists will be on the beach if they've got any sense. I don't suppose we'll get many in until after four. I might even shut the door for an hour or two at lunchtime if we're not busy. You can take your time; there's nothing on the list that'll spoil.' Alice pushed the list across the table. He put it in the breast pocket of his shirt, tapping it to acknowledge it was safe with him.

'Okay, see you later, love.' he said, pressing a fleeting kiss on her forehead.

Alice reached up, fondly touching his face. 'Oh, and tell your mother I'll take her some saffron buns next Wednesday when I make a batch. She'll need to make a bit of room in her freezer so she can keep some back in case anyone calls round. She was complaining the other day she didn't have anything to give visitors. She's too old to be baking, especially with that damn oven of hers.'

'Why doesn't she just buy them?' John asked. 'I could get her some if you like?'

'What, bought saffron buns? Wash your mouth out, John Taylor!'

He noticed when she smiled his wife's blue eyes were as bright as the day he'd married her, only she didn't smile much anymore. Perhaps his plan would change that. Once she got Carly back, maybe she'd be able to smile again?

He left her busying herself with the washing up and took the road out of town towards Hayle. Passing through familiar streets, he took the left-hand turn by the park, up towards Phillack where his eighty-five-year-old mother lived alone since his father died five years before. The terraced cottage had belonged to his grandparents. His mother and father retired there when he and Alice took over the pub.

As he opened the gate, he felt a pang of guilt for not having visited for a while. He'd left it to Alice. He found it too difficult to talk about Carly. The gossipy raking over of his daughter's disappearance was more than John could deal with, even though he understood that for his mother, it helped her reinforce Carly's miraculous rescue. The trouble was, John knew it hadn't been a happy ending. He couldn't tell her the truth because she'd want to know what he was doing about it. Then he'd have to admit he was doing nothing; that he was a coward.

He felt a whoosh of stale air and the weight of his impotence as he opened the weather-peeled front door with his key. The place dozed in a deep moth-balled sleep; like a princess waiting to be woken; his mother the kindly old retainer. He paused for a second to watch the dust motes dance in the front room to his left, used only for best.

His mother would be at the back of the house, in the box room off the kitchen. The Cornish range, its cast-iron face stern, polished handles gleaming in the pokey darkness, churned out a steady heat all year in the room she called the snug.

'Ma ... are you there?'

There was no answer. His mother wasn't in her usual chair, but there was a cup of tea on the table next to it, so she hadn't gone far. He sat on the sofa opposite, moving a newspaper to one side to make room. The walls were covered in family photographs; history towering over him, like a shrine to his failure.

His thoughts were interrupted by the sound of the back door closing and his mother walking in, carrying a bowl of sun-warm tomatoes, freshly picked from her greenhouse.

'Hello my 'andsome,' she smiled, clearly delighted by the unexpected visit from the son she rarely saw these days. 'I didn't hear you come in. I was up the garden. I'll put the kettle on. You'd like a cuppa, I expect, but I'm afraid I've got no cake to offer you.'

'Alice said she'll bring you some saffron buns on Wednesday, so keep your freezer free.'

He could hear himself repeating his wife's words and knew, had his mother not mentioned cake, he wouldn't have remembered.

'Smashing. I like to have something in if visitors come, but it's a bit much for me to bake these days and the shop ones aren't right, they don't use enough saffron, it's all yellow colouring, I reckon.'

He quickly steered her away from the subject before she got onto the sacrilege of vegetarian pasties, which was another of her bugbears.

'Is Dad's old dinghy still moored down on the Saltings?'

She came back into the room carrying a paper bag full of tomatoes for him, which she placed on the table.

She was a small, sturdy woman with none of the brittle, papery frailty of old age. She stood solid in the doorway, her knuckles swollen out of shape by arthritis, exacerbated by years of ringing cloths and pulling pints behind the bar. It was a body used to hard work and committed to fighting time with every sinew it could muster. Her face was remarkably smooth and her hair, steely grey, retained a stray flash of dark chestnut here and there. She wore an apron, and John realised he'd rarely seen his mother without it.

'Yes, still there,' she replied. 'The engine is up the shed.'

'I might take it out for a bit of fishing myself. Now I've not got the pub, I've got more time to spare. I thought I'd take her out for a spin to see how she goes before I start thinking of buying a new rod.'

'It'll be good for you to get out on the water. Your father always liked to get out on a fine day. He said there was no better medicine; it made him think straight when he had something going round in his head. Maybe you could take Carly, and she could do me a picture, that would be nice. I could do with a new picture to put up. She's always loved the sea, that girl. A chip off the old block. How is she ... Carly?'

'Fine, fine; a day at a time, you know.'

He didn't want to talk about what Carly was up to. He'd never actually lied to his mother about her and was amazed she hadn't already heard, given the gossip-mongering that went on in the village but he guessed she saw fewer people these days, and a lap dancing club in Penzance was off the radar for the church ladies and her knitting circle.

'You must bring her over next time you call; I haven't seen her for weeks.'

'Oh, you know what teenagers are like, always busy with their friends. Is there fuel in the engine?' he asked, changing the subject.

'Yes, and a billy-can full as well. Your dad kept it so he didn't have to waste time when he wanted to get an early start.'

'I'll just go up and have a look.'

'What about your tea?'

'I'll have it when I come back down,' he said kindly, kissing her on her warm cheek on his way to the back door.

The timber shed stood at the top of the sloping back garden. Its silvered wood looked in want of a coat of creosote. He pulled back the latch. Inside, his father's tools hung regimentally around its walls; shovels, hoes, garden forks all polished and ready for action, redundant and useless. *Like me,* John thought.

His mother employed a handyman from the village to mow the lawn, keeping only the greenhouse as her domain.

He scanned the dimly lit space for the engine. He spotted it propped up in the corner, a navy-blue tarpaulin casually tossed over the blades to protect the legs of anyone who should accidentally stumble upon it. To its side, a green plastic petrol can, which he lifted and felt by its weight was full, just as his mother had said.

Wrapping the tarpaulin around the small engine, he carried it and the can of fuel through the house to the car while his mother looked on from the kitchen.

Returning to the front door, he could see her running a tea-towel through her hands at the end of the passageway, the sunlight from the street streaking her face.

'Your tea's going cold,' she said, screwing up her eyes against the glare, 'and you've left your tomatoes behind ...'

He didn't reply.

All she could see was the silhouette of her son in the doorway, the light bright behind him. It was a vision she'd see every day for the rest of her life. What she couldn't see was his face or the tears streaming down it.

THIRTY-FOUR

John drove to the Saltings, to the quay where his father's boat was moored. He parked the car and carried the engine and the petrol down the pebbled beach.

Fitting the outboard motor, the way he'd done a hundred times before, he placed the can in the boat, pushed it out and jumped in. When he had enough clearance, he started the engine and headed away from the shore out of the estuary, watching the sea change from turquoise to intense cobalt blue as the water deepened.

He breathed in, filling his nostrils with the cleansing fresh air that once would have been the smelling salts to all his ailments. His old self would have welcomed its magical power, but he didn't want his head clear today. He was happy to revel in the muddled thinking that had invaded his brain and hung like sea mist the night before at the club. Since then, all his senses had been dulled. Even now, as he steered the dinghy further and further out, the sound of the outboard motor seemed reassuringly distant like a buzzing fly in a windowless room.

Eventually, he cut the engine and sat for a while looking back towards the coast where his life had once been. That world, like Carly, was lost to him now. Alice would be better off without him. He'd made everything worse. With him gone, Carly would come home, she'd see the need to be there for her mother; to comfort her. He was sure of it.

They'd been wrong to try and move on, thinking if they didn't talk about her ordeal, the memory would fade more quickly. Carly needed help; professional help. Otherwise, why would she be behaving in this way?

Alice would get it for her when she came home and

everything would be alright again. They'd be able to put the past behind them, but not if he was there as a constant reminder of her struggle and his inadequacy. There was no going back, for either of them. No wonder she was punishing him; she had reason to be angry. He'd let her down.

John moved to the front of the boat. Picking up the can of fuel, he unscrewed the lid and began shaking it around the deck and over the top of the engine. He felt into his top pocket and pulled out the shopping list Alice had given him and the matches he'd brought for the task.

Lighting the paper, he let it drop to the deck of the dinghy and watched the blue flames lick around his feet. He supposed there must be pain, although he couldn't feel it. When it finally hit, the heat was so intense and the agony so great, it was too much to fathom. His engulfed body fell to the floor of the boat. With one last effort, he turned his eye towards the sky; took his last breath and let go.

Later that evening, Alice rang her mother-in-law who confirmed John had called that morning and taken out his father's boat. Alice alerted the coast guard, who after a search extending into the early hours of Sunday morning, found the burnt-out wreckage of the dinghy and her husband's charred body.

THIRTY-FIVE

Karenza sat with Alice most of the evening after she called to say John was missing.

When the burnt-out boat was found, her friend deflated like a cartoon character flattened by a train. Finally persuading her to take one of the sedatives prescribed by her doctor during Carly's disappearance; she wandered home. It was two in the morning and, frozen with fatigue, she was looking forward to her bed.

As she walked along the squeezed streets bordered on both sides by revamped fishermen's cottages she couldn't help but wonder how many fretful nights had been spent within them. How many women before Alice had waited for their man to return from the sea and how many had felt the same loss? The town wore the sunny face of tourism these days but the shabby chic painted walls were only a couple of Farrow and Ball coats away from the sea-damp hovels they had always been. When the town woke to the news of John's death, old wounds would be ripped open; old tragedies re-lived.

She'd expected the house to be quiet but as she opened the door she could hear the TV. Dropping her bag, she marched into the living room to turn it off; ready to have a go at whoever left it playing to itself the next morning.

Treeve was there; a three-quarters drunk bottle of cheap vodka and a shot glass resting on the coffee table in front of him.

'Treeve?'

She picked up the bottle, holding it towards him, tilting it slightly as she did so to show how little was left. She sensed the despair in his blurry eyes wasn't just about the booze.

'Have you been with Alice?' he asked.

'Yes, they've found a dinghy and a body; and they're sure it's him.' Her voice broke with the finality of it.

'I know, I was on the quay when they dragged him in. The word is he topped himself,' slurred Treeve grimacing. His mouth opened as if he were about to say something but nothing came.

Karenza's anger at finding him drunk waned as his head fell into his hands, and he began to groan.

'It's my fault. It's all my fault.'

'What's your fault?'

She crouched down to his level; turning his head towards her, so she could look him in the eye. She resisted the urge to pull back when his hot vodka breath hit her.

'John Taylor's death. It's because I made him watch Carly.'

'*Watch Carly*, what are you talking about?'

He flicked his head away, grabbing for the bottle, pulling the shot glass towards him.

Karenza knocked it out of his hand.

'What are you talking about?' she shouted.

He gazed at the glass as it rolled across the floor, tears clouding in his eyes.

'I made him watch Carly dance naked. I held him and made him watch her.'

'When, when did you do this?' she asked, sluggishly trying to make sense of what he was telling her.

'Friday night.'

Karenza slumped down in the chair next to him as it dawned on her what he meant.

Slowly, struggling now and again to keep the thread, Treeve told her the whole story; how John had come to the club to try and stop Carly's performance. As she listened, Karenza knew Jem had done this, and they had to get away from him.

Carly was beyond saving, Alice had said as much, and John had lost the fight. She had to protect her own.

'You've got to leave that job. It doesn't matter about the money. There are other jobs. Jem is evil; pure evil. Just go there tomorrow and tell him you quit.'

'I can't do that,' he slurred.

'Why on earth not?'

She wasn't sure whether his listlessness was down to the drink or just him. He was hopeless. She asked him again, 'Why ... why can't you?'

In desperation, she picked up the glass from the floor and poured him a shot.

She held it at a distance from him as a prize for the information he was having trouble parting with. 'Why?' she demanded, sliding the glass towards his hand.

He necked it in one.

'Because he needs me to do this job for him. He needs the Auntie Lou, and I know too much about it for him to just let me leave.'

'The Auntie Lou, why does he need your boat?'

He had been working on the boat off and on for weeks now. Karenza assumed it was part of his plan to get it ship-shape and back on the water so he could re-apply for a fishing licence. She'd not considered where the money was coming from to do the work. She assumed he'd been able to put a bit by from his wages, and during the day had free time to spend working on her.

She hadn't asked too many questions because she wasn't that interested. She'd been glad he was occupied because it meant she'd been able to avoid 'the talk'; the conversation that would end with her asking him to pack his bags.

Little by little, as she fed him shots, he told her how there was a shipment of cocaine coming in, and he was meant to take the Auntie Lou out to sea to collect it from another boat. He was to drop it at another location, to be taken ashore by dinghy.

After that, he didn't know what was happening to it.

'Why didn't you just say no, for god's sake?'

'You don't say no to men like Fielding.'

'Why didn't you say you'd sold the Auntie Lou, or she was beyond repair ... anything?'

'I don't know. I don't know,' he moaned.

'Then, you have to say no now,' she said, sympathy waning.

'I can't, I've taken the money for the boat repairs, and he's made it clear there was no way out now I know about the drugs.'

'What do you mean he's made it clear?'

'For Christ's sake, Karenza, what do you think I mean? To use his words, *I wouldn't be needing a boat or anything else where I'd be going.* He also made it clear if I ran or grassed him up, he'd go after my family. That means you and the kids, Karenza. You're the only family I've got.'

She didn't have the heart to tell him they weren't his family, that the very thought of her family being tied to him filled her with dread. He was just a bloke she'd been stupid enough to fall for. She no longer felt anything for him other than a dull sense of responsibility for having led him on in the first place and for encouraging him to work for Jem because she'd been too gutless to dump him. His revelation he'd played a part in John's humiliation made her feel sick and ashamed. How could she look Alice in the eye?

Her head thrummed as she struggled to fathom what to do.

Then it came to her. She had options, of course, she did. She *did* have family to ask for help. She certainly didn't want to worry her dad, but Ross was in the police. She needed protection, and he was it. Treeve had got himself into something; now Ross would get them out of it. He'd know what to do.

'Look, you can't be part of this. There can be no winners here. If it goes well, you're bound to Jem forever. If it goes wrong, you go back to prison. Either way, you lose, not to mention the danger this family is in. I'm going to speak to Ross. I'm going to tell him what you've told me.'

'You can't, you can't!'

'I know you don't like him,' she said sharply, ignoring his pleas, 'got some stupid macho thing going on between you two, but this is serious.'

Treeve leapt up from his chair and grabbed her by her wrists.

'No, Karenza, you can't please ... please, don't. They'll get me wherever I am, whatever I do. They'll know it was me who grassed them up because they'll find out your connection with Ross,' he pleaded.

He looked petrified. Karenza had never seen her bulking boyfriend in such a state, the force of his grip travelling up her forearms.

'Okay ... okay, calm down, I won't tell Ross. I won't tell anyone,' she shouted, breaking away. 'We'll just have to get through this as best we can and when it's done, think of a way to get out of this,' she mollified.

Treeve would have to be kept in the dark. He was not up to subterfuge, and if he caved in and told Jem of her intentions before Ross had the chance to sort this, God only knew what might happen. She'd have to wait until she could see Ross on his own. It would be humiliating to ask him for help. He'd think her a fool, or worse still irresponsible for getting herself mixed up with someone who had put her and his children in danger, but at least he could be trusted to help, and what choice did she have?

Like her father said, everything Jem touched turned bad. She should have followed her instincts and ditched Treeve when he'd taken the job. She'd been a coward, and she was paying the price. Now his mess was her mess too.

THIRTY-SIX

Josie got the text from Loveday early Sunday morning;
Call me.

After their row, she hadn't expected to hear from her and had spent the last two nights lying awake wondering whether she should cut her losses. Self-preservation had kicked in on Friday night, and since then, she'd been clinging on by her fingertips. The relief at seeing the text made her determined to tell Loveday everything no matter what the consequences. Anything was better than the emotional limbo she found herself in and the risk of another chunk of her life being wasted on a man she didn't love.

She texted back, arranging to meet later that morning for coffee in St. Ives. She thought if she confessed in a public place, she'd be forced to hold herself together.

Loveday was already there when she arrived; nursing a cappuccino. She looked beautiful but forlorn, dressed in a grubby t-shirt and jeans as if she'd pulled on the first thing to hand. Wanting to take everything in, every nuance, just in case this was the last time she saw her, Josie paused by the entrance and reflected how her lover was incapable of hiding her feelings. Some people wore their hearts on their sleeves. Loveday carried hers like a motto through a stick of rock. It was possible when she told her about Theo, that would be it. Terrible as the thought was, she would commit it to memory and face what she'd done.

She walked across the black and white chequered tiles, touching Loveday's shoulder as she slid into the chair opposite. She'd half expected her to flinch at her touch, but she didn't.

'Hi,' she said coyly as the waitress approached to take her order, 'tea please, lemon no milk.'

Loveday looked up fleetingly.

Josie took a deep breath, determined to begin her confession before the waitress returned, and she lost her nerve, but Loveday interrupted.

'Something terrible has happened, and I thought you'd want to know?'

'What's happened?'

'It's John Taylor, Carly's father, they found his body at sea last night. He set fire to his boat. He killed himself.'

'How come you know this?'

'Renna phoned me, she was with Alice Taylor last night when they found him.'

Josie remembered Friday night; the poor man's humiliation. Jem had a hand in this; she knew it. 'Look, Loveday, John Taylor came to the club, you know the way you told me he'd done before, only this time, rather than get rid of him, Jem forced him to watch Carly strip. The man looked dreadful, and now he's done this. Jem might as well have lit the match.'

Loveday stared at her; eyes wide as saucers, lip trembling.

'He'll get away with it the same way he always has for everything else he's done over the years.'

'No, he won't, not this time.'

'You know him better than anyone, you know he never pays.'

'Maybe not until now, but things are going to change. He'll pay this time, he'll pay for everything, I promise you.'

'And what do you imagine you can do?'

'It's not what I can do, it's what *we* can do; you and me. We're going to take the bastard down.'

'And how are *we* supposed to do that?'

Josie was frustrated at Loveday's lack of belief in her. It was now or never.

'What I'm about to tell you is between us, right?'

'Okay.'

'Promise. Say it, say you promise.'

'I promise, okay, I promise.'

Josie told her about the drug deal; how she planned to take the cocaine and how the loss of it would lead to Jem being hunted down by the people he worked for.

'How on earth can we possibly pull this off?'

'I don't know *exactly*, but I do know where the coke is going to be dropped and roughly when it's going to happen.'

'That's a start I suppose, but how can we get hold of it. What's more, what are we going to do with it if we get it? Unless you're going to shop Jem to the police?'

'If I did, we'd have bigger enemies than Jem to worry about. No, it's got to look like Jem's done the dirty on his people; that way they'll deal with him without the police becoming involved.'

'And when is this going down ... isn't that what drug dealers say?' Loveday smirked.

Josie didn't bite. 'Treeve's picking the stuff up in a week's time in the early hours of Sunday morning.'

Loveday's face darkened.

'Renna's Treeve?'

'Yeah. He's picking the stuff up from a Spanish trawler in his boat.'

'The Auntie Lou?'

'I don't know. If that's his boat, then yes.'

'Does Renna know about this?'

'Of course not. *I'm* not meant to know about this.'

'Then, how do you?'

'I overheard Jem talking with Theo Morgan.'

'Theo Morgan?'

Josie had confided in Loveday about her affair with Theo; that they'd had more than a fling. Loveday's voice rose a pitch or two.

'When?'

'Look, does it matter when?'

Loveday, leaning back in her seat, began to stir her lukewarm coffee first clockwise then in the other direction.

'It matters to me,' she said.

'Theo's in Cornwall. I went to visit him at Sennen Cove with Jem. I overheard them planning the whole thing. I was listening and heard them talking.'

'So, Jem was with you?' she said, looking for the answer in her cup.

'Yes, Jem was with me.'

Loveday lifted her eyes, and the anxiety clouding her face moments before dissipated slightly.

'And you've not seen him since, I mean on your own?'

For a moment, Josie faltered, wondering if it was better for everyone if she lied. *Why inflict pain; what purpose did it serve?*

'I saw him on Friday. I was with Theo.'

The truth tumbled onto the table.

Loveday's spoon clattered into her saucer.

'I knew it, I knew there was something, and did you sleep with him?' she shouted, teeth bared.

Josie reached for her hand to calm her down; aware of heads turning in their direction.

'Listen to me, please,' she whispered.

Loveday snatched her hand away.

'You did, you bloody did. It's written all over your two-timing face,' she spat.

Flashing a look close to loathing, she scraped her chair across the tiles, jumped up and ran to the door.

Josie threw a ten-pound note on the table and followed her; 'Wait.'

She caught up enough to grab Loveday's arm and pull her into a narrow side alley off the main street. Not ideal for conversation, but it would have to do. At least there were no windows. No prying eyes to tell tales.

'Let me at least explain,' she pleaded.

Angry tears tracked Loveday's cheeks. She wiped the back of her hand across her nose. She was shaking as Josie took her hands to steady her.

'I could have lied to you back there. It wouldn't have been easy, but I could have done it. But then what would that have said about us?'

Loveday bent her head and shrugged.

'Look, I didn't sleep with him. I let him ... touch me ... kiss me, that's all.'

'And that makes it alright does it?'

'No, of course it doesn't, but I only did it to get information, to find out about the drugs so you and I can be together. I did it for us, don't you see?'

Loveday wrenched her hand away, her face defiant; her voice rising to a scream.

'For us! You made out with your old boyfriend, for us! What exactly am I to you anyway; a bi-curious interlude; a distraction from your miserable marriage?' she mocked. 'Well, you wasted your time because there is no us. Go back to Jem or Theo or who the hell you like, we're finished!'

'But you don't understand,' Josie shouted after her.

It was too late; Loveday had disappeared, and this time Josie knew there was no point going after her.

Her mobile vibrated in her bag. It was Lorraine.

'Josie, can you come to the club?'

The same worried tone she'd heard from her the day she relayed her concerns about Carly.

'Is this about Carly's father?' she asked.

'Yeah, how did you know? Her uncle just telephoned. He asked to speak to Carly, but before he did, he told me her father's body has been found in a burnt-out dinghy off the Towans.'

'How did she take it?'

'That's just it; I don't know. She ran up to her bedroom after and won't open the door. Her uncle said he was on his way but has been held up at the police station. Her mother is in a terrible state; poor man's running around trying to sort everything.'

Josie imagined how difficult it must be to be the bearer of such terrible news in any circumstances, let alone when it's met with silence at the other end of the phone.

'He wanted to tell her before she heard from anyone else because it's all around the town John Taylor killed himself. I suppose that's where you heard it?' said Lorraine.

'That's right,' Josie lied.

'I couldn't reach Jem, and you were so good with her the other night.'

'It's alright. I understand. I'll be there as soon as I can.'

THIRTY-SEVEN

Lorraine was waiting for her in the bar.

'It's okay,' Josie reassured her, 'you go, I'll try and get her to open the door so her uncle can at least talk to her when he finally gets here.'

Lorraine didn't need a second bidding.

Josie had no idea what she was going to say to the girl. She couldn't begin to imagine what was going through her head.

Pausing outside her door, she steeled herself to knock.

'Carly, it's Josie, can you open the door for me? I know you've had terrible news and probably want to be on your own, but I need to know you're okay. If you could make a sound, maybe knock on the door or something. Can you do that for me?'

She listened. There was no response for what seemed an age, then the gentlest rap on the other side of the door.

'Well done; that wasn't so bad, was it? Now, how about opening the door?'

She was relieved as the bolt slid back and the door shuffled open.

Josie was shocked at how young and frail Carly looked; legs bare, baggy jumper reaching down to her knees. All of the lithe physicality present when she danced had vanished like stardust.

Josie enfolded her, holding her close for a second before leading her to the bed. They sat together in silence until Josie found the right words to say. She couldn't tell her what she felt; that Jem had driven her father to this, but not to worry, she had hatched a plan to make him pay.

'I'm so sorry about your dad, Carly. I imagine you want to go home to be with your mum.'

Carly stared down at her hands, lying limply in her lap like broken birds.

'I'll help you gather together a few things, and then when your uncle comes you'll be ready to go.'

Josie got up to make a start, but Carly didn't move. She stared into space, the skin under her red-rimmed eyes, translucent, as her body trembled with silent sobs.

Josie grabbed the holdall sitting on top of the wardrobe and began opening drawers and packing enough for one night. Someone could take the rest of her stuff over to her in St. Ives tomorrow once she'd broken the news to Jem she'd gone. She put the uncomfortable prospect aside and distracted herself with the task in hand.

'There, that should be enough,' she said, turning to look at Carly.

She was lying on her side; knees pulled up to her chest, head buried in her pillow. Josie moved around to the other side of the bed and gently pulled the long tear-damp tresses away from her face. She was fast asleep.

THIRTY-EIGHT
Carly

When I wake, Josie's gone.

I feel under my pillow for the knife I grabbed from the bar when I put the phone down. I feel the blade, sticky with the juice of cut lemons.

'Your father is dead. I'm afraid it looks as if he took his own life.'

I play the words over in my head. It doesn't make them any more real, but I know they're true, and it's my fault.

Jem may have started this, but I dealt the lethal blow.

Pulling my jumper up, I lift the knife and begin to cut the words into my thighs. The lemon juice stings, but it's nothing compared to my pain.

They'll expect me to go home; to be a comfort to my mother, but what would that achieve? The wound would fester. I have to see this through if my dad's sacrifice is to have any meaning at all. No, I'll bide my time; embrace the tormentor and nurture the monster until he repays the favour.

When Jem comes to my room, I will be dressed and unpacked. The holdall will be back in its usual place on top of the wardrobe and I will see his relief and understand the measure of his need.

THIRTY-NINE

Karenza could tell the minute Loveday walked through the door something was wrong. Her friend was an open book; a fun plot with a scatty heroine. Today, it was a different story; a tragedy by the looks of it.

Gil took one look at her friend's manacled smile and muttered under his breath, 'Take her upstairs. I'll be alright here for half an hour. I'll give you a shout if we get a rush on.'

Loveday led the way up the ancient wooden staircase to Gil's living quarters. The narrow corridor branched at the top; right leading to the bedrooms set aside for the Air B&B guests, left to her father's sitting room. She cleaned it every week and ducked as she entered to avoid bumping her head on the lintel above the doorway. Karenza did the same. The whole place was a higgledy-piggledy mix of rickety steps and impossibly narrow corridors.

'Can I get you a coffee?'

'Have you got something stronger?'

'I think Dad keeps a bottle of whiskey in the sideboard.'

She knew her father had begun taking a shot every night before he went to bed to help him sleep after her mum's death. She retrieved the bottle and poured two glasses.

'It's Josie and me, we're finished.'

'I thought you were getting on so well. It's not Jem, is it; he's not found out about you two?'

'No, nothing like that. He doesn't know. In fact, he doesn't even seem to give a crap anymore. He's too wrapped up in all the Mermaid stuff.'

'So what then?' she asked.

Loveday flung her head back against the sofa dramatically, raising her eyes to the ancient beams.

'She's been with someone else; some bloke from her past.'

'Who?'

'He's called Theo Morgan, and he's down here because he's heading up a drug deal Jem's involved in.'

Karenza's mind shifted back to her conversation with Treeve. Her best tactic was to play dumb until she had the whole picture. If she went off on a tangent, questioning Lowdy about the drugs, she might clam up. She needed to get as much information out of her as possible. The more she knew about this thing, the more likely it was she'd be able to save Treeve from further involvement. She'd already got a name, *Theo Morgan*.

'How exactly do you know that Josie slept with this ... what's his name?'

'Theo, Theo Morgan; because she told me so ... well she didn't admit sleeping with him, only fooling around, but it's only a matter of time. Then she had the nerve to say she'd done it for us, so we could be together!'

'What did she mean by that?'

'She says she has a plan to get rid of Jem once and for all.'

Any conversation about getting rid of Jem Fielding got Karenza's attention.

'How?'

'By taking the drugs,' said Loveday. 'She met with Theo to find out the details so she can intercept the drugs and make it look like Jem's taken them.'

Karenza's mind was working overtime. They were Jem's drugs; he couldn't exactly steal them from himself.

Loveday continued; 'If Jem's bosses can be made to think he's cocked it up or worst still, taken their drugs, to sell on for himself, they'll deal with him if he doesn't run first. Either way, we'll be shot of him forever.'

So, Jem wasn't in charge.

'What else do you know about this drug deal?' Karenza asked, suddenly aware they were sitting in her living room talking about smuggling cocaine as if it were part of regular Cornish life, along with Flora Day and clotted cream.

Loveday rolled her glass between her palms.

'Lowdy, is there something you're not telling me, something I should know?'

Loveday hesitated; took another sip, and let it all out.

'They're going to use the Auntie Lou, Treeve's been chosen to collect the drugs at sea and bring them around the coast to be picked up by Morgan's boys. They'll take them to Newlyn to be packed in fish boxes and taken out of the County ... I'm so sorry.'

'It's not your fault. You didn't force Treeve to get a job with Fielding.'

Loveday clammed up immediately; her eyes stapled to the floor. Karenza could tell there was something else.

'What is it?'

'But I did encourage him to stay there.'

'What do you mean?' asked Karenza, suddenly confused.

'The night he came out of prison, when he was bragging about having landed a job earning good money, everyone else said he should listen to you and steer clear of Jem, but I'd had too much to drink and started thinking it might be good to have a friend on the inside, working for Jem; someone who'd turn a blind eye about Josie and me; someone to watch our backs.'

'Jesus, Lowdy.'

'I told him he should ignore you; you'd get over it, and he should do what he thought was best for him, regardless of what you thought.'

Karenza knew deep down, her friend's encouragement had little or no impact on Treeve's decision. After all, the following morning he'd all but decided to turn down the job with Jem. It was her who had persuaded him otherwise. She'd landed them in this mess because secretly she wanted him out of her life and saw the job with Jem as an obvious route.

Morally she should put Loveday straight, but tactically it was a bad idea. She needed her to feel responsible for Treeve's fall from grace for a little while longer. She had to meet with Josie Fielding and needed Lowdy to arrange it and the only way her friend would swallow her pride and contact her former lover was if she felt culpable.

'You selfish bitch. If you hadn't persuaded him to go against me and to work for Jem, he'd be here in the pub, working for Dad and me and my family wouldn't be in danger.'

She was on a roll, continuing quickly before she changed her mind.

'Worse still, all this was for some half-ass relationship over before it's hardly begun.'

She felt she may have gone too far with the last onslaught if Loveday's wretched expression was anything to go by.

'I'm so sorry, I feel like crap about it. I knew no good could come of working for Jem, but we were desperate.'

'It's too bloody late to be sorry. 'It's about salvaging the situation now; about making sure Josie's plan goes ahead. I need you to arrange a meeting with her for me.'

'I can't. I said I'd never speak to her again. You can't expect me to go cap in hand?"

'I can and you will; you owe me and if you don't do this, that's it, we're done. I'll never speak to you again. I'll cut you dead if I see you in the street.'

Loveday crumbled, nose running, tears rolling down her face.

'Alright ... alright, I'll do it,' she choked.

'Today; do it today. Tell her I need to speak to her ASAP. We haven't got time to muck about.'

FORTY

Karenza walked Loveday off the premises. She had to trust Josie even if her friend didn't. If not, god only knew where they were heading. She started making the list in her head;

ONE: Talk to Josie Fielding to check out her plan.

TWO: Get Ross on board.

THREE. She had no idea what three was. Everything depended on ONE and TWO.

She didn't want to go to her ex with her tail between her legs, begging him to get Treeve out of trouble. She wanted to go with a plan; give him all the information to put Jem away and move on with some dignity.

THREE: Move on.

She didn't intend for anyone else to pick up the tab for her mistakes anymore. She had to re-make her bed.

Her eyes rested on her father.

Gil Martin glanced up as she walked to the bar.

'What's up with madam then?'

'Oh nothing, the usual; woman trouble.'

'She ought to be ashamed, in tears about her bloody love life when a man is dead. She wants to walk in Alice Taylor's shoes for a while, then see what she's got to cry about, stupid girl.'

Karenza bit her tongue. She didn't want an argument, and her father's mention of Alice led conveniently to her next request.

'Dad, I know I've been tied up with Lowdy, but I promised Alice I'd go and see her when my shift was over. I've not exactly been much help to you today, but I feel I should go.'

'Don't worry about me,' he said, voice mellowing, 'you go on and pass on my condolences. My heart goes out to that poor woman.'

'Thanks, Dad, I'll make up the time, I promise,' she said, kissing his whiskery cheek.

***

She'd expected John's brother, Peter, or his wife, to answer the side door leading to the flat above the gallery and was surprised when Alice appeared in her dressing gown.

She wore the grey mask of the day before, now furrowed from a night wrestling with her pillow; eyes hollow and dry; too tired for tears.

On seeing Karenza, she turned and silently walked back upstairs, leaving her to shut the door and follow her.

'Have you slept at all?'

Alice slumped onto the sofa.

'Not really.'

'Look, I'm going to make you a cup of tea, and then you're going to take a couple more of those pills the doctor gave you and go back to bed.'

Alice didn't reply. They were close enough to enjoy the luxury of not having to speak at times like this, and Karenza let the silence settle as she washed up the few dirty cups littering the kitchen table before returning with the tea.

Alice took it, holding it between her cupped hands.

'I feel so guilty,' she muttered.

'Alice, there's no need to talk, not now, please just drink up and let's get you to bed. I'll direct the calls to the answerphone so you won't be bothered, and I'll stay until you're asleep. By the time you wake, Peter will be back.

'He offered to stay, but I didn't want him to. I wanted to be alone.'

'But he's coming over later?'

'When he's dealt with the paperwork,' Alice slurred as if she was having trouble converting the words in her head to speech.

Karenza guessed she meant the identification of John's body.

'Then I'll stay until he gets back. I expect you'll go home with him then?'

Alice jolted, slopping tea into her lap, although she didn't seem to notice.

'No, I want to stay here. It's not right to go there.'

Her voice was full of panic. Karenza didn't understand. Alice had always got on well with John's family. They were good, kind people.

'Why on earth not? You can help each other through this terrible thing. Only for a few days maybe, until after the funeral?'

Her response was emphatic.

'No.'

'Is it Carly. Do you want to be here when Carly comes home?'

Alice nodded.

'I understand,' she said, taking the cup from her friend's hand, 'then I'll come here and stay with you; until she arrives.'

'No, I want to be on my own ... I deserve to be on my own.'

'Don't be silly, Alice.'

Karenza put her arms around her. She hadn't noticed how much weight Alice had lost over the months since Carly first went missing. She'd covered it up with layers of tops and jumpers. In only a dressing gown, she felt as if her brittle bones might crumble if held too tightly and felt insubstantial after Lowdy, whose lean and muscular body had been wiry with emotion.

'I should have told him. I should have told him long ago ... I should have told him Carly wasn't his.'

The revelation landed like a slap.

'I had all those years to tell him. Before she was born, I was so scared he'd leave me and then, when she came, and she was so beautiful, so precious and he loved her so much, how could I tell him?' she sobbed.

Karenza listened, not knowing what to say; wanting to pretend she hadn't heard it at all.

'Then when Carly couldn't speak, and the doctors were asking questions about whether there was anything in our family history, I thought I should say then, in case it would help, but when they found there was nothing physically wrong, I was so relieved, I let the moment pass.'

'You don't need to tell me this, not now, not when you're so tired. You're not thinking straight,' soothed Karenza.

'Yes, I am,' Alice snapped. 'I need to tell someone. You're my friend. I need to tell someone, and you're here. You said you were here for me?'

'I am,' Karenza relented, 'I am here for you.'

'As time went on, it became too difficult to tell him, and then, when she was taken, we needed to be strong, we needed each other, and I couldn't risk it. Once she left home, I thought what's the point, now he need never know, but that was wrong.'

'Why was it wrong? What purpose would it have served? John loved Carly, and you loved John.'

'But don't you see?' whispered Alice. 'That's why it was wrong because he loved her too much. If I'd told him he wouldn't have loved her so much, and then he wouldn't have killed himself.'

'Alice, that's not so. You can't know John would have loved Carly less? We don't know why John did this, we only know it's not your fault; or Carly's. It's nobody's fault.'

Karenza heard the words slip easily from her lips, but in her head, she heard the words she couldn't use to comfort her friend.

It's not your fault; it's Jem Fielding's fault; Treeve's too, for making John watch.

Alice looked exhausted, and Karenza was beginning to feel the strain herself. Being the confidant of your friends was not all it was cracked up to be. It was not an easy ride, especially when you had problems of your own to deal with.

'Let's get you to bed.'

She pulled Alice to her feet and led her to the bedroom, settling her like she would a child between the sheets, smoothing her hair away from her forehead.

'I'm glad I've told you.'

'I'm glad too, and I promise you, I won't tell anyone about this.'

'Why haven't you asked me?'

'Asked you what?'

'Who Carly's father is?'

'Because it's none of my business. It's in the past. Let it stay in the past, Alice.'

'I want to tell you, I truly do, but I don't know. I don't know who he was.'

Alice's eyes were semi-closed now; her speech slow and laboured.

'I never knew his name,' she yawned.

As she fought sleep, Karenza watched her pass through a landscape she'd visited many times herself over the years, where the twisting tendrils of memory and dream looped.

'Carly was conceived on my eighteenth; two weeks before me and John got engaged. I never told you that before but you probably remember that year; settled hot weather and long lazy days. The year you and Ross got married.'

Karenza did remember; she had never been as happy since; least not that particular brand of happy - in love and thrilled at being pregnant for the first time.

'A group of us had bought tickets for Boardmasters. It had been a great birthday, camping up on the cliff overlooking the beach, wandering the festival, getting henna tattoos and getting high,' she smiled wistfully.

Karenza had been to the festival many times and knew exactly what she meant; the lightness of youth.

'Sometime during the evening I got separated from my crowd and strolled down to the beach to look for them. At one end, a small group gathered around a fire, listening to a girl with blonde plaits play guitar. Her voice was high and folksy; like a young Joni,' she said squeezing Karenza's hand. 'They had a laid-back vibe, and I liked it; sitting around the fire with a bunch of hippies. It felt like my Woodstock. Then someone suggested we go for a swim. They all just stripped off, but you know me; I didn't like to. I didn't know them, so I gathered up the clothes and when Joni girl asked me to watch her guitar, I was quite relieved.'

Karenza loved her friend dearly. She'd always had a reputation for not having a reputation growing up. She could see how she'd gravitated to the group of hippies. She'd always struck Karenza as more flower child than Spice Girl.

'I left the clothes in a little pile on the shoreline and wandered back up the beach to the fire. It was then I spotted him. He was playing the guitar I was meant to be watching and he was good; not the strummed chords of before. His fingers seemed to bring the thing to life.'

'What did he look like?' Karenza asked, curiosity kindled despite herself.

'I guess about twenty; jeans, white shirt loosely pulled apart. Tanned but only a faint glow, which made me think he wasn't local; not a surfer out in the sun every day. I wondered if he was one of the festival performers and he'd seen the fire and the guitar and decided to sit and play for a while. As I got near, he looked up. His coppery hair curled at the nape of his neck as if he'd been swimming. He motioned me to sit and began to sing.'

Karenza noticed Alice's cheeks redden.

'By the time he'd stopped, I was sobbing and had no idea why. I tried to stop feeling a complete idiot, thinking it was the booze or the weed I'd smoked earlier, cos I'd never smoked pot before. He didn't seem to care. He put the guitar to one side and reached across to me. I remember the touch of his fingers was icy on my wrists.'

Karenza noticed her touch her wrists as she looked off into space, recollecting every magic moment.

'I kept thinking; *What am I doing, what about John?* but the thought floated away like a feather. I felt as if my head would burst. I felt so hot, what with him and the fire. Then we were doing it, and it was so natural as if we'd known each other forever. I couldn't seem to get my bearings. I could see the light from the clifftop; hear the thump, thump of the music. I tried to focus but could see nothing but him; it was like diving into murky water.'

She paused.

'Go on.'

'I heard voices. Joni girl was standing over me; plaits dripping water onto my face. I could see her lips moving, but I couldn't hear a thing. Then suddenly John was there, trying to make me sit up. I remember I was cold, and someone pulled a blanket around my shoulders. I heard him shout; "What did you give her, what's she bloody taken?"

"Nothing, I promise you,' said one of the girls. "We were in the water. She decided to look after our stuff. When we came back, she was lying on the blanket, completely out of it."

I remember needing to vomit and there being a bitter, salty taste in my mouth as I spewed mostly water; at least half a pint. When I finally finished, I felt a bit more like myself. I was able to get to my feet and make my way with John's help back up the cliff path to the festival. As I was leaving, the girl with the plaits gave me a little kiss on the cheek, and I remember whispering so John couldn't hear; "He was playing your guitar, and it was so beautiful. He was so beautiful." Do you know what she said?'

Karenza transfixed, shook her head.

'"Who was? There was no one here with you. You were alone." That night I slept in the van, nestled tightly next to John. The next morning, I felt strangely refreshed, if a little embarrassed. John put my sickness down to the booze or a bug. I wouldn't be the first to go down with a sickness bug at a festival after all. As we packed our stuff and dismantled the tents, I scanned the crowd for the boy, but he wasn't there, and I guessed he'd left the night before. When I started putting on weight and went to the doctor to see if the pill was to blame, he told me I was pregnant; that unfortunately, the pill was not one hundred percent effective, especially if you were suffering from a stomach bug like the one I'd had that summer. When I told John the news, he naturally assumed the baby was his and was delighted. The wedding was brought forward, and we were married two months before Carly arrived.

When I saw her pale green eyes and that halo of golden hair I knew the boy was her father and later when the doctors told us about her, I tried to remember if the boy had spoken to me that evening, and do you know what. He never said a word.

FORTY-ONE

Josie got the call from Loveday the evening after their bust-up in St. Ives. The conversation was clipped and awkward.

'I'm glad you called,' she said.

'Well, don't get your hopes up, this isn't about us. It's about Renna. I know you won't like it, but I've told her about Treeve and the drugs,' she paused, 'and about you and Theo Morgan. She wants to meet you.'

Theo's name speared from Loveday's lips; an arrow designed to wound.

Had it been anyone else, Josie would have shouted at them for their feckless indiscretion, but she knew Loveday would slam the phone down if she gave her the slightest excuse, and she couldn't afford to let that happen.

'Okay,' she said calmly, 'what does she intend to do with all that *dangerous* information?'

'All I know is, she wants to meet up with you, and I owe her big time, so I agreed to set it up.'

Josie guessed the purpose of the meeting. It had been a mistake to tell Loveday about Treeve. She was a loyal friend and wouldn't want Karenza involved in anything that could compromise her safety. Treeve's involvement did that, although what his girlfriend expected her to do about it, she didn't know? She had no intention of tackling Jem about Treeve if that's what the woman was going to ask her to do. Jem didn't know she had any idea about the drug deal, other than the few snippets of information she'd learnt from him. If he thought anyone else knew; that Treeve had told Karenza or she'd spoken about this to anyone, there would be consequences.

'Where?'

'You can meet at mine if you like?' and then, 'it's more convenient for Renna,' as if she didn't want to be doing Josie any favours.

'Fine; did you tell her anything about my plan?'

The phone went quiet for a moment before Loveday answered, and Josie noticed the pique in her voice vanish, as it maybe dawned on her what she'd done.

'Yeah, I did. I probably shouldn't have, but it just slipped out.'

Damn it, thought Josie What the hell do I do now?

'I see, well then, we'd better meet as soon as possible. You arrange it, and I'll be there.'

Josie put the phone down wondering what the hell she'd started.

Why didn't she do herself a favour and take Theo up on his offer and have done with all these infuriating women?

She knew why; because she loved one of them and no matter how reckless and downright foolhardy, she was, she couldn't get her out of her mind. She just wished Loveday was capable of understanding danger. You didn't play games with Jem; at least not games you weren't certain of winning.

That said, he'd been much better tempered of late. He was so wrapped up in the club. The business was booming, and he had plenty to be pleased about. He spent increasing amounts of time with Carly. She'd seen Jem and Carly sitting together; her listening, him talking, animated and happy, and noticed a look in his eyes she'd never seen before. She'd wondered if it was the fact the girl couldn't answer him back?

At home, he'd talk about the show and Carly, then take himself off to bed. Josie hadn't pushed her luck. She hadn't mentioned she knew the man he'd forced to watch Carly dance was John Taylor and certainly had no intention of bringing up his suicide.

She had to be the dutiful wife for a little longer, and his obsession with the girl made it a whole lot easier. She'd let him take pleasure in the silence while it lasted.

FORTY-TWO
Carly

I take great trouble selecting the pink-throated shells; clams small enough to fit in a fist.

Along the outer edge of each, I scroll a single word. The same two words I whisper to myself when no one is around to hear. On the first, I have painted 'Spring; a peppering of tiny flowers celandines, forget-me-nots and yellow gorse; a carpet of new beginnings'.

On the second, a fishing boat on a choppy sea, dolphins riding in its wake reminding me of the scrimshawed whales' teeth in the County Museum. This one is for my father; this one is his truth, and it will be buried with him.

It's sad they snatched him from the sea to be given to the mud. The sea would have suited him better. Had they left him where he was, the cool green seaweed could have taken root in his mouth as his bones turned to coral. How beautiful he would have looked; his tears, salt upon the sand.

Mum believes he'll live again. She's right but not the way she thinks. He'll be food for the worms and the creatures that crawl, then for fungus and mould. Green shoots will twine around what's left of him and push through the soil towards the light, upwards and upwards until he completes his resurrection.

All living things feed off the dead of others one way or another.

FORTY-THREE

Ross drove Karenza to John's funeral. She'd hoped it would be a chance to talk to him about Treeve, but it was clear her ex wasn't in the mood for talking. Even allowing for the grim circumstances, he was morose. This was no time for confessions.

They were early, having overestimated the tourist traffic. Rather than mingle with the crowd gathering in gossipy reverence or stand in steely silence next to Ross, Karenza wandered up the steps to the graveyard.

John's coffin would be walked the short distance from his mother's cottage through the village to its final resting place. Alice had said it seemed right to leave from there rather than the flat, where they hadn't lived long enough to call home.

The churchyard had a shaded, leafy tranquillity, not at all like the windswept cemetery where her mum lay. She'd been here as a child with her nan. She recalled the squeak of the rusty tap; the tinny splash of water hitting the bottom of the watering can. There was a melancholy ritual about it; removing the droopy dead flowers from the brass-lidded vase; arranging their perky replacements.

The hum of voices ceased, and assuming the funeral party was in sight she found Ross and they made their way inside, finding a pew midway down the aisle.

The mid-afternoon sun fractured the stained-glass, casting colour wheels across the flagstones and the backs of the wooden pews as the organist began. She closed her eyes, relishing the coolness in the summer heat and the smell, a kind of musky perfume, which as a child she'd put down to God. She'd always liked lifting the red velvet cushion off its brass hook and kneeling to pray. It felt like a special thing to do; speak to God. She didn't go to church anymore, other than to weddings and funerals or on Christmas Eve after the pub shut, but as a child, she'd felt comfort in it.

They stood as the mourners stuttered down the aisle. Alice, tightly wedged between John's mother and brother Peter, looking for all the world as if she'd clatter to the floor if they stepped away. Cloaked in voluminous black folds she looked like a broken-winged blackbird fallen from its nest.

Peter's wife and children followed with a small entourage of other family members but no Carly. The girl's absence was noted as heads swivelled and turned, searching for her. Karenza guessed most would not know Carly had left home before her father's death.

The service, despite the vicar's best efforts, was wretched. The congregation did their best to mumble through the chorus of 'For Those in Peril on the Sea' as voices cracked and coughed away stifled grief. They listened to Peter's faltering voice speak of the big brother who'd taught him to sail and then to the sermon about death being a transition; a journey to somewhere else.

Karenza felt anger at the need to skirt around the truth. The man they were saying goodbye to had been so desperate, so unhappy, he'd killed himself. Not only that; he'd done it in a terrible, brutal way, and none of them and certainly not God had looked to stop him. John's misery had been caused by Fielding, and those who knew the truth didn't have the guts to do anything about it.

When the service ended, they were forced to wait while the large crowd of mourners slowly shuffled out. Only family was to stay for the internment. The rest were invited back to John's mother's house for the wake. Queuing to exit, they heard a commotion outside; raised voices and wailing; the high-pitched cry of a woman. Ross immediately slipped into police mode, grabbed her hand, pushing past the bottleneck out into the sunlight.

Once there, it was clear what was causing the uproar.

Carly stood someway off, beside the open grave prepared to receive her father. She wore a long, white cotton dress billowing in the breeze around her slender body, giving her the incongruous appearance of a summer bride. Yet, somewhat surprisingly, it wasn't her odd attire causing the furore. Through the arched lynch-gate, Jem leant nonchalantly against a bright red convertible.

Alice, on seeing him, had bolted down the path and needed to be restrained. She was being walked back up by Peter, who had a tight grip around both of her arms. The vicar stood in catatonic disbelief that the whisp of a woman who had sat so resolutely throughout the service had turned into a screaming banshee. He of course, had no idea of her reasoning, neither could he fathom why an inappropriately dressed young woman was standing motionless beside the pit where he was shortly to commit John Taylor's body. His eyes flitted back and forth between the two women as he clung to his bible as if waiting for divine intervention.

Ross left Karenza's side and, without comment, walked towards Alice. Peter, on seeing him, loosened his grip as Ross took the distraught woman into his arms. As he whispered comfort, Karenza could see Alice nodding, and when he finally broke away from her, the woman lifted her head and walked unaided back up the path towards the rest of the mourners. Relieved, the vicar gave a little nod to the funeral director who signalled for the coffin to continue its journey to the graveside. Alice and the family followed on behind.

The rest of the mourners milled around for a minute, but sensing the show was over and there was food and drink to be had, slowly moved away down the path towards the road. Karenza joined the throng, meeting Ross halfway down.

'I think you'd better stay to make sure Alice is okay,' he said discreetly.

'I'm not family. I'm not sure it's my place?'

'Renna, you're one of the few people who knows what's really going on here. You know about Carly and Fielding, and your friend needs you.'

'Where are you going?' she asked, feeling abandoned.

'I'm going to have a word with him,' he said, nodding towards Jem, who was now sitting in his car watching the procession of mourners walk away down the hill.

'Be careful, Ross.'

Ignoring her, he walked back down the path.

Karenza made her way up to the top of the graveyard, where Alice stood next to Carly. She had hold of the girl's hand; her head resting on her shoulder, eyes closed in prayer. Carly, head thrown back, squinted up through the trees, her face bathed in dappled light.

The broody, sullen Carly, Karenza had watched evolve in the months after she'd been pulled from the mine shaft was gone. This girl brimmed with life. She shimmered in her diaphanous dress like a Greek goddess. Karenza felt a shudder as if someone had walked over her grave.

Just before the coffin was lowered, Carly lifted her arms high above her head, her hands cupped; holding something. As the vicar and those around her looked on in bewilderment, she leant forward and placed whatever it was on the coffin lid. Karenza couldn't see clearly from where she stood, but a few minutes later, when she moved forward with the others to take a handful of the earth to scatter into the grave, she saw the object was a beautifully decorated shell. Karenza had seen people place mementoes on coffins before. There was nothing particularly odd about that. It was the way Carly held the shell up to the heavens; in a show of sanctification that was strange. From the look on the other mourners' faces, they were equally unnerved.

Karenza moved closer. She could just make out a tiny intricate seascape and writing along the pink lip of the shell. One word in bold italics, **SACRIFICE**.

The letters tumbled like scrabble tiles in a bag. It was a terrible word; loaded with pain, but it was the perfect word to sum up what John had done. He had paid for Fielding's monstrous actions with the only thing he had left; his life. Alice, head still resting on her daughter's soft white shoulder, began to smile as the pair gently swayed to a rhythm only they seemed to hear.

Once the gathering was dismissed, Carly unceremoniously dropped her mother's hand and began to walk slowly away. Karenza expected Alice to try and stop her; grab her, or shout after her, but she did neither. It was then she noticed Alice was holding a shell like the one resting on John's coffin; hers elaborately decorated with vines and flowers.

'Alice, are you okay?' she asked, reprimanding herself for her clumsy, insensitive words. Of course, she wasn't okay. How could she be?

'Yes, I'm fine now … now I've seen Carly,' she replied quietly.

'Is she coming home now to be with you?'

'No, I don't think so,' she said blithely looking around, 'no … she's gone.'

'Gone where?' Karenza was trying desperately not to judge but was finding the girl's behaviour reprehensible.

'Back with Jem to the club,' Alice replied flatly, looking down at the shell in her hand.

'You should have told her that her place is with you; that you need her?'

Alice didn't reply; only looked at Karenza in a way that made her feel stupid for suggesting such a thing, before turning her back on her.

As Alice took her brother-in-law's arm and walked away down the path, Karenza caught a glimpse of what was written on the shell she carried;

RETRIBUTION.

FORTY-FOUR

Karenza reached the road just in time to see Carly slipping into the seat of the Aston Martin next to Jem and them speed away. She watched as Ross's eyes followed the car's progress until it rounded the bend out of sight.

'Come on,' he said, his face grim, 'I don't feel like sausage rolls and talk of old times, let's go.'

She did not argue with that. Once in the car, she could keep quiet no longer.

'What did you say to Jem?'

She watched his brow furrow.

'Nothing much. I just asked him what his intentions were for Carly.'

'What do you mean, his intentions? He's not some Victorian suitor, he's a common pimp. You and I know he's only got one intention and that's to sell her to the highest bidder. I don't know what's wrong with everyone; first Alice, now you; have you both gone mad?'

'I know what you're saying, but I think in this instance you're wrong. He seems to genuinely care for the girl. She enjoys the dancing, and I don't think he's going to let any harm come to her.'

'What are you talking about; he's the reason for all this, for John's death? If he hadn't taken Carly, none of this would have happened, and John would still be alive.'

'John's not alive because he couldn't move on.'

'Things would have got back to normal if Jem had been forced to make Carly go home.'

She knew this was a backhanded dig at Ross for coming home without Carly the day John had been arrested, and she regretted saying it the moment it left her lips.

'We have no evidence Jem took Carly. How does that old song go? *Don't look back, you can never look back.*'

Karenza knew the song, but they weren't wearing wayfarers; weren't extras in an eighties video. *You should always try to right your wrongs. Re-write the shitty lyrics.*

Karenza's mind was no longer on John and Alice. It was firmly on herself and the hopes she'd harboured for her and Ross. Looking at his stony face, she felt deflated and miserable.

Ross, other than in her misjudged fantasies, had no interest in revisiting their relationship. He wanted to move on. She, like John, hopelessly longed for an irretrievable past.

FORTY-FIVE

Ross decided to have a drink in the pub after he'd dropped Karenza home. It had been a traumatic day; a day of goodbyes and stark reality.

He'd been completely floored when he'd got the call from the station saying they'd found John's body. He was as close to John as he'd been to any other man, but John hadn't confided in him. He knew since Carly things had soured between them.

Everyone was slipping away; John, Karenza, his kids. Everything was changing, but he was stuck and useless, unable to control events. On top of it all, some bastard had given his fifteen-year-old daughter MDMA. Karenza was right to be angry with him.

His father had been an old school copper, on the beat, then later, CID, but he'd never had to deal with the stuff he had to stomach these days. Ross had never seen his father afraid. He, on the other hand, spent most of the time petrified, frightened for his kids, for his wife, and himself; perched on a precipice. He couldn't protect them, that was clear. He hadn't been able to stop Karenza hooking up with a loser, operating on the fringes of criminality. He hadn't even been able to protect himself from Treeve's punches.

For a while, when Treeve was in prison, he'd felt in control. He'd been able to visit her and the kids and feel at ease. Her expectations had lessened and Piran and Livvy were growing up; choosing their own paths. He could dip in and out without fear of ruining things for them. His two youngest had moved up to Bristol to live near Trudy's parents. She had a new bloke who seemed prepared to take all three of them on. He'd checked him out on the police database, and he seemed sound enough.

He'd lost ground today. Karenza had rattled on about Carly and Jem and why he hadn't been brought to justice. He'd lied to her, saying you couldn't go back to how things were, that change brought consequences. In truth, he desperately wanted his old life back. He wanted to be with Karenza and the kids, but he guessed now Treeve was back he was surplus to requirements. He'd heard he was working for Jem, but he couldn't very well attack him for it. After all, to his immense shame, so was he.

He'd been in Fielding's pocket since shortly after he'd split from Trudy. Feeling sorry for himself, he'd gone to one of Jem's clubs in Plymouth and made the mistake of getting paralytically drunk. He'd woken the next morning in a strange bed with a young woman he had no recollection of ever meeting. When he left, apologising profusely, she was fine. She'd smiled saying they'd met in the bar and she'd offered him a bed for the night. He'd been too embarrassed to ask if they'd had sex, but the fact, they were both naked suggested they probably had. She seemed quite happy either way, and he assumed she was of a less inhibited generation who didn't think it a big deal.

The photos sent to his phone the next day said otherwise. They told the story of a bruised and battered girl who, according to the text, had been raped and held captive by him in her flat until the next morning. The text from Fielding said the girl worked for him, and with some persuasion on his part, was prepared not to report the incident in return for Ross agreeing to provide certain services to her employer. If he didn't agree, he could, of course, take his chances with the justice system, but the girl was prepared to give a witness statement and had photos of her own, taken on her iPhone of him naked next to a bedside table upon which could be seen, a considerable amount of white powder. She'd say the cocaine was his, and there had been a violent change culminating in the beating she'd received after he'd snorted it.

The incident had happened at a time when Trudy was already flexing her muscles about access to the kids. He knew he could wave goodbye to them and his career if the allegation were to come out, whether he was found guilty or not. People would think there was no smoke without fire, and his family would forever be the subject of cruel taunts and smutty jokes.

Now Treeve was working for Jem, he was on tenterhooks all the time in case Jem realised the connection and couldn't resist telling Karenza. He wouldn't say why he'd become crooked, of course; that he'd been set up and blackmailed. He'd merely drop the hint he was in his pocket and occasionally tipped him the wink; like he had when he'd kidnapped Carly, telling him the girl remembered nothing.

He, unlike Treeve, had no excuse for not knowing what he was getting himself into. He'd attended police briefings about Fielding; even been on the task force set up to investigate him and realised with hindsight, that was probably why he'd been targeted.

Ross had foolishly hoped the man would simply drift into obscurity and he could avoid being compromised, but then Fielding had taken Carly and put pay to that. Even though in the end he'd had to do very little because Carly remembered nothing, he still felt guilty letting Fielding in on the fact there was no evidence to incriminate him. Then, when Carly had gone to Jem's place, he'd felt sure the truth would come out. If matters had escalated that day and John had not calmed down, Fielding would have taken pleasure in rubbing salt in the wound by letting John know not only had he lost his daughter but his best friend and the man in charge of the inquiry, was bent. Jem had got away with it, of course, just as he always did, and it was John who had got the caution, just like it was John who was dead.

He had to be realistic and try to move on. He'd watch the kids to make sure there wasn't another incident like the one with

Livvy the other night, but he wouldn't interfere.

Gil pulled him a pint.

'You alright lad, bad old business eh ...?'

'Yeah, it is, but he had his reasons, I suppose, and who are we to judge?'

'I know, but when you get to my age, every little squeeze of life is worth having, especially if you're like me and believe this is all there is.'

'I suppose.'

'I would give everything for an extra day, an extra minute even, with my June. You can say an awful lot in an extra minute. Don't waste your minutes boy, they soon become days and before you know it, you've wasted a bloody lifetime not saying what you feel.'

FORTY-SIX

As planned, the women met at Loveday's flat in St. Ives the day after John Taylor's funeral.

Climbing the narrow stairs, Josie felt anxious and a little sad. There was a real possibility there was no going back for her and Loveday, and the staircase held memories. They'd climbed it on the day they'd first acknowledged their feelings for each other. They'd paused and kissed on the very step she now stood to ring the bell.

Loveday answered the door, casting a cursory glance in Josie's direction, before silently stepping back.

Karenza sat on the sofa.

She was as Loveday described her, dark-haired and pretty with pale grey eyes that looked tired as if she could do with a good night's sleep.

On seeing her, she got up and moved forward as if to shake hands; then seemed to change her mind.

'Karenza? I've heard a lot about you from Loveday,' Josie said. She never used the name she'd heard her lover called by her Cornish friends. She didn't like it. Lowdy sounded like a nickname Jem would give to one of his heavies, a name for a *geezer*.

'Do you want something to drink?' asked Loveday sulkily, pouring herself a large glass of wine.

'Just a small one, I'm driving,' she answered. Loveday still hadn't met her eye, and taking her drink, Josie moved away to sit next to Karenza.

Loveday remained propped against the breakfast bar, uncommunicative and sullen.

It was Karenza who broke the ice.

'I don't really know where to start, so I'm just going to come out with it,' she said, 'if you decide not to listen or want no part of it, I understand. Lowdy has told me about your life with Jem, so I know the risks for you.'

Josie was beginning to warm to Karenza; she had guts.

'Go on,' she said, taking a sip of wine and sitting back to listen.

'I know about the drugs, and that you've got a plan to intercept them and get your husband to take the blame.'

Josie looked at Loveday.

'Don't blame her for telling me, she had to. We've been friends for years, but even then, she wouldn't have told me had Treeve not been involved, so don't you dare say this is none of my business cause it is ...'

Josie got up and walked towards the window. She looked down at the cobbled street below, full of holidaymakers milling about, oblivious to the unravelling above their heads.

'Look, if you think I can in some way influence Jem not to do this or to pick someone else other than your boyfriend to help, you're mistaken. Things have gone too far. They need his boat, so they need him and please don't think he could run. This is not a normal job he's taken, and now he knows too much. There would be consequences you couldn't begin to imagine.'

'I know there's no easy way out, but there's the way you've talked about with Lowdy.'

Josie could tell this woman had guts, a steel backbone in times of crisis.

'I'm listening.'

'I know Treeve's meant to collect the drugs and drop them inshore so they can be picked up,' continued Karenza 'but what if he only drops some off? What if the rest are dropped off somewhere else, to be picked up by us?'

'Why leave any?' Loveday asked, confused.

'Because that'll keep them occupied for a while,' said Josie. 'They'll think some have gone adrift or sunk. It's a distraction; it'll keep them looking. If there were none, then they'd know immediately something was wrong, and we'd be pressed for time.'

'Exactly,' said Karenza.

'I see,' said Loveday, looking between the two women; seeing more similarities in the pair of them than differences.

'In the meantime, we'll pick up the rest and then deliver the haul to the police,' said Karenza

'Oh no, you've got this all wrong; we can't involve the police,' protested Josie. 'Sure, they'll arrest Jem, if he doesn't get away first and if we're lucky he'll be sent down, but it won't end there. The others will know they've been grassed up, and there will only be a few candidates. Your Treeve will be at the top of the list. Do you think they'll let that go? No way. You don't know these people. You tell the police, and you might as well sign Treeve's death warrant, and if they find out about your involvement; you might as well sign your own and your kids as well whilst you're about it.'

'But you don't understand.' said Karenza, 'I mean, perhaps get Treeve on witness protection or something. You see my ex-husband Ross is a policeman. We can trust him not to tell anyone where he got the information from. It can be an anonymous tip-off as far as anyone knows.'

Josie got up again and went to the kitchen to pour herself another glass of wine, knowing she'd need it for what she had to say next.

'You haven't got a clue, have you?' she said.

Karenza glared at her; indignant. 'Well, no, I don't mix with the same crowd you do. I'm not fully up on how drug dealers and pimps react, but I know the kind of man I can trust!'

Josie couldn't stop herself from retaliating.

'You misunderstand me. You can't tell your ex-husband because he'll tell Jem. He's on Jem's payroll. Your precious Ross is bent; has been for a couple of years, so he's the last person we can trust, and I hope for all our sakes you've not said a word to him?'

'Josie, what the hell?' Loveday shouted.

'It's true; like I would make it up. Jem's bragged about it to me; how he's got this local DI, Ross Trenear who watches his back for him, who tips him off.'

Karenza looked between Josie and Loveday, her face vacant as if she'd missed the punchline to a bad joke and that any minute they'd explain she'd heard wrong. When they didn't, she made for the door.

'I've got to go. I'm sorry ... sorry I wasted your time.'

Josie grabbed her arm as she brushed past her. She felt sympathy for the woman but wasn't prepared to risk her safety for her.

'Have you told him; tell me now if you have?'

'No, no, I haven't,' Karenza spat, pulling her arm away as she flung open the door and stumbled down the stairs to the street below.

'Karenza, wait!' shouted Loveday after her.

'Leave me alone; just leave me alone ... go back to your girlfriend, or whatever she is to you.'

FORTY-SEVEN

Karenza only just managed to make it around the corner before vomiting.

Like a tree hit by a storm; trunk tilting, roots exposed, she rested against the wall, afraid to move in case she fell. It was minutes before she was able to control the shaking enough to lift her mobile and text Ross;

Come to the house NOW, it's an EMERGENCY.

She weaved through the throng of tourists, brown-limbed and cheerful with all the time in the world, knowing she'd give anything to trade places with any one of them.

Once home, she poured a glass of wine and waited for Ross to arrive. She knew he would be there as soon as traffic allowed; she wasn't one for histrionics, her text would be taken seriously.

She'd felt intimidated by Josie, tall and elegant in her crisp white blouse.

She'd pictured her differently; a gangster's moll straight out of a Martina Cole novel; damaged goods, tough as nails, but with a heart of gold. She was none of those things. More Martha's Vineyard than East Ender, wholesome and athletic; her fine blue eyes and graceful charm had thrown her. What she'd said about Ross had cut her to her core.

They'd been kids when they got together. Ross a few years older and in her mum's book a 'nice boy'. She hadn't much cared whether he was nice or not. He was fit and athletic; a surfer in a town where everyone wanted to be one, but most just wore the wet suit and carried the board. He dated the popular girls; the ones who she and her friends aspired to be with tousled hair and flat navel-pierced stomachs. She'd written his name all over her exercise books and scribbled about him in her diary. Years later, to her embarrassment, he'd rolled about laughing when he'd read the toe-curling entries out loud.

When he left for university, she assumed, like all the other broken-hearted girls in St. Ives, he'd probably never come back or if he did, he'd have some uni type in tow. So, when he returned in the vacation and took a summer job as a barman in her dad's pub she thought she'd died and gone to heaven.

She'd scour the rota for his shifts, making sure that she was waitressing at the same time. Her father clocked something was up when she volunteered to work Saturday nights. Before, she'd have moved heaven and earth not to work when her girlfriends were out partying. For Ross, it didn't matter, his Saturday nights began at eleven just like Piran's did now when the pub closed, but at sixteen with an eleven-thirty curfew, her evening was all over by then. Even if she went straight from work to join her mates she'd be lucky if she had half an hour before they'd be throwing sand on the fire and winding their way home along the cliff path.

When she and Ross began to hang out together, sitting on the harbour wall when the pub closed, eating fish and chips and listening to the music spilling from the late-night bars, she'd thought she might never bother to go out again.

At first, she'd been in awe of the beautiful boy sitting next to her as he shared the things he got up to at college. He wanted to become a policeman. His dad was in the Devon and Cornwall force and pulled a few strings so Ross would be posted back to Cornwall at the end of his training.

She'd hung on his every word, longing for something more; loyal, devoted and resilient. Eventually, her resilience paid off and in his third season working in the pub and the year he graduated, she won him over, and they began to properly date. When he finished at Hendon the following year, and at the end of his training, they'd got married in the church in the middle of

St. Ives. As the crowds gathered to throw rainbow confetti, she remembered Loveday kissing her cheek and giggling, 'God girl you've only gone and bagged Ross Trenear!'

She'd had to pinch herself and continued to feel grateful for the next ten years until she woke up from the fairy-tale and realised Ross wasn't always Prince Charming and that being a policeman's wife was often thankless and lonely. After sharing him with his friends, the force and the sea, there wasn't much left for her and the kids. When he wasn't on duty, he was surfing, and when he was at home, he was tetchy and short-tempered, setting impossibly difficult boundaries that he left her to enforce.

She'd tried to get him to confide, but he seemed to have no need for her or wish to invite her in. She eventually came to realise he didn't know how to lean on anyone. He'd never had to. Life for Ross had been charmed. Everything he touched turned out the way he wanted. He was bright, good-looking and popular, and all his dreams had come true. Yet it seemed to her that despite rising through the ranks, despite their son and daughter and her devotion, he wasn't content with his lot in life, so she'd thrown in the towel and asked for a divorce.

He, to her surprise, had said yes without much discussion. When the decree absolute came through she'd cried for the best part of a year and then let him go.

When he crashed through the front door shouting her name fifteen minutes later, she still hadn't fully recovered.

'Renna?'

On seeing her calmly nursing a glass of wine, his tone switched to annoyance.

'What the hell's going on?' he demanded. 'Your text sounded urgent as if something terrible had happened and here you are in the middle of the afternoon drinking.'

Retrieving his keys from the worktop where he'd dropped them, he turned to leave.

'Sit down,' Karenza said quietly.

'No way, I've got stuff to do at work.'

'Sit down, Ross!'

He looked at her face, full of accusation and anger and did as he was told.

'What is it?'

'Tell me about Jem Fielding.'

Her words sounded slightly slurred. She knew he'd guess the glass of wine wasn't her first that day. It was unlike her, and a niggling unease began to show on his face.

'If you're on about John's funeral again, I told you before, I was just trying to keep the peace. Carly's an adult. She can keep company with whoever she likes.'

Karenza looked him in the eye. 'And what about you, Ross, who do you keep company with these days, who's your new *bestie?*'

His face blanched as the penny dropped, confirming her worst fears.

'I'm talking about you being crooked, bent ... on the take, all those clichés you always said disgusted you. The words that mean you're in the pocket of that filthy piece of shit,' she tremored. 'All my adult life, I've looked up to you. Even when we split up, even then, I thought it was my fault. I thought you were in the right; that I should have tried harder. I always thought, no matter what, me and the kids could rely on you.'

'It's not what you think. I'm not on the take. I'd never do that; you have to believe me. Look at me; look at my car, my flat; do I look like someone being bankrolled by a gangster ... do I?'

He was right. Ross was hardly living the high life. Financially, it was a struggle for him to maintain a roof over his head and pay his way with the kids. She had to give him a little leeway on his maintenance now and again when he fell behind.

'So, why?'

He sat down. 'Because he's got something on me, and it's enough to ruin my career and make the kids' lives a misery and I care about you and them too much to let it come out.'

She'd never seen him cry before, not in all her years of knowing him. Throughout their marriage, she'd longed for him to show some vulnerability. Enough to let her know she was needed; that he wasn't totally self-sufficient, but she didn't want this. Now, as he broke down, she didn't know what to do or say.

'Tell me,' she soothed, reaching across and taking his hands in hers, 'tell me everything.'

Ross told her the whole story. How he'd been an idiot to go to Jem's bar and how he'd paid the price. Karenza had no idea why he'd let himself be taken in so easily or why things had gone so far. She did know he hadn't raped and beaten that girl. He didn't have a violent bone in his body. She also knew she had to help him out of this mess.

FORTY-EIGHT

'I can't believe it. I can't believe Ross would be tied up with Jem,' said Loveday, flustered by what she'd heard.

'Yeah well, we don't all have the luxury of principles.'

'How did it happen. I can't see Ross risking everything for money. I know he's not flush but even so. I just don't get it?'

'It may not be money. Jem's got a hundred and one ways to keep someone in their place. He knows how to get at you; how to keep you dependent on him.' Josie could see Loveday's mind working overtime, trying to justify Ross's behaviour.

'Look, it could be anything. Jem might not even have used whatever it is yet. He keeps information on lots of people; compromising information, sometimes for years. He's clever at gathering dirt to be used at the optimum time. It'll be something he's holding over him; keeping close to his chest until it suits him, and when it does, he'll call in the debt. All I know is, it's enough for him to be sure Ross will turn a blind eye when he needs him to.'

'But what could ... ?'

'Look, Loveday, it's not important what it is. What is important is that you trust Karenza not to tell Ross about our plans. Do you trust her?'

'I suppose, or at least I believed her when she said she hasn't said anything ... it's just—'

'It's just what?'

'She'll want to know the truth. I think she'll need to talk to him now you've told her about Jem, she'll want to confront him.'

'But she can't. If she does and he lets on to Jem, he'll know it's come from me.' Josie jumped up and grabbed her coat. 'Come on, take me to her place. I need to speak to her before she makes a big mistake. One we won't be able to fix.' The two women made their way to the quay. Josie could see why the locals called the tourists 'emmets' the Cornish word for ants, as they jostled for space in the narrow streets.

As she always did, Loveday let herself in, Josie behind her. Moving through to the kitchen they stopped in their tracks. Ross and Karenza were sitting at the table holding hands. Ross followed Karenza's gaze towards the door. When he saw Josie, he pulled away.

'What is this; what's she doing here?'

'Have you said anything?' asked Josie, knowing full well there could be only one reason for Ross to be there so soon after their meeting.

'Nothing about our discussions, but I have talked to him about Jem.'

'Shush for god's sake, that's his wife,' Ross said, pointing at Josie, 'that's Jem Fielding's wife.'

Karenza touched his arm reassuringly. 'I know. You've got to trust me, Ross.'

Casting a wary look in Josie's direction, Ross sat back in his seat.

'Come in,' she said to the two women in the doorway, 'take a seat. We need to talk.'

She relayed the story Ross had told her earlier. At one point, he got up and walked to the other side of the room, turning his back to them, but he didn't try and stop her talking.

When she'd finished, Josie turned to Ross.

'I can tell you right now if you have no recollection of hurting that girl, you probably didn't.'

'How do you know; how can you be so sure?' Ross stared wide-eyed.

'I've been married to the man for fifteen years, and I know a set-up when I see one,' she replied.

Gratitude welled in Ross's eyes. He gave a self-conscious cough as he turned away.

'Jem's done this before,' she continued, 'sometimes he gets the girls to say they've been raped. Other times he tells the men the girls they've been with are underage.'

'You mean, it's all made up?' asked Loveday naively.

'No, not quite, that's the clever bit,' she looked at Ross. 'The minute you went into that club, you were a marked man. They probably slipped something into your drink. The problem is it's easy to get the dose wrong. It sounds to me; you were too far gone for it to go the way they'd planned.'

'You mean, I wouldn't have been able to perform ... sexually?'

'I'm guessing not. Jem videos all the girls. Most of the tapes are deleted, but the ones with mileage; ones of people he can blackmail, planning officers, teachers, lawyers, policemen, people he can use, he keeps.'

'So, mine would have been useless because I didn't ...' he looked at Karenza, 'I couldn't ... '

'Because you didn't have sex,' interrupted Josie, 'I guess that was the case; otherwise they wouldn't have taken the photographs. They wouldn't have needed to beat the girl up and blame it on you.'

'Are you sure?' asked Karenza.

'Prostitution is an ugly business. No one wants to admit they've paid for sex; it's humiliating, and the threat of exposure will make people do anything; usually, the sex is enough.'

'So, there's no tape of me then?' asked Ross

'I didn't say that. My guess is there will be a tape, but it will just confirm you were in the room with the girl. The photographs came afterwards, once Jem's boys had worked their magic on her face.'

'Where would Jem keep the tape?' asked Karenza. She liked

Josie; she recognised her strength came out of adversity. It was hard-earned. She looked all glamour and polish, but underneath she was a real woman. She would be happy to call her a friend.

'It'll be where he keeps all the others; in the safe at home. The photos will be there too.'

'And are you telling us the only thing stopping Ross breaking free of your husband is that tape and the photos?' quizzed Karenza.

'What about the girl?' asked Ross.

'I wouldn't worry about her. Jem wouldn't let one of his girls give evidence. Most of them are addicts and unreliable witnesses anyway, but mostly he'd be afraid they might prove loose-lipped and talk about other things he wouldn't want the authorities to know. Trust me, it's the tapes he relies on and, in your case, the photographs. These girls come and go, he never keeps them in one place for too long. They're usually illegals, smuggled in and out; they don't ever use their real names.'

'Could you get the tape and the photos for us?' asked Karenza.

'I could,' said Josie, suddenly realising this was an opportunity to get Karenza back on board with her plan, 'but it depends on your willingness to help me in return.'

Josie liked Karenza's plan and was surprised it was better than her own. Intercepting the drugs on route to Newlyn or once the shipment had been loaded into the vans was high risk. Theo's boys were likely to be heavily armed. She'd have to hire muscle of her own, and although she had contacts, there were issues. She'd have to draw out substantial amounts of cash from her accounts to pay for the hired help, and that would leave her short if she had to get away fast. There was also a chance those she employed thought better of crossing the likes of Theo and Jem and shopped her at the last minute. No, Karenza's plan was less messy, and if they could use people not connected with

Jem's business, they'd have a better chance of success. Josie couldn't afford for her to bail now, she needed her. Whether Loveday wanted to be with her or not, she wanted to be free of Jem. She would do anything to make sure she didn't miss this opportunity.

She looked at Ross and thought, I have no choice; I just have to risk this. I have to believe he wants his life back as much as I want mine.

'It depends on you promising to help me with the plan to intercept the drugs and get rid of Jem.'

Ross looked confused. 'What drugs?'

Josie continued, grateful for the confirmation Ross knew nothing yet; that Karenza had told the truth and this wasn't some scheme to set her up and shop her to Jem. She needed to keep the momentum now she had his attention.

'Jem has a shipment of cocaine coming in next Saturday night. It's coming by sea, being picked up and taken out of the county. It's not Jem's deal, he's just the middleman, and if it goes wrong, he'll pay. I want it to go wrong. I want us to take the drugs and make it look like Jem did it.'

'How much cocaine are we talking about here?' asked Ross the policeman in him suddenly coming to the fore.

'About 100 kilos, give or take.'

'Christ, that's huge!'

'It's likely to be a one-off and our only chance to get rid of the little shit.'

'Who's in charge then, if not Jem?'

'Someone from out of county, Theo Morgan. He's high up in the organisation, and it's his last job. It's high stakes for everyone involved.'

'And how were you planning to do this?' asked Ross.

'Well, I had an idea, but your ex-wife's is better.'

Ross shot a glance at Karenza. 'Why are you involved in this?'

'The drugs are being picked up by a fishing boat out at sea and then dropped just off shore for Morgan's men to pick up in smaller boats and take inland.'

'And?'

'Treeve's the one picking it up out at sea. He's using the Auntie Lou.'

'You're kidding me. That bloody idiot.'

Karenza immediately looked defensive. Josie understood why. Ross no longer had the right to criticise; he lost that the minute he walked into Jem's club. The woman didn't need Ross to tell her Treeve was an idiot; she knew already. She could see where this was going and had no intention of letting the conversation disintegrate into a pissing contest between the men in Karenza's life.

'Let's just calm down,' she said, 'Treeve's not the enemy here. He's a victim like the rest of us.'

Josie could tell Karenza didn't like being chastised. She'd probably had enough of people telling her to be sensible. Where the hell had sensible got her, sensible was only any use if everyone else bought into it too?

'I thought, and it's just a thought, we could pick up the drugs and drop them somewhere else, or some of them at least. Then I was going to tell you,' she looked at Ross 'that was until Josie put me straight about you and Jem.'

Ross looked shamefaced.

'Anyway, it doesn't matter because Josie picked up it wouldn't work because they'd know Treeve had grassed them up and lead them back to me and the kids.'

Josie interrupted. 'Also, we can't rely on Treeve not telling Jem the plan. Once you've had a taste of what it's like to piss Jem off, it's a hard thing to do; trust me, I know from experience. He'll not double-cross him lightly; knowing what it would mean for Karenza and the kids.'

Ross bristled at the mention of his children. He clearly didn't trust Treeve to keep his family safe. Josie didn't blame him. Treeve was a hulking beast, but he wasn't the brightest and could easily be tricked into spilling his guts. He'd trip himself up without even knowing it, and that would be their downfall.

'But if we don't tell Treeve' said Karenza, 'we can't do this. We need him to navigate the Auntie Lou, none of us can do it.'

They began to argue; their voices rising; frustrated they'd discovered a major flaw in the plan. The conversation descended into chaos. Loveday niggled at Josie about Theo. Ross criticised Treeve's ineptitude while Karenza half-heartedly defended him.

Then a voice boomed from the doorway.

'Shut up, the lot of you. I can navigate the boat. I know those waters like the back of my hand, I'll do it.'

FORTY-NINE

They fell silent as Karenza's father walked across the room and extended a calloused hand to Josie; 'Gil Martin, very pleased to meet you, Mrs. Fielding.'

'Josie, please call me Josie.'

He turned to face the others; face like thunder.

'Before we go any further, we have to lay down some ground rules.'

'Dad, are you sure you want to be involved in this?'

'I'm already involved. I'm here to make sure this thing works, and the first step on that score is to keep that daft sod Treeve in the dark.'

'I second that,' Ross chipped in.

Gil threw a disparaging glance in Ross's direction.

'You've not exactly covered yourself in glory; what the hell were you thinking?'

No explanation would suffice. Ross knew it and looked away.

'Well, it's done now, water under the bridge; this is about putting right what we can. Isn't that so, Josie?'

'Yes, that's right,' Josie replied, startled the question had been cast in her direction.

Up until that point, she had not felt confident this group of people had it in them to pull this off. Even Ross on meeting him wasn't the level-headed hero she'd been led to believe by Loveday. She was beginning to think she was expecting too much of them. These were ordinary people living unremarkable lives in a small Cornish town. Why would they be able to handle this? She, on the other hand, had lived this life for longer than she cared to remember and, to some extent, she was immune to stuff that would send normal, decent people running for the hills. There wasn't much she hadn't seen hanging on the arm of her husband. She'd witnessed degradations these people couldn't even imagine and had first-hand experience of a few of them.

It annoyed her back at Loveday's flat when Karenza took the high ground. She'd felt the need to bring the woman down a peg or two; to let her know her precious Ross was not whiter than white; that everything wasn't rosy in her garden. It was spiteful. When Karenza left, she'd panicked. It was only now Gil Martin was in the mix that feeling was slowly subsiding; hesitant confidence returning.

Gil looked around the faces at the table. 'I want no more arguing between us. Any problems we've got with each other we take up again when this lot is finished. Until then, we watch each other's backs. We talk to no one, and you girl,' he looked at Karenza 'start locking that front door. I could have been anyone listening, one of the kids or Treeve or worse. This isn't a game.'

Karenza nodded.

'Now, we're thin on the ground, so each of us will have a job solely our responsibility,' counselled Gil.

'Like what?' asked Loveday.

'Well, I'm going to be in charge of the boat. I'm gonna have to get on board to check her out before the job.'

Josie spoke up, buying into Gil's ethos, 'I've got to keep tabs on Jem and Theo; make sure nothing unexpected comes up we're unaware of.'

'Exactly,' said Gil

'You don't think you'll need someone with you on the boat?' asked Ross. 'Treeve's a younger man than you, it's possible he'd have been able to pick up the packages, loaded them on board, and unloaded them at the drop-off point on his own, but I think you'll struggle.'

'I'm afraid you're probably right,' sighed Gil.

'I could help,' volunteered Ross.

'No, that's impossible. If, for some reason, things go wrong, you can't afford to be found on the boat. Anyway, you're better off ashore co-ordinating things, keeping an eye on the authorities, warning us if the coastguard or your lot get a whiff of this before we're good and ready.'

Ross had to agree it made perfect sense.

'I can go with you Dad,' piped up Karenza.

'You'll have to hide,' said Josie 'there's not meant to be anyone else on the boat, and the Spanish boys will pick up on anything unusual; anyone who's not meant to be there, especially a woman.'

'That's true, it's too dangerous, maybe I'll have to do it on my own ... take my chances.'

'You can't Dad, there's no way you could get the stuff to the drop-off point and get back in time to unload before anyone notices. It'll take two of us to ditch the stuff, to do it quickly and get away before Morgan's men move in to pick it up and realise they've been short-changed.'

'Okay, but the slightest hint of any trouble, you contact me so I can put a stop to this. If something happens, I call in the authorities there and then, no matter the cost; understood?' said Ross.

'So how are we going to deal with Treeve?' asked Loveday.

'Rohypnol, it's immediate, effective and easy to administer,' offered Josie as the silence stretched and eyes widened.

'She's right,' said Ross, 'I should know.'

Loveday laughed, and for the first time, the mood in the room lifted, allowing each to let their guard down and talk freely.

The conversation went on until the early evening when Karenza said they'd have to leave because the kids would be coming home. By then, they had a plan, a cobbled-together, opportunist, Whisky Galore sort of plan, but a plan nonetheless, and for all of their sakes, they knew they had to make it work. There was no room for error; it could cost them their lives.

Part Two:

The Sisterhood

FIFTY

Over the next few weeks, things were fine-tuned. Each of them concentrated on their tasks, liaising with the others only when necessary. It was considered too risky for Josie to meet with Karenza, so Loveday took on the role of go-between.

Josie watched her come and go at the club and wondered if they'd ever be able to rebuild what they'd had before Theo. She hoped so, but there was no guarantee. Loveday remained frosty with no sign of any thaw. Whatever she was doing now was for Karenza rather than her. Strangely that made her love her even more.

Josie stayed on the alert for anything unusual. Carly remained a welcome distraction. She'd heard from Lorraine that Jem had taken Carly to John's funeral and had been amazed he hadn't sent one of his boys instead. He was besotted with the girl and prepared to take risks because of it.

She'd been able to meet with Theo. They'd had lunch in Truro, away from Jem's circle of influence. Theo remained earnest and adamant about his plans to take her away with him, and to some extent, she was relieved that for once, she hadn't been played. It hadn't been a ploy to get her into bed. She made it her business to drive the conversation towards the drug deal and, as a result, now knew most of the details and timings. He confirmed Treeve would be given the co-ordinates on the day of the drop and let slip the pickup point was just off the Gurnard's Head. Theo's boys would do the pick-up and take the gear back to Sennen Cove.

She'd made it clear she wanted to leave with him quietly. Jem would only be aware after the event, so they wouldn't have to worry about him losing it and doing something stupid.

Theo understood, he knew Jem was a loose cannon, and no one could predict how he would take the news. Josie knew in normal circumstances he would have told Jem and thought to hell with the consequences. He was higher up the pecking order, and if push came to shove, the powers that be would support him every time. Many of them knew her history and what she'd had to put up with and wouldn't be a bit surprised she'd gone back to Theo, but these weren't normal circumstances. For the moment, Theo needed Jem on side and couldn't risk complications. Any muddying of the waters could jeopardize the job and his future. As far as he was concerned, once it was over, he wouldn't give a damn, and his bosses could deal with Jem directly if they wanted to make this a regular thing.

He and Josie would be in Barbados and wouldn't care either way.

He told her his boys had already moved to the holiday house in Sennen Cove and suggested he and Josie ought not to meet there again. In consequence, they hadn't had the opportunity for intimacy since their first encounter, and strangely, he hadn't complained. It seemed to her the deal was all-consuming for him too. They did make plans to leave together the day after the drop. Theo had chartered a plane out of the county and intended to take her with him. She was to bring nothing with her. He said he'd replace everything; new clothes; new home; new life with him in the Caribbean. He didn't even bother to ask whether there might be things she wanted to keep, bits of her life she didn't want to discard like old tat. She was glad her future didn't lie with Theo. She was sick and tired of being told what to do by men. There were times she felt guilty about leading him on, but others, when his head pivoted as a pretty woman walked by, she felt he deserved everything he got.

She passed on all the information she accumulated, so Gill and Karenza could time how long it would take to get from the

Gurnard's Head back to St. Ives and unload the rest of the gear. Every fact was cross-checked where possible.

She also passed a phial of Rohypnol to Loveday to give to Karenza.

'She can slip it into his drink, and it'll knock him out, leaving him with no memory of what's happened. Jem keeps it at the club to give to the girls when he wants them to be extra compliant for punters with unusual tastes or to drug the men he's marked as potential blackmail victims, like Ross,' she said, handing it over.

'Will this little bit be enough?' asked Loveday holding the clear liquid up to the light.

'Trust me, it'll be plenty, even for a bloke like Treeve. Karenza must give it to him as late as possible on the night of the drop. Then Ross and you can tie him up and take him to the club, while Gil and Karenza go to meet the trawler.'

Josie noticed Loveday wince at the thought.

'Look, this is for Treeve's protection. He must be found unconscious at the club. It needs to look like Jem has drugged and tied up his own man.'

'I know ... I do know that. It just suddenly seems so real, now you've given me this.'

She put the phial in her back pocket and left to meet Karenza.

Josie spent any spare time she had putting her own house in order. It was an exercise she'd started months before, soon after her trip to Spain with Loveday.

She'd begun accumulating money of her own. Jem had always given her cash; crisp bundles of it but kept careful tabs to check it was either spent or handed back. He thought nothing of sending her off on a shopping spree with thousands in her pocket, just so long as when she got home, she could show him the receipts for the Dior blouse or the Balenciaga bag. He liked her to be decked out in designer brands; it reflected well on him.

She'd spotted an opportunity to utilise her extensive wardrobe by chance when the wife of one of Jem's golf club buddies let slip she'd bought a genuine Prada bag online from a site with loads of nearly new designer gear up for grabs.

When she got home, Josie took a look for herself. The site was called 'Designer Gear 4 U', and there were pages of genuine, nearly new items for sale. It wasn't like eBay. Instead, you created a profile, uploaded the photos of what you wanted to sell in your 'shop' and off you went. It seemed like a good arrangement to her. She had enough spare stuff to stock several shops. She was interested in the prices being achieved and the fast turnaround.

For a Chanel bag, ticket on, bought for 5k you could get 3k; ticket off 2k.

She'd started selling the vast array of designer clothes, bags and shoes Jem had bought her over the years. They disappeared bit by bit from her wardrobe. She kept enough not to raise suspicion so the rails still looked full, but huge amounts of her second-hand, hardly worn items had gone.

She'd taken several shopping trips and spent thousands. She brought the items home, showed them to Jem, wore some with the tags still in and then sold them on the site for less than she'd paid, but still a good price. The money was paid directly from the site into an account she set up for the purpose. Doing this, she'd accumulated more than two hundred thousand pounds in only a few months. Although it wasn't much by Jem's standards, it was enough to start a new life. She could be her own woman.

Jem didn't seem to notice her depleting stock of glad-rags. She hadn't been required to accompany him to any charity balls or golf club get-togethers for months. His pink and yellow Pringle jumpers sat sulkily in his wardrobe like slices of stale Battenberg as he spent more and more time with Carly.

FIFTY-ONE

By the day of the drop, everyone knew their role and the timings off pat.

Josie knew Jem would be picked up early by Mike, and if everything went to plan, might never come back. She thought she'd feel more, but when the crunch came all she felt was relief the day had finally arrived.

As soon as she saw the electronic gates clunk behind them, she moved into gear.

Her main job was to feed snippets of information throughout the day to Theo, which when cobbled together would point the finger back at Jem and make it look as if he'd set the whole thing up.

She'd bought a second-hand Louis Vuitton suitcase and filled it with the kind of clothes Jem would wear. It had to look like he'd packed properly. Anyone who knew him would smell a rat if the case wasn't packed in cruise mode, shirts folded and wrapped in cellophane; black and brown loafers and a pair of deck shoes, everything needed for a getaway to sunnier climes. In the side pocket was a money belt full of cash and a bag full of toiletries, including a couple of grams of coke. When she'd finished, she put it in the back seat of the Aston. She'd drive the car with a suitcase full of Jem's clothes to the rear of the club where Ross and Loveday would fill it with the cocaine they'd brought from St. Ives, and that's how it would be found by Theo once she'd tipped him off. By then, he'd realise only half of the shipment had been picked up by his boys. When he found Treeve tied up in one of the private booths, he'd assume Jem intended to frame him and to finish him off later. Anybody looking at the evidence would conclude Jem had done a runner following her tip-off, and when they found the drugs in the back of his car, they'd know she'd been right to shop him.

The first job of the day was to retrieve Ross's tape from the safe set into bookshelves running along one wall of the library.

When it had first been built, she'd taken delight in visiting second-hand book shops buying books to fill it until she realised there were to be no real books.

'What do you mean, they're not going to be real?' she'd asked

'They'll be covers; all classics, the brown ones, the red ones, but then inside, you only get the first few pages, and the rest is blank.'

'Blank?'

'Yeah, blank, like I said blank, is there a bloody echo in here, or are you being thick on purpose?'

'So, you've ordered books with *covers* but no text.'

'Exactly, all new and all matching, two hundred of them. I can't stand the smell of old books. They come next Wednesday.'

She remembered how she'd taken herself to her bedroom, picked up a pillow and screamed into it.

As she lifted *The Old Curiosity Shop* from the shelf labelled 'Dickins' and reached behind to tap the combination into the safe, she wondered how bleak and tedious it must be to spend your entire life an ignorant, unfeeling bully.

Then again, the way he treated Carly; she wondered if she'd witnessed a glimmer of some higher feeling the girl released in him. Maybe Carly was his Little Nell and their story, a book waiting to be written. She quashed the ridiculously romantic analogy. If she needed a real comparison, Jem's world was Wonderland. She was Alice and he was the maddest of Mad Hatters.

Peering inside the safe, she could see the box of tapes, labelled with dates and names. She picked up the one marked

'Trenear', then moving the others around so the gap was less obvious, put the box back. She felt around for the large brown envelope taped to the side she knew was full of stills from the videos. Retrieving it, she shuffled through the predictably sordid contents and found the ones of the girl's bruised face and put the others back.

Done, she thought, now she'd given Ross his life back.

FIFTY-TWO

Karenza woke to the sound of Treeve brushing his teeth. Reluctant to leave the comfort of the duvet, she rested her head against the headboard. Catching her reflection in the mirror, he turned to face her. Treeve was ignorant of all the details. He had no information other than he was to stand by for the co-ordinates. Karenza pretended to agree they should tell no one especially not Ross, and go along with the job on the condition that after it was over, he'd hand in his notice and use the money he'd made to go back to fishing.

He'd been working virtually non-stop on the Auntie Lou since John's funeral, and Karenza sensed after what had happened, he was glad to be released from his shifts at the club. He'd been able to take the boat on short trips around the coast to try her out for the past few days. She'd persuaded him to take her dad with him on the pretext of smoothing over the cracks in their relationship. Gil had no interest in establishing a rapport with Treeve. His sole purpose for being there was to familiarise himself with the boat.

When she'd broached the subject, Treeve was keen on the idea. He wanted a second opinion on the work he'd done and thought it would be an ideal opportunity to clear the air without Karenza's over-anxious presence. She'd encouraged his misconceived notions of a 'mano-a- mano' talk. Treeve took Gil out two days in succession, and the older man spent the entire time nodding and smiling to every boast the younger one made while taking in every inch of the boat. When at the end of the second day, Treeve handed him a roll of notes in repayment of his debt, Gil took it. He told her afterwards he hoped once this was all over, she'd kick the bloody idiot out. Despite this, he had no wish to see the big lummox hurt, and so when Josie came up with the plan of drugging him and tying him up, like the others he'd embraced the idea.

'Morning, I didn't know you were awake. I couldn't sleep so thought I might as well get up. Sorry, I woke you.'

'No, it's fine. I've turned the alarm off. It was nearly time to get up anyway,' she smiled, stretching.

She didn't confess she'd been woken yet again by Piran stumbling home in the early hours and, unable to get back to sleep, lay awake watching Treeve toss and turn all night. She needed to have a word with the boy. She wouldn't be surprised if he had a new girlfriend on the go. Not that she minded, he seemed happy enough despite looking like death warmed up.

She'd spent the day before, going back and forth to the zip pocket of her handbag retrieving and returning the small phial of clear liquid Loveday had delivered from Josie. It looked so innocuous, only a couple of teaspoons worth, but apparently, it was enough to knock Treeve out for several hours. The effect would be instantaneous.

She had to wait for the right moment to give it to him; once she had all the details of the drop so they could put their plan in motion.

'I'm gonna grab a cup of coffee and then go check the boat one last time,' said Treeve pulling on his jacket.

'Okay, but before you go, can you just run a few things by me again?'

'Karenza look ... '

'I know you don't want to talk about it but please, Treeve. If something goes wrong and you don't come back you surely don't expect me to be quiet about it. I need to get the details straight in my head.'

'I've told you all I know. I'll get a call about an hour before I meet the Spanish trawler. I'll get the co-ordinates then, along with the details of the place I drop the drugs off. Once I've dropped them, I mustn't hang around. I'm to come straight back, moor up, and that's it. I just keep my head down until further notice.'

'When will you get the call?'

'I don't know, I told you that ... ' there was a hint of impatience in his tone. 'It'll be after dark, at high tide. I'm guessing the early hours of tomorrow morning. Until then, we should go about our business as if it's just like any other day.'

'But it's not like any other day.'

'I do know that, but for my sake, can we pretend we're ordinary people getting on with our ordinary lives?'

Karenza heard his desperation and knew she should feel pity but couldn't. She felt nothing; that ship had sailed.

FIFTY-THREE

They stayed up watching mindless Saturday night telly waiting for Jem's call.

Piran and Livvy were staying with friends; Livvy getting her first overnight pass since the incident at the festival.

The call came as Treeve thought it would, at about one o'clock, Sunday morning.

As soon as he came off the phone, Karenza was on his case.

'What did he say?'

'The job's on. He'll text me the co-ordinates and the password in the next few minutes. I'd better get my gear,' he said, racing upstairs.

She watched the phone while he was gone, eyes glued to the screen; willing the co-ordinates to appear. She was torn whether to go and retrieve the Rohypnol or wait for the information to arrive. Then another thought crossed her mind. What if Treeve didn't want a drink; they were already awash with tea and coffee? Booze; it would have to be booze. He wouldn't turn that down.

When he returned, he was dressed head to toe in black. She and her father would be wearing almost identical gear; no high viz tonight.

The phone tremored, practically jumping out of Treeve's hand.

'Is that it?'

'Yeah ... it is,' he said, distracted; trying to work out where he had to go from the co-ordinates.

She walked to the kitchen, returning with a large shot of vodka.

'Here,' she said, 'take this; Dutch courage.'

She'd poured the entire contents of the phial into it.

Treeve knocked it back in one.

'Thanks,' he said, handing her the glass.

She scrutinised his every movement, not knowing what to expect. She'd visualised him becoming dizzy, grabbing the arm of the chair, crashing around the room before falling flat on his face, like in some cheesy whodunnit. He did none of those things.

She bit her lip, resisting the urge to ask if he felt alright as he walked to the hall and crouched to thrust a large torch into the rucksack he'd packed with everything he needed for the job.

'Phone?' he said, 'for the password Jem gave me. I've got to text it when I've picked up the stuff.'

He'd dropped it on the kitchen table after he'd taken the message. Karenza went back to fetch it. As he slipped it into his pocket, he slumped slightly to one side; knees buckling.

Karenza watched from the doorway, knowing she shouldn't intervene. He tried to straighten up, but there was no strength in his legs, and he fell back onto his backside; legs out in front of him, eyes glazed, trying to speak.

Had she not known what was happening, she would have thought he was having a stroke. The symptoms were like those she'd seen in the advert on the telly teaching you to spot the signs, but she had no intention of calling for an ambulance. Instead, she reached into her back pocket for her mobile and called Ross.

'It's done.'

He and Loveday arrived in a matter of minutes, armed with plastic cable ties to bind Treeve's wrists and ankles. Ross took a reel of silver duct tape from his pocket and, as Loveday steadied Treeve's head, stuck a strip of it across his mouth.

'What if the drugs make him sick? What if he chokes; he could choke, couldn't he? 'Karenza fretted.

'Okay, I'll leave it off in the car, but it goes back on when we get to the club. I didn't feel sick when they gave the stuff to me, and I'd had a skin full. For once, he's sober, so as long as we lay him on his side, I'm pretty sure he'll be fine,' Ross reassured her.

Ross didn't have any of her qualms; hell-bent on getting the job done.

'Renna, I said he'll be alright,' he said sternly, 'get your stuff; your dad's waiting.'

She hadn't moved; hadn't been able to take her eyes off Treeve's limp body being hauled around like a sack of potatoes since they arrived.

'Karenza,' Ross shouted.

'Do you need my help to lift him?' she asked.

'No, you go, we'll manage.'

Shaking, she pulled her coat from the rack and reached across Treeve's slumped body to pick up his rucksack. 'Okay, I'm going,' she muttered, leaving them to heave him into the boot of Ross's car.

***

Her dad was waiting for her next door when she arrived.

'You ready?'

'Ready as I'll ever be.'

'Right then, let's get this show on the road.'

She followed her father through the shadowy cobbled streets down to the pier where the Auntie Lou was moored, trying to imagine this was just another fishing trip, like all the others she'd been on with him over the years, but her roiling stomach told a different story.

'Now before we set off, have you got everything?'

'I brought Treeve's bag.'

'Have you got his phone with the co-ordinates?'

Karenza stopped in her tracks.

'No ... no, it's in his pocket ... damn it. How could I be so stupid?!'

'Calm down ... take a breath,' Gil said, his voice calm. 'Go back, quick before they load him in the car and leave for Penzance.'

'I've thought about nothing else for weeks, planned it over and over in my head, and I've already mucked up; what if they're already gone?'

'Never mind the post-mortem ... go!'

She raced back along the pier to the cottage. She tried the front door ... locked! It was never locked; leastways never used to be before all this. She ran up the side alley, around the back. She couldn't see Ross's car.

'No ... please no,' she muttered, fearing they'd already left with Treeve's phone in his pocket. Without the co-ordinates and password, they wouldn't know where the pickup point was. Theo told Josie it was off the Gurnard's Head, but that was all. They wouldn't have a clue; it would be a stab in the dark. Why the hell hadn't she asked Treeve the details before he passed out? She'd been too busy watching his reaction to think straight.

She spotted headlights coming along the back alley towards her and shielded her eyes from the glare. The lights dipped, and the car stopped. She heard the car door open and close, and then to her relief, Ross's voice.

'What the hell, Renna; why aren't you on the boat?'

'I've forgotten his phone; it's got the co-ordinates and password on it.'

Ross marshalled her to the back of the car and opened the boot. Loveday sat huddled in the passenger seat looking as sick as Karenza felt.

She took a sharp intake of breath at the sight of Treeve curled up, feet and hands tied; out for the count.

'Which pocket?' asked Ross.

222

'In his jacket, I think, inside top.'

Ross reached in, retrieving the phone.

'Now go, we've already wasted too much time ... and be careful, Renna.'

Her heart jolted.

'I want you to take this with you just in case.'

Reaching into a bag stuffed down beside Treeve, he pulled out what looked to Karenza like a toy gun.

'I don't think the kind of men we're dealing with are going to be frightened by a toy.'

'It's not a gun, you numpty,' he laughed, 'it's a Taser, police issue. It's set up, with the cartridge in place, so all you have to do is pull the trigger. It'll give you a few minutes to get away from trouble if you're cornered, that's all.'

Karenza had seen Tasers in crime dramas on the TV and was immediately alarmed at the thought of firing one herself.

'It can't kill anyone, can it?'

'No, but it will incapacitate them. It makes their muscles go to jelly for a few minutes, that's all.'

She could tell by his face, it wasn't quite true. She knew Tasers had been known to kill people in certain circumstances; she'd seen it on the news, but she also understood if he thought she might need it, she probably should take it.

'Okay ... and I just press the trigger?'

'Yes, but don't hesitate. If you're in danger, use it. Now go.'

She turned and ran, clinging on for dear life to the phone with one hand and the Taser with the other.

Her dad was on the boat waiting at the bottom of the ladder for her to get on board. She thrust the Taser into her pocket and jumped the last couple of rungs.

'I hope from the look on that face you got it?'

'Yeah, I caught them just as they were leaving.'

'Good, now come on we've got time to make up.'

FIFTY-FOUR

Gil stood at the controls of the Auntie Lou. He'd plotted the co-ordinates from Treeve's phone into the navigation system. Josie's info was spot on. They were to rendezvous with the Spanish vessel half a mile off the Gurnard's Head, an outcrop of rocks shaped like a fish between St. Ives and Sennen Cove, which the Cornish called 'Ynyal' meaning 'the desolate one'. Karenza looked back towards her hometown from the sea, imagining the journey the drugs had taken to get there, and thought how small the world was and how easy it was for some gangster on another continent to bring down her universe.

She took a seat by her father, not trusting her sea legs. Already feeling queasy, she knew when they neared the pickup point, she'd have to hide under a tarpaulin down below and wanted to get as much fresh air in her lungs as possible before that. Whether it was the roll of the boat or nerves making her stomach churn, she wasn't sure.

Unlike her, Gil looked calm; in his element at the helm of the boat.

'You alright, maid?'

'Yeah Dad, I'm okay; just nerves.'

'It's a bit late for that now.'

She knew he was right, too many people were relying on them, Josie, Ross, and even if he didn't know it, Treeve.

'I know, I know, it's just ... I'm a mum, I've got two kids. What the hell am I thinking of?'

'Listen, love, we're doing all this for those kids; so they're safe. Now get a hold of yourself, you're no good to anyone in this state.'

Her father's voice was emphatic and did the trick.

'Alright, sorry. How long 'til we get there?'

'That's more like it, *how long 'til we get there, how long 'til we get there?*' Her father's comic mimic of her little girl whine made Karenza laugh despite herself. She remembered how she'd been impatient as a child when her dad took her out in his boat. He'd always said she'd make a terrible fisherman.

'Not long. We'll spot 'em long before we get to them. We'll be able to tell what we're dealing with.'

She watched the clouds lace across the moon and thought how on any other night she might consider the scene romantic as her mind strayed back to Ross and the way he'd looked at her when he'd told her to take care, like he really meant it.

The revelation was glorious but sad at the same time. All that hurt and wasted time; lives pulled apart only to arrive back where they'd started all those years before.

She'd intended to move on for everyone's sake and had, until he split from Trudy, all those old feelings flooded back. It felt strange being back in love; not the same as before. This time he needed her as much as she needed him.

'There she is, straight up ahead,' Gil shouted.

Karenza jumped. She could see the lights on the top of the mast about two hundred metres to the East of the Auntie Lou.

'She's about the same size as us,' said Gil. 'That's good. It means there's likely only to be one or two of them in the crew.'

'What does it matter?'

'If it goes wrong, it'll be an even fight.'

She didn't want to crush his optimism by pointing out that their 'gang' consisted of an old man and a petrified middle-aged mother of two.

'It doesn't matter how many of them there are; they're drug dealers. It only takes one man to shoot you.'

'I get your point. You'd better go down below and keep out of sight.'

Karenza did as she was told, her stomach swimming with a different sort of sickness now; she recognised as fear. She felt the Taser in her pocket and wondered whether she'd ever have the guts to use it.

FIFTY-FIVE

The urge to vomit intensified with the weight of the reeking cover. Karenza was grateful the boat had been out of action lately, so she didn't have to suffer the putrid smell of fish guts as well as engine oil. Head resting on the swaying lower deck, she could hear the water lapping now Gil had cut the engine. The sound of muffled voices and the rhythmic bump of the Auntie Lou as she buffeted the bow of her Spanish counterpart confirmed they'd come alongside. Her heart thumped an irregular rhythm of its own; unnatural and dangerous.

She was finding it hard to breathe through the suffocating humidity of the tarpaulin, now dripping with condensation. Sticky rivulets of sweat trickled between her breasts and her jumper stuck to her back. Wriggling onto her side, she poked her fingers about in the dark, trying to get some fresh air. Her shoulders were tight up against some empty pallets, and she knew if she moved, they could topple and give her away.

Inching forward, she found the corner of the cover and made a small triangular opening close to the deck. Laying her head next to it, she breathed in cool fresh air. Peering through the gap, she could just about see her father through the half-open cabin door. He looked remarkably relaxed, his grey stubble catching a silvery glint now and again in the light from the other vessel.

She shuffled to her left, trying to get a better sightline, but it was impossible lying on her side. Her right arm was starting to numb, and by the time she glanced back, a man had joined Gil on board; young and stocky with dark curly hair.

Karenza guessed he was there to help with the transfer of the holdalls from the other vessel. They must have thought her father couldn't manage, and that scared her. Surely, they'd think it odd Jem had sent someone his age, to deal with the drop alone. She felt the weight of the Taser in her pocket, remembering Ross's words; *'you just have to pull the trigger.'*

The two chatted as they hauled the bags aboard; shouting now and then to an unseen third man on the other boat.

She felt cornered and vulnerable. The Auntie Lou was tethered to the other trawler. If anything went wrong there would be no point running; there was nowhere to go. She'd have no choice, if she was found, she'd have to use the Taser and take her chances in the water, leaving her father to fend for himself.

Even as she thought it, she knew she'd never be able to do it.

The sweating had stopped but she now ached with the cold clamminess of a bad bout of flu. Her fingers, locked in the same position for too long, felt numb and arthritic.

The lingo bouncing between the Spaniards and her father seemed, by its tone, good-humoured as she strained to hear what they were saying.

She was concentrating so hard she started at the sound of footsteps coming down the stairs. Had the battery light above the door gone on? She hoped not.

Black boots walking towards her, then darkness as her view was suddenly obscured; the small air gap she'd made, stopped up by a bright blue bag.

Her father's voice whispered: 'Are you alright?'

'Yes,' she whispered back.

'Hold tight, we're nearly finished. The bags are all aboard. I'm just moving them below. Not much longer now.'

'Okay,' she quivered, eyes stinging with tears. She could tell herself as often as she liked to stay calm, but it made no difference. She felt like a rabbit in a snare, trapped and defenceless.

She listened as Gil moved back and forth from the steps to the place where he was piling up the holdalls. When he'd finished, she heard him shut the cabin door behind him.

She could hear nothing beyond the closed door and was beginning to think that perhaps the other vessel had gone. Then suddenly, raised voices; a rolling jumble of muffled words building to shouts and curses recognisable in any language.

The door of the cabin flung open; her dad's familiar footsteps, followed by another. The stifling heat began to prickle at her skin again. She gripped the Taser.

Her father's voice; close; standing guard directly over her.

'Not to worry, amigo,' he said, 'I can do that. It's fine ... really.'

The other man in the room sounded young; *the man she'd seen earlier?*

He was closer still; kneeling, his head near to her own. She held her breath, sure he was bound to hear her. She gripped the Taser, her sweaty hand shaking; throat dry and sore. If she didn't get some air into her lungs soon, she'd faint. The tarpaulin was a lead weight; like a stone placed on her chest. She wouldn't be able to keep it together much longer. Any minute, the creeping claustrophobia could send her screaming from her hiding place, no matter what the consequences.

'I tie it back on ...' the young man said. 'I should be with my girlfriend tonight, not here. My sister, that man, her husband, he Bastardo!'

He shouted something else out in Spanish to the man on the other boat, whose reply didn't sound like he had a sense of humour.

'Look, friend, I'll do it,' her father said, 'I've got some rope on board. You just tell your brother-in-law you've done it; he won't know the difference, it'll be okay.'

There was another shout from the other vessel.

'*Vamos idioto, Adios al viego amigo!*'

'*Gracias,*' said the young man.

She heard him rise and move towards the stairs. '*Gracias, amigo.*' he said again.

Thank God, she thought, oh thank God.

'You're welcome,' replied her father, following him back on deck.

The man had been inches from her face, had he moved any closer he would have felt the heat rising from her steaming body.

With massive relief, she listened to the engine of the other boat start up and fade as it motored away.

Even though she wanted to move and believed it to be safe, she couldn't. Her whole body was shaking, convulsing as if she'd been shocked. Her temples pounded with the thump of her heart.

When her father lifted the tarpaulin, she lay for a minute on her back taking in huge gulps of air like a floundered fish.

'Come on, girl, up you get. This is no time for lazing around.'

'Why did that bloke come down here?' she panted. 'I was certain he'd find me.'

Gil reached down to help her to her feet. Her legs felt stiff and heavy as concrete as the feeling slowly returned to them.

'A buoy fell off one of the bags as they were passing them over and they had to fish it out of the water. The one onboard the other boat seemed to be in charge and he made the other one, his brother-in-law, as it happens, come down to tie it back on. I told him I'd do it. You sure you're okay, maid, you look a bit green around the gills?'

'You'd be too if you'd been under that stinking tarpaulin for all this time,' she said, trying to forget she'd nearly lost it and had been seconds away from blowing her cover and firing the Taser, now safely back in her pocket.

'I know. Well done. I mean it. It must have been hard not

knowing what was going on,' he smiled, 'but we did it, maid. We did it!'

She wanted to cry; to wail like a baby; bury her head in her father's chest, and beg him to take her home.

'Well, we've done half a job,' she coughed, wiping her nose with the sleeve of her jumper. 'Now for the next bit. Where's Treeve's phone, we've got to send the password to Jem confirming we've picked up the stuff?'

'We'll need to get a bit closer to shore to get a signal. I guess nobody thought of that,' said Gil, retrieving the phone from his pocket.

Karenza looked at her watch. The whole exercise had taken precisely forty-two minutes. It was, without doubt, the longest forty-two minutes of her life.

FIFTY-SIX
Carly

Tonight, the waves call me; its briny scent pricking my nostrils. I lick my skin; savouring its salty tang. The men who come to watch me suck me dry like starving babies. They will have to find comfort somewhere else from now on. I have danced my last dance.

Out of my bedroom window, I watch Josie park Jem's car. I'd like to paint her. There's plenty to find behind the mask she wears; loathing for the monster she married, of course, though since Loveday, hope too.

I've known Loveday all my life. Time after time I've watched her rip the plaster from love's weeping wound with a grin. I hope she has finally learnt a hard-earned smile has greater meaning.

I've watched the women plot and scheme from afar while I've silently bided my time. I am the invisible member of their sisterhood; my job to distract the enemy and listen at doors.

It's how I learnt Treeve was part of Jem's plan and realised Karenza was involved; the daughter, the mother, the wife, with no time to be herself. She, like me, has found her strength through her hatred of Jem. Hers a blowtorch; mine a flame to catch a moth.

Finally, all the strands are coming together. I will stay as close as possible to Jem tonight. My power lies in his insecurity; his weakness is my strength. He trusts me because he needs to trust someone, and he has no one else.

FIFTY-SEVEN

Josie parked the Aston in Jem's usual space in the alley around the back of Mermaids. Leaving the boot unlocked, she walked over and punched in the security code to open the door to the basement of the club. Once inside, she turned on the booth lights. The bulbs above the doors gave the room an eerie green glow. It was a depressing sight, those grubby rooms where the girls took the men for private dances. When occupied, they'd hit the switch swapping a green light for red, alerting everyone the booth was busy. What little privacy they had, came from pulling down a tatty bamboo blind hanging in the small window at the top of each door.

She opened one of the booths as quietly as she could. She didn't expect anyone to be around. The staff, including the girls, had been sent home early. Jem was upstairs, waiting for the call from Theo, confirming the cocaine had been landed and was on its way to Newlyn.

Each of the booths contained a leather couch, a side table, on which stood an iPhone docker, a bottle of baby oil, a box of tissues and a frosted glass bowl containing a wide variety of condoms. Josie shuddered at the sight of the tawdry tableau.

Josie picked the booth nearest the door for Treeve. The less distance they had to carry him, the better. Standing on the bench, she unscrewed the lightbulb from the ceiling. If anyone should turn the light on, the booth would remain in darkness. No one would think anything of it, the bulbs blew all the time, and maintenance only came in on Monday mornings. Once done, she returned the bench to its rightful place and left the booth to wait for Loveday and Ross to arrive. She reached to turn off the lights, flinching as she felt icy cold fingers on her wrist. She froze, expecting to see Mike or worse, Jem, and rummaged for a plausible excuse for being there at that time of night, but as she turned, she saw the person lifting one finger to her pursed lips in the semi-darkness was Carly.

'Shhh.'

She'd forgotten she lived there and had never heard a sound come from her lips before. She remembered what Lorraine had said about Carly and that night in the bathroom. It was abundantly clear she understood whatever Josie was doing was secret and was warning her. She turned to go back upstairs. Josie was bewildered at first, then strangely reassured to know Carly was on her side. Her phone vibrated; Loveday. She lifted it to her ear.

'We're on our way.'

FIFTY-EIGHT

Karenza read the text from Jem, scrolling past the co-ordinates to the word in capitals below; **SIREN**.

How bloody predictable, she thought, talk about a one-track mind. As her father steered the boat closer to shore, she texted the word back to the sender. New co-ordinates came back immediately.

'There, done; here you are, Dad,' she said, holding up the phone to her father. 'Was Josie right, are we heading back toward Zennor to drop the bags off?'

'Yes, Treen Cove; proper Mata Hari that one.'

Gil stood at the helm looking every bit the captain of all he surveyed.

'Do you think those men suspected anything, what with you being older?'

'Here, I'm not as ancient as you may think. They just wanted to get it over as quickly as possible, just like us. Just a couple of *Pescadores* subsidising their fish quotas is my guess.'

'Do you think we can pull this off, Dad?'

'We'll give it a damn good crack, that's for sure.' he smiled as he pushed at the throttle to give the engine a bit more juice.

Fifteen minutes later they picked up the lights from Zennor. Karenza wondered whether Theo's boys were coming from Sennen Cove to pick up the drugs or from somewhere else. She knew from Josie they were taking them back there before making their way to Newlyn, *but what if they were keeping watch from a vantage point ashore.* She shivered.

'Could someone be watching us ... from the shore, I mean, with binoculars?'

'No, we're too far out, and we've got no lights on.'

'But Zennor looks so close.'

'It's deceptive. On a clear night, like tonight, it looks closer, a bit like the moon. Look at it,' he stared upward, 'it looks like you could reach out and touch it.'

Karenza followed his stare. The moon hung in the sky, nearly touching the indigo water as if at any moment it might drop like a Christmas bauble with a plop right into it. They continued past Zennor, away from the lights, towards Treen Cove. When Gil was certain he was in the right spot, he cut the engine, heaving the anchor overboard.

The cove had a strange, unsettling atmosphere. By day it was a tourist attraction for those who revelled in old tales about smugglers and Cornish wreckers. The cliffs were riddled with man-made caverns dug out to store contraband; tobacco, lace and barrels of brandy smuggled from the continent. A network of tunnels designed to keep the customs men guessing had, a century later, been used by local fishermen as natural refrigerators to store shellfish. The cliff loomed dark and forbidding. It was a calm night, one where you'd expect to hear only the slap of water on the boat's bow, but what little breeze there was, funnelled a mournful high-pitched wail around the cove.

'There she is, the Siren calling,' joked Gil.

Karenza knew the Zennor myth well. She'd always thought of the mermaid as a beautiful, beguiling creature, but the sound she was hearing conjured up a vision of something different, something desperate. She shook the thought from her head.

'Shall I bring the bags up, Dad?'

'Yes, but they'll be too heavy for you on your own. We'll leave the one without the buoy there. We'll keep that one and four others, but we'll bring up the rest.' They brought up the bright blue bags with their buoys attached, and one by one, Gil tossed them overboard.

'Aren't they meant to be tied together, to make them easy to find?'

'But we don't want them easy to find, do we? We want Theo's boys to have to look for them. At first, they'll think they've come loose of each other, and some have floated away. It'll take them a while to realise they're not there.'

'Buy us time?'

'That's the idea.'

She was amazed at how he had thought of everything.

When they'd thrown over all the bags they intended to, Gil started the engine, slowly moving away from the cove where the holdalls now bobbed up and down in the black water. Karenza began to relax and feel that maybe, just maybe, she and her father together had managed to pull this off? She hunkered down as best she could from the cold. Gil reached into his inside pocket and pulled out a silver hip flask.

'Here, maid, take a sip to keep out the cold, we're nearly home and dry.'

Karenza took the flask from him; feeling the burn of the whiskey as it hit her throat.

'Ughh, whiskey,' she grimaced.

Gil smiled. 'That'll be the pirate in you. I suppose you'll be wanting rum the next time we do this?'

'Next time! You've got to be joking!'

Karenza scanned her father's face. He looked happier than she'd seen him look in ages; youthful, full of vitality.

'Dad ... what do you think about mermaids?'

'I've never caught one if that's what you're asking?' he laughed.

'You're a funny man,' she smiled back.

'Is this about the boy again?'

She'd told her father about how she'd had a row with Piran about him going to watch Carly dance.

'Well, partly, I suppose.'

'Cut the boy some slack, love. It's natural he should be curious at that age. He's not a kid.'

She knew deep down he was right, of course, but she had been disappointed.

'Joking aside, why is Jem's club so popular, since the mermaid thing? I just don't get it.'

'Beggared if I know, I'm too old for all that. The old boys when I was fishing used to say the Siren was everything men love and fear all wrapped up.'

'How so?'

'When men are at sea for months, they try not to think about women too much. It makes 'em itchy; causes agro. It's the reason why, back along, women were never allowed onboard ship; they were unlucky.'

'You think the whole mermaid thing was made up to warn men off women when they were at sea?'

'Weren't difficult; we're scared to death of the lot of you,' he laughed, 'leastways scared of you clipping our wings.'

'Macho claptrap.'

'Perhaps so, but there it is.'

'Well, I'll let you into a little secret, our wings get clipped too.'

'I suppose they do; women give up plenty, but you're better at coping with it than us.'

'Maybe we've had more practice?'

'True enough. It's the women you can depend on when push comes to shove. There's a reason why most figureheads on boats are women. They're the ones that guide you home.'

'Perhaps I'd do better with men if I expected less from them?'

'There's a sobering thought, given your choice of men. Look, love, your lot are a mystery to most of us, and it's natural to fear what we don't understand. Women can be lovey-dovey one minute, shouting the odds the next. Most of us men are happy to walk that knife-edge.'

'It's a crappy job, but someone's got to do it,' Karenza smiled.

'Anyhow, the mermaid thing is a load of old rubbish,' said Gil, his voice lowering to little more than a whisper, 'but when I was young man and found myself at sea alone on the boat and I heard that wailing ... calling me, I sometimes thought if I looked overboard, into the dark water ...'

He grabbed Karenza's knee, making her jump, and she felt like a kid again coming home from a fishing trip with her dad.

Nearing St. Ives, Karenza went below, to cut the remaining bags free of their buoys and empty their contents into three black bin bags.

Josie had warned her the Aston's boot was not the biggest and they'd probably need to ditch the bags the cocaine had been landed in. Karenza tried not to think about what she was doing as she lifted the cellophane-wrapped bags of cocaine out of the holdalls.

She could see Ross through the cabin window waiting for them on the pier, the boot of his car open. He was alone. Loveday, she assumed had stayed at the club with Josie. As they came alongside the harbour wall, Gil threw the rope to Ross for him to secure the Auntie Lou and come aboard.

'Everything go okay?'

Karenza could tell from his flushed face and excitable tone that he was both pleased and relieved to see them.

'Of course, what did you expect, boy?' Gil winked at Karenza.

'Right then, let's get this stuff to Penzance.'

Looking around to check that the coast was clear, they lifted the bin bags full of cocaine from the Auntie Lou into Ross's boot.

'You go on, Renna; I'll clear up here before I go home. You go on to Penzance with Ross. We've made good time, but the sooner this is over with, the better.'

'Okay Dad, if you're sure. I've put the blue bags in a pile beside the buoys.' She kissed her father and jumped in the passenger seat, next to Ross.

As the heater began to bring a welcome tingle back to her icy toes, she felt strangely excited. It was a sharp contrast to the abject fear she felt on board.

Ross looked at his watch. 'Josie's waiting for a call from us to tell her that we've got the gear and are on our way. She's gonna wait about thirty minutes before ringing Theo. That'll be around the same time as his boys get back to Sennen Cove.'

'Was Treeve okay?' she asked.

'He was sleeping like a baby when I left him with Josie at the club.'

'I just hope everything goes smoothly at that end.'

'Why don't you call Lowdy? She'll be glad to hear your voice.'

He was right, Karenza could hear her relief at the other end of the phone.

'Josie's in my car waiting to put the call through to Theo. The Aston is open, so you can just drop the stuff into the boot.'

'Okay see you in a bit, and Loveday ... thank Josie for this and don't let that one go, she's a keeper.'

FIFTY-NINE

Josie was glad when Loveday's phone finally rang. It was exhausting watching her wandering around the car kicking the tarmac. When the call ended, she stubbed out her cigarette and walked back to the car.

'What did they say?' Josie asked as Loveday climbed back into the passenger seat.

'They've dropped off some of the gear and Renna and Ross are on the way with the rest. Gil's tidying up at the other end.'

'Good, I'll give it thirty minutes then call Theo.'

For Josie, the night's events had pulled things into sharp focus and shuffled her priorities. The more time she spent with Loveday the more she wanted her. Loveday had softened too but despite this, she still noticed the pucker of jealousy on hearing Theo's name.

'Do you think we ought to check on Treeve?' Loveday asked.

'No, we don't want to go back more than we have to. We don't want to run into Jem.'

'So, you'll never get the satisfaction of telling him what we've done?'

'No, I suppose not.'

'Or about us?' she added.

'What does it matter if there's no *us* to tell him about,' Josie said, turning towards her, 'unless of course you think there is?'

'I suppose ... I mean, I think so. I want to move on and I think I can ... if you still want to?' Loveday said, sheepishly.

'It's all I've ever wanted.'

Josie leaned across. As she touched Loveday's cheek the awkwardness between them melted away.

'Okay,' said Josie, pulling back and taking a deep breath.

'Let's not get ahead of ourselves, we have to focus; time to ring Theo.'

She put her phone on loudspeaker.

'It's Josie. I know it might be nothing but you told me to watch Jem and let you know if he was deviating from the plan or acting strangely. Well, something odd seems to be going on with him and I thought you ought to know.'

'What's he done now?'

'I've been trying to get hold of him and he's not answering his mobile or the phone at the club. Then, I went to the wardrobe to hang up some shirts and noticed some of his clothes are missing and one of the suitcases. I checked the safe and his passport's gone too. I've been online to check the bank accounts and Theo ... he's cleared them out.'

There was a brief moment of silence on the other end of the phone, then an explosion as Theo bellowed; 'I'll wring the treacherous bastard's neck. He's a dead man.'

As his words thundered, the reality hit her. He would do it, Theo meant what he said; he would kill Jem if he got hold of him and she realised in that instant it wasn't what she wanted. No matter how much she hated him; how much he'd done over the years to make sure of it, she didn't want his death on her hands.

She flung open the car door.

'You wait here.'

'Why, where are you going?'

'I'm going back to the club to warn Jem.'

Loveday jumped out of the car.

'Why would you do that? You just said it wasn't a good idea to go back.'

'I don't expect you to understand, but I don't want him dead. I've thought about it, even *prayed* for it, but when push comes to shove, I want him gone, not *dead*. You heard Theo. To be a party to Jem's death would make me no better than him and I don't want to be like him.'

'You can't stop it. They'll catch up with him eventually.'

'I know, I know but this way he at least gets a fighting chance of getting away.'

'And a fighting chance at coming back to get us if he finds out what we've done.'

'Trust me, he's no idiot, he'll want to disappear. He won't risk coming back. He doesn't care enough about me to risk himself. I want whatever happens to him to happen away from this place. We want to live here afterwards, remember. We don't want his ghost haunting us.'

'If you're determined to do this, I'm coming with you.'

'No way, you stay here. You being there will be one more thing to worry about. I promise I won't be long. I just need to tell him Theo rang me to say something had gone wrong and he thinks he's behind it.'

Loveday moved towards her, arms outstretched, trying to marshal her back into the car but Josie pushed her away. 'No, Loveday I mean it. I have to go back.'

SIXTY

Josie made her way through the semi-darkness up to Jem's office. He was sitting at his oversized desk when she entered. At first, she thought he was pouring over the books, massaging the figures so the taxman didn't get his share. Jem's social conscience began and ended with Jem, but as she got closer, she could see he was brushing the remains of a line of coke into the drawer. She had no idea why he was being coy. His recreational drug-taking was as much a part of their life as his violence. Coke to keep him awake; ketamine to make him sleep, Viagra to keep it up. She could tell from his pupils the drugs were kicking in, and from the cloud crossing his face, she was unwelcome.

'What are you doing here? I told you I had business to deal with tonight.'

'I know, that's why I'm here. It's about that business.'

He raised his hands to his head, smoothing back his hair with his palms. Lingering at his temples, he closed his eyes as if to shut her out.

'What are you on about?' he blinked, clearly disappointed she hadn't disappeared in a puff of smoke.

'I'm here to warn you.'

'Warn me about what? Look if this is more of you nagging on about the protests about Carly stripping, I've told you before, it was a one-off; a mistake. The locals will get over it, they'll have to, cause there's plenty more to come, and if they don't like it, too fucking bad.'

He got up and made his way around the desk towards her, running his finger along the highly polished surface with the smug satisfaction of a man who thought he'd arrived.

'Theo called me,' she blurted out, 'to say something's gone

wrong. Some of the drugs are missing, and he blames you. I've come to warn you.'

The corner of his lip twitched the familiar warning sign she'd come to read as danger. She'd expected him to look shocked, or at least concerned, but instead, his face twisted with the possessive jealousy that was the hallmark of their marriage.

'Why would Theo call you; why, if he thought something's gone wrong, didn't he call me?'

He spat the words with such ferocity she instinctively stepped back, struggling to keep her nerve. 'I don't know, maybe he thought I might know something?'

In her panic the words spilt out before she could fully engage her brain. The conversation had taken a completely unexpected turn. Jem, oblivious to the threat he was under, seemed instead fixated on her and Theo, and she knew she was in trouble.

'What the hell have you two been up to? Have you been at it behind my back? Yeah, that's it, and now you're cooking up some plan to get rid of me. That's what this is.'

With one swift move he reached up, grabbing her by her hair; his face contorted. He wound the fine blonde tresses around his fist, winching her head down and in, close to his chest, until her neck was bent back; her face forced upwards to his.

'Have you been screwing Theo Morgan?'

'No, I swear.'

'Liar,' he snarled. 'I can practically smell him on you, and now the pair of you are fitting me up.'

A spray of vitriolic spittle landed on her cheek.

'No ... no, I promise ... I promise.'

He forced her onto her knees, pushing her head down so her nose scraped the floor. Instinctively, she lifted both hands above her head, trying to protect herself from what might come next.

'You'd better tell me the truth.'

'Nothing, nothing's been going on!' she pleaded; eyes

smarting, pain spiking through her neck. 'I wouldn't ... I couldn't. I'm ... I'm in love with someone else. I'm in love with Loveday.'

He let go of her hair, but she stayed put until she saw his highly polished loafers take a step back.

'You're what?'

Struggling to her feet, she touched her burning scalp and watched as loose strands of hair webbed between her fingertips before floating slowly down to settle on the gaudy carpet.

'What did you just say?' Jem demanded.

Josie turned to face him and, sniffing back resentful tears, took a deep breath. Her head was throbbing.

'I said, I'm in love with Loveday Solomon.'

'The cleaner, you're in love with the cleaner?'

SIXTY-ONE

Loveday sat in the car for as long as she could bear to. She tried ringing Josie, but the call went to answerphone. In the end, she couldn't stand to wait any longer and followed her to the club. Once there, she tracked the sound of shouting up to Jem's office entering just after he shrieked the word '*cleaner*', and just before he began to laugh. Spotting Loveday he choked out the words;

'Here she is, right on cue, Mrs Mop.'

Loveday searched Josie's face for clues of what was happening. Seeing her tears, she snapped.

'You shut up, you pig; I know what you are. You're a bully, and you don't deserve her. At least I love her. You don't know what love means. You want to own her.'

'Not anymore, I don't, not now, she's been with you,' spat Jem, 'You can have her. It's disgusting, fucking disgusting.'

Josie felt a weight lift. Jem didn't care; they could be free. She'd done her bit, warned him about Theo. Whether he believed her or not was up to him. She needed to grab Loveday and get away before he changed his mind.

Loveday's face darkened. '*Disgusting ... disgusting?* You're the disgusting one, thinking you can use your wife as a punching bag and sell your filthy drugs down here. Well, we're not going to stand for it. We're doing something about it!'

The look of moral affront slid from Jem's face; his eyes narrowing.

'What are you on about, you mental bitch?'

Josie grabbed Loveday. 'Nothing ... come on, we've got to go,' she whispered, then turning to Jem, 'she didn't mean anything, Jem, she's emotional.'

Loveday shrugged her off. 'We've taken your filthy drugs, so you can't sell them, and we've dropped you in it. It's payback time, you piece of shit. Hope that's *disgusting* enough for you?'

Jem ran at Loveday, knocking her backwards like a sumo in a wrestling bout, leaving her reeling on the carpet. He spun around and grabbed Josie by the throat.

'What have you done? What does the filthy cow mean?' He grabbed her arm, forcing it with a crack, behind her back. 'Tell me now or I'll break it. You and I know I mean it.'

'Okay, okay ... We've ... taken some of the drugs,' she stuttered.

'Who's we?'

'Me and Loveday.'

Jem bent her arm back further.

'And who else? You couldn't do it on your own. Who else?'

'No one. I promise,' squealed Josie, wincing with pain.

Still shaking, Loveday ran towards him, fists clenched.

'You come any closer, and I break her neck,' Jem shouted at her;

'Who else, I said, is Morgan in on this?'

Loveday staggered from the room down the stairs to find help, just as Jem pulled Josie's arm so far back, she thought it had been pulled clear of its socket.

SIXTY-TWO

'Thanks,' said Ross.

'What for?'

'Putting your neck on the line to get me out of the hole I've dug for myself.'

'You're welcome, but it wasn't just for you. It was for Treeve and Alice and John; for all of us; the whole county, come to that. That scum had to be stopped from peddling his crap to kids like our Livvy.'

'Well, I think you're incredible ... foolhardy and mad, but incredible nonetheless,' he grinned.

'It was Josie. She's the one who had the idea in the first place. I just climbed on her bandwagon. I saw a way out for Treeve, and then when I heard about you and Jem, I didn't have any option. I knew we'd never be free of him, and I couldn't risk the kids.'

'I'm only sorry I couldn't see a way out for myself, other than perhaps the same route as John. What about old Gil then?' he said, clearly wanting to change the subject.

Karenza could read him like a book.

It made her think of Piran and his late-night exploits, of young love that left you breathless and torn, and she wondered why it was so hard to ever get that feeling back.

'I know,' she said. 'He was in his element out there on the boat. I was petrified, but not him. He acted like a pro, even chucking in a bit of the lingo. It was *amigo* this and *amigo* that!'

She told him about the young Spaniard coming down below and how she'd been only seconds away from revealing her hiding place and using the Taser he'd given her.

'It was Dad who kept me calm.'

'I'm just glad you're both safe.'

'So, am I,' she smiled, seeing a glimmer of the old Ross; the confident, together Ross she'd fallen in love with all those years before

Rounding the corner, St. Michael's Mount rose out of the sea. A monastery fortress on its island, a place for contemplation and prayer for centuries. Nowadays it teemed with tourists in the summer. You could walk across the causeway from the mainland, but you always had to keep an eye on the tide in case it turned, and you were stranded. Like life, you had to take your chances while you could.

The depressingly tatty guesthouses hemming the road were shuttered; disappointed '**Vacancies**' signs swaying in the on-shore breeze. The town looked worn out, and as they passed the railway station where she'd collected Treeve the day he came out of prison, she wondered how many people ended up there because they got on a train and just kept going? It was literally the end of the line.

The place had lost its identity, abandoned to the bed and breakfast hostels, left behind in the clamour for government money. It felt forsaken. The main street was a mix of small independent shops, selling mostly cheap tourist tat. The plucky shopkeepers fighting against the tide of pound savers and charity shops, changing their stock so regularly there was a pervading pop-up quality to the place.

They swept into the harbour road, past the Jubilee Pool, the elegant nineteen-thirties lido nodding to a more glamourous, palm-treed past then down the pokey narrow back lane to the rear of Mermaids. There, parked where Josie said it would be, was Jem's Aston, its bright red paintwork gleaming under the only unbroken street light.

'You keep watch,' said Ross, 'there shouldn't be anyone around, but just in case.'

Karenza took up her position by the club's back entrance, where she had a good line of vision across to Ross and down both ends of the narrow alleyway should anyone come from either direction. As she leaned back against the door, it swung open.

She glanced across at Ross. He was busy removing the packs of cocaine from the bin bags into the trunk of the Aston, stacking them so they looked as if they'd been carefully concealed around the spare tyre. She had time to pop inside and check on Treeve. Josie had told her where they'd put him. She'd trusted Ross and Loveday but thought it wouldn't hurt to look in on him, herself.

She pushed the door. The basement room was in darkness. She could hardly see anything at first. Slowly, her eyes adjusted.

At the far end of the room was a staircase leading up to the main bar. A small shaft of light shone from behind the frosted window in the door, highlighting the stainless-steel handrail.

To her left, she could just make out a series of doors, each one had a little window with a lifeless lightbulb above. She guessed these were the private booths Josie had spoken about. She remembered they'd put Treeve in the one nearest the door. She understood why; his bulk meant he wasn't easy to carry.

She felt her way to the first booth. As she opened the door the sauna-like heat hit her. The stench of body odour and the sickly cloying fragrance of cheap air freshener filled the suffocating space, along with a faint whiff of urine. She guessed Treeve had soiled himself where he slept. She pulled out her phone. Flicking her finger across the screen, she shone the torch into the darkness.

Treeve was slumped on a narrow bench against the wall, his hands and feet bound with plastic ties put there by Ross. The silver strip of duct tape across his mouth gleamed florescent in the blue torchlight. His eyes were closed, his body lying on its side, hands tied in his lap, feet bound together resting on the ground. She'd been in a state of panic when she'd seen him bundled up in the boot of Ross's car, but she'd managed to persuade herself it was just as if he'd passed out after a night out on the lash. Here, in this seedy dump, it was all too tawdry and real. Here was the man she had woken next to the morning before, drugged, bound and gagged and she'd helped put him there. Moving closer, she could see the wet patch darkening his jeans and felt a wrench of guilt. Her fingers traced the contours of his face. He was as warm as toast. She rested her head against his chest and listened to the rise and fall of his breathing. She knew this was for the best. They'd been right not to tell him what they were up to. It was better he wasn't involved. She knew his limitations. He had to be found by Theo like this, so he looked like Jem's victim. It would look that way to the police, too, when they finally came. They'd think Jem had taken Treeve's boat and used it against his will. Nevertheless, she hated to see him like this. Of all the things she'd done that night; collecting the drugs, cowering under the stinking tarpaulin, this was the worst.

She reached across to his mouth and gently pulled back the corner of the duct tape, revealing his lips. She let the sticky tape flap down to one side. His lips parted and a steady snore rumbled that would have resulted in an elbow in the ribs had they been at home in bed. The familiarity of the sound made her feel better. She was just about to put the tape back when the door suddenly opened, making her jump to her feet. It was Loveday.

'Come quickly, it's Josie. Jem's going to kill her.'

SIXTY-THREE

Karenza followed Loveday up the stairs through the door to the empty bar. Except for the ultraviolet strip light running along the edge of the stage, it too was in darkness. Loveday pulled her up the second flight of stairs.

'Come on, he's got her!' she screamed.

Karenza could hear a man's voice. He was shouting as Loveday burst through the door, dragging her behind.

The room looked to Karenza like an upmarket gentleman's club, with its wood-panelled walls and leather buttoned sofas, but the similarity ended there. The man holding Josie by the neck up against the stripy wallpaper was no gentleman.

Jem turned as they entered but didn't release his grip.

'Here she is, the cavalry. Hey, Josie, *'your girlfriend's back, and I'm gonna be in trouble,'* he sang.

'Leave her alone!' shouted Loveday, less convincingly than before, clutching at her ribs.

'Or what? She's still *my* wife last time I looked,' he snarled, 'and if you pair think you're gonna get away with this, you're more stupid than I thought.'

Josie's face flushed purple as her fingers clawed at Jem's knuckles, clamped tightly around her throat. Her feet pawed the ground as he lifted her from the floor.

Loveday ran at him, jumping onto his back. He swung his free arm, throwing her to the ground. He released his grip on Josie's neck, and her legs buckled as she fell to her knees, coughing for breath. 'Don't touch her,' she croaked, her voice rasping and strained.

Jem towered over Loveday; his fists clenched. 'You think I won't hit you cause you're a woman, well that's never stopped me before; ask her!' He pointed to where Josie lay crumpled on the floor. 'If you're so keen to grow a dick, you'd better be able to take what comes with it,' he sneered.

Loveday jumped to her feet, framing up to him. 'Go on then, big man, bring it on ... you coward.'

Jem took a swing at her, landing a blow on her cheek, and she fell backwards. He lumbered forward, crouching over her, waiting for her to get up so he could take another swipe. Karenza slipped from her hiding place by the door.

Moving from the shadows, she pulled the Taser from her pocket, holding it down by her side out of sight.

'Get away from her!' she shouted, remembering what Ross had said, just *pull the trigger, just pull the trigger*.

Jem turned, 'Who the hell are you? What's this, a bloody threesome?' he sneered, pleased with his joke.

Karenza didn't know why she said it, but without hesitation, she blurted out, 'I'm Karenza Martin, you hideous pig. Treeve is my boyfriend, and Alice Taylor, Carly's mum, you know Carly, the girl you abducted, and whose father killed himself because of you, she's my friend. That's who I am.'

Jem looked as if he'd been slapped with the mention of Carly's name. He backed away from Loveday, towards Karenza, a nervous smirk playing across his face.

'Well, well. At least you're a red-blooded woman with the right kind of balls.'

Karenza's hand began to shake as he moved to within only a few feet of her, talking all the time.

'At least you're not one of them,' he said, gesturing towards Loveday and Josie. You don't need a prick cos you've got yourself two already; a bent copper as an ex-husband and that giant kid you call your boyfriend. You ever thought of getting yourself a real man? It seems, due to unforeseen circumstances, I'm available if you're interested?'

The desk lamp sent contorted shadows across his face, violence crackling from his body like static as he stretched out his arms and walked towards Karenza as if he was going to grab her in a bone-cracking bear hug.

'Shut up, bloody shut up,' Karenza shouted, voice shaky and unconvincing.

He kept walking.

'Or what? Like I said to these two, what are you going to do about it?'

In the time it took him to turn his head and let out a snigger at the two women on the ground, Karenza raised her hand from her side and pulled the Taser's trigger.

Two barbs catapulted from the green cartridge and fixed into Jem's chest. He looked stunned as he twitched and convulsed, then collapsed; eyes wide and vacant.

SIXTY-FOUR

Loveday struggled to her feet, holding her hand to her face as a large bruise began to swell her cheek. 'Come on,' she said, grabbing Josie from the floor. 'We've got to get out of here before he comes round.'

Karenza froze. She looked at Jem and then the Taser in her shaking hand.

Loveday shouted, 'Come on Karenza, we've got to go.'

Still carrying the Taser, Karenza followed the other two women back downstairs to the basement just as Ross walked through the door.

He looked at the fired Taser in Karenza's hand.

'What's going on, I turned around and you were gone?'

'I came in to check on Treeve, but then Loveday needed me to help Josie.'

'To help her do what?'

'To get away from *him*,' said Loveday.

She went on to tell Ross how Josie had gone back to the club to warn Jem about Theo but had ended up blurting out about their affair.

'Why Josie, why did you come back, everything was going to plan?'

'Because he's been my husband for all these years, and despite everything, I thought I owed him the chance to run. I hate him, I *really* hate him, but I don't want to see him dead. I just want to see him out of my life,' she panted, 'but then when he started taunting me everything came out, *everything*. I told him about Theo and Loveday, and that's when it really kicked off. Then, when he saw Loveday, he lost it.'

'What do you think he'll do?' asked Karenza.

'Nothing for the next ten minutes,' said Ross, 'but after that, who can tell? It depends on what he thinks Theo will do. If he thinks he won't wait for an explanation, my guess is he'll make a run for it while the going's good.'

Ross looked at his ex-wife and couldn't help but smile. 'Well done,' he grinned.

'It wasn't funny,' Karenza said.

'It certainly wasn't for him,' said Ross, then, spotting Loveday's shiner.

'God, are you okay? That looks nasty.'

'Yes, it's fine, he caught me right on the bone, that's all. It looks worse than it is.'

She didn't say the crunch she'd heard as Jem's fist connected meant he'd probably broken her cheekbone.

Josie cupping her face, planted a gentle kiss on the livid bruise.

'Come on, we need to get clear of here before Theo turns up,' said Ross quietly, feeling suddenly awkward for intruding on the moment.

'What about Treeve?' said Karenza. 'We can't leave him here alone, not with all that's happened.'

'Does Jem know he's here; did you say anything about that?' asked Ross.

'No, we didn't tell him, but he knows Treeve is involved because Karenza's here,' said Loveday.

Ross frowned. 'Is Theo on his way?'

'Yes,' said Josie. 'I called him. He knows something's up. He bought the story Jem was up to something when I told him the money was missing and he'd cleared out his clothes. He's coming from Sennen.'

'Good, then let's leave Jem to him. You did your best, Josie, but we can't risk our own safety for that monster upstairs. We go with the original plan. Treeve stays where he is to be found by Theo when he gets here. Josie, I'm afraid you're going to have to stay behind to make sure of it. You'll have to fight his corner if Jem chooses to front it out. Are you okay with that?'

'Of course. Let's stick to the plan.'

Loveday chipped in, 'I don't want you to stay. I'm frightened for you; I've seen what he's like first-hand now. He's an animal.'

'Look, we've come so far. We can't go back now. It was a shock for you, I know, but I've seen worse and survived. If he was going to kill me, he'd have done it there and then, and now Karenza's tasered him, I don't think he'd be up to it.'

'Okay, that's decided,' said Ross, 'just keep your head down and make sure you've got somewhere you can bolt to if he comes looking for you before Theo arrives. One way or another Jem's on the hook. The drugs are in his car. He'll never be able to explain his way out of that.'

Josie turned to Loveday. 'You go with Ross and Karenza. I promise I won't take any chances.'

'As soon as you see Theo coming, you text me; understand?' said Ross his voice deadly serious now, 'just in case we miss his arrival.'

I dare say Theo's boys are in Sennen by now awaiting instructions because everything's gone tits up. If Theo thinks Jem's involved he won't risk any further contact with any of his crew, even the van drivers.'

'That makes sense,' said Josie. Theo will call in another team from out of county to move the gear.'

'Karenza, you come with me,' said Ross. 'You sit in Loveday's car until it's safe. I'll keep an eye on the club and Josie, you'd better know if anything, and I mean anything, goes off plan I'm calling this in right away.'

He turned to Josie, noticing the bruise on her neck for the first time. 'Remember, any trouble from Jem or Theo, get out.'

'Theo won't hurt me; he's no Jem,' she replied, pulling the

collar of her blouse up to cover the marks, 'but I take on board what you're saying.'

She looked admiringly at Karenza. 'You go, you've done your bit. I never thought you had it in you! I'll make sure your fella's okay, I promise.'

It was only after they'd gone Josie remembered Jem was not the only one in the building. Carly was there too.

SIXTY-FIVE

Jem dragged himself sideways along the carpet to his desk. Reaching up, he groped for the scissors he knew were there. He pulled them onto the floor and, with a trembling hand, cut the wires hanging from the Taser barbs. Slashing away his shirt, he revealed the two shafts protruding from his chest. Grabbing each in turn, he let out a gut-wrenching battle yell as he yanked the barbs free, throwing them across the floor.

He lay still for a second. *How had this happened,* he wondered. *How the hell had Josie and that dyke pulled this off, not to mention the bitch who'd Tasered him?* He lifted his hand to his chest. It felt tender, but he didn't have time to examine it.

It had been bad enough when he'd thought Josie was carrying on with Theo. He'd always thought Theo thought of her as a favourite toy he'd lent him, one he could take back any time he chose. He'd always expected in the back of his mind, one day the school bell would ring signalling playtime was over. He'd never dreamt she'd ditch them both for a woman. He hadn't seen that coming. *That bloody holiday,* he thought, *and did Mike know, had he told everyone and were they all laughing at him and, come to think of it, where was Mike? He was meant to pick him up outside the club, then drive him to the warehouse in Newlyn, so he could supervise the packaging of the gear. Was he in on this too?*

He checked his rant to self, realising it wouldn't matter what anyone thought of his sexual prowess, his bollocks were the last of his worries. Keeping his life would be an achievement. He'd been stitched up to be the fall guy when it was discovered the drugs were missing. Theo would see to that.

Flinching with pain, he pulled himself up onto the chair. Reaching into the pocket of his blood-spotted shirt, he retrieved the key to the desk drawer. Unlocking it, he pulled it out and turned it over, sending the contents scattering across the polished surface. Taped firmly to the underside was an envelope. He tore it away and ripped it open. Inside was an electronic key card.

Still shaken, he walked to the back of the room and swiped the card through the reader on the wall, opening the door concealed within the wood panelling. Reaching for the light switch, he stepped inside.

The tiny space contained a rail of clothes for when he spent the night at the club. Wincing, he pulled off his shirt. Tossing it into the corner, he picked a dark blue replacement from the rail.

On the back wall was a small safe. Jem tapped in the combination.

Resting on the shelf was a passport and a small black book, which he knew contained a list of internet accounts and their passwords. Next to them were four stacks of cash, banker's bindings still attached. Each held five thousand. Twenty thousand wouldn't get him far, but it would have to do. At least it would buy him time. He had accounts all over the world, most of them in Josie's name, but she didn't have the passwords. As long as he had access to the internet, he could move money around until he found somewhere to settle; somewhere he wouldn't always have to be looking over his shoulder. If he was lucky, he could get a safe distance from Theo, then contact those further up the chain of command to put his side of things; how he'd been stitched up. Right now, no one would be listening, but once he told everyone what those bitches had done, things would change. He remembered the look Morgan had given Josie in Sennen and couldn't wait to see his face when he found out about Loveday, that Welsh git had been pissing up the wrong tree.

He thought about how he'd pay someone to kill the bloody

lot of them. No one was going to set him up and get away with it. He'd make them all pay, especially Josie, but all that relied on his survival.

He'd have to change his plans. He'd call one of his connections and arrange to charter a private plane out of Newquay to the south coast and then across the channel. The problem was Mike. *Where was Mike?*

His phone rang, making him jump. He answered, lifting it to his ear, saying nothing.

'Jem ... Jem are you there, you weasel? Where's my gear?' It was Theo. 'Jem, answer me. If you've cocked this up, I swear to God, I'll be feeding you to those fishes you like so much, Jem ... Jem?'

Jem hung up. 'Shit!' he shouted aloud, banging his fists against the window. He needed more coke.

He walked across to his desk and retrieved a small plastic bag from the mix of things scattered across it. Trying to control the shake in his hand, he tipped the contents out. Lifting the antique silver paper-knife Josie had bought him for Christmas, he read the inscription;

TO MY BIG MAN,' Love Josie xx

What the hell did that mean? BIG MAN. Had she been trying to be funny? He'd show her what a big man was capable of. He'd show her a big fucking gun when he caught up with her. Cow!

He was about to throw the knife across the room when he remembered why he'd grabbed it in the first place and began cutting the fine white powder into three thick parallel lines. He felt for the note he'd used earlier. Rolling it back into a thin tube, he used it to sniff up the white powder.

He pinched the bridge of his nose; the sudden burn making his eyes smart. Then the rush; predictable; reliable. His chest was killing him, but this would be enough to keep him going for now; enough to get away.

He turned sharply as the door behind him opened. He thought for one terrible moment it was Theo there to finish him off, but it was Carly. He had no idea why she was there. He looked at her and wondered for a split second whether he should ask if she wanted a line, but then felt bad about even thinking it. He ran his finger along the last of the powder rubbing the remnants into his gums. He felt better, stronger; in control.

The anxious throbbing in his chest subsided and he found himself walking towards her, turning as he did to take another look out of the window to see if Mike was there with the car. He wasn't.

The phone rang again. Theo.

Carly took his hand, pulling him behind her.

Jem protested, 'What is it, what do you want?'

She turned and, pleading with her eyes for him to follow, pulled him forward with both hands. He couldn't resist.

'Okay, Okay. I need to get my money, my stuff ... STUFF.' he said pointing to the open door in the panelling.

Back at the safe, he pulled a small holdall from the floor and placed his passport, the money and the notebook inside.

Bending down, he lifted the carpet at one corner and began to prize away a small section of floorboard. He reached down and pulled up a thin rectangular case. He flipped open the lid to reveal a row of small videotapes just like the one Josie had taken from the safe at the house.

Jem was astonished at Trenear's stupidity at thinking he'd only have one copy. He could still make use of them. He could live for a long time off the filth he had on people, including that smug copper.

Retrieving his jacket from the back of the chair, he walked to the window one more time. Still no sign of Mike.

As he glanced back at Carly, the longing for her he'd felt the first day he watched her dance and which had grown into so much more since, overwhelmed him. At that moment, as his eyes locked into hers, he forgot about Mike, Theo and Josie and knew he had to follow her. It might be his only chance to escape, perhaps his last chance of happiness too. He didn't know why, but he was convinced that as long as he had her, everything would be okay. He would take her with him and be able to start again, and this time it would be different because he had her on his side.

SIXTY-SIX

Carly led Jem down the narrow stairway to the basement. The bulbs above the booth doors were on, except for the one nearest the exit, where Josie sat with Treeve.

'Why the hell don't they turn the lights off? Do they think I'm made of money?' Jem grumbled.

Josie's heart pounded at the sound of his voice. She looked across at Treeve and, for the first time, noticed the tape on his mouth had become unstuck. Carefully, staying close to the floor to avoid being spotted through the window, she shuffled towards him. As she reached across to replace the tape, to her horror, he stirred, letting out a low gravelly moan. Grabbing the loose end, she pulled it back across his lips, holding it in place. The Rohypnol was beginning to wear off, and she knew if he woke, he'd be disorientated and bound to make a noise. She also knew she wasn't strong enough to restrain him if he did.

Jem paused, hearing the noise. It sounded like it was coming from one of the booths. There shouldn't be anyone there, but he was certain he'd heard a muffled groan. He walked to the door nearest him, next to where Treeve lay. Not fancying another Taser attack, he gingerly pulled back the door. Though relieved to see it was empty, he was certain he'd heard something, and he moved on to the next cubicle. He was about to open its door when his mobile rang again. Theo's number flashed in front of him; Jem switched it off.

Carly pulled at his jacket. He hesitated for only a second before forgetting about the mystery noises and moving to the exit.

Josie heard a tap on the window of the booth. Looking up from the floor, expecting to see Jem's fuming face peering in at her, she saw a hand. Small and delicate, the smooth palm pressed against the glass seemed to glow in the ambient green light. Although it hovered there for only a second, it was long enough for Josie to know with absolute certainty it was Carly, and like earlier, the gesture confirmed the girl was on her side.

With a flick of a switch, the place was plunged into darkness as Josie heard the door to the alley close.

SIXTY-SEVEN

Jem spotted the Aston parked in its usual space.

'What the hell's that doing here?' He walked towards it and tried the door. It was locked. He looked around, checking he wasn't being watched. He had a spare key in the office. He could get it, and he and Carly could make their getaway, but something wasn't right. Suspicion niggled like a hamster on a squeaky wheel. Who'd driven it there and why?

Peering through the window and spotting the suitcase, he knew the Aston was a trap. Josie must have fitted it up with the case, no doubt full of his clothes, to make this look like he was on the run. He tried the boot. It was unlocked. As it sprung open, he scanned the carefully stacked cocaine Ross had stowed there and, totting up its value, realised it was a sum worth killing him for.

'Damn,' he spluttered, as it dawned on him just how thorough the women had been; setting this up to look like he'd planned this.

He'd be a sitting duck if he used the car and had no intention of falling in with his wife's little scheme to get him killed.

He shut the boot, ran his fingers one last time along her lovely shiny bonnet and followed Carly towards the quay.

'Where are you taking me? I need to get to an airport.' He pointed to the sky and mouthed the word again.

She ignored him, sauntering along the quay as if they had all the time in the world. At the end of the jetty, she untied a rope attached to a dinghy with a small outboard engine.

'No, no, we can't,' Jem protested, turning to walk back, calling over his shoulder, 'Come on, Carly, we've got to go. We've got to go!'

The screech of wheels stopped him in his tracks. He looked up, saw Mike's car and assumed he'd finally turned up. The car did a swift U-turn as if coming back to pick him up. He felt an immediate sense of relief, but as the BMW drew closer, he could see Mike was in the passenger seat, and Theo was driving. What's more, the car had mounted the pavement and was heading straight for him.

He turned and ran back towards Carly who'd remained sitting in the dinghy as if expecting he'd be back.

'Go ... go,' he said, leaping awkwardly into the boat.

He heard a car door slam and the sound of hollow steps on the timber jetty.

'Now ... for Christ's sake, go!' he shouted at the girl.

Calmly, without regard for the danger they were in, Carly started the engine, leaving the two men standing in their wake, Theo's curses drowned out by the roar of the motor as it cut a trench through the water. Mike and Theo turned to tiny dots, then disappeared. Jem took a breath. He had no idea where the girl was taking them and didn't care, as long as it was as far away from Theo as possible. Despite the chill, a toasty warmth embraced him as his eyes turned to Carly, and he reflected she must have feelings for him, maybe even the same feelings he had for her, after all, she'd just saved his life. The thought spawned a sense of wonder that allowed him to forget his predicament for one magical hope-filled moment.

SIXTY-EIGHT

Josie waited a few minutes until she was sure the coast was clear and then, leaving Treeve, made her way out of the booth upstairs to Jem's office.

She spotted the cut Taser wires on the floor and put them in the bin. The concealed door at the back of the room was ajar, and she could see the safe door was open. She sent another text, this time to Theo.

Jem's gone. He's emptied the safe in the club and I've found one of his men tied and gagged in the basement. Please, get here quickly. Jx

A text came back almost immediately.

Be there in five. Spotted Jem on the run. Got away.

Josie made her way back to the stairs, pausing to glance at herself in the large ornate mirror hanging by the door to check her look. She needed to appear suitably shaken. She pulled a face that would do the trick and thought when Theo arrived, she might add a few tears for good measure. Hopefully, this would be the last time in her life she'd have to call upon her acting skills. After today she could finally be herself.

She opened the door to the alleyway just as the black BMW rounded the corner and drew up outside.

'Here goes,' she whispered.

Both men jumped out of the car. Mike was the first to speak.

'You okay, Josie? We just saw Jem. He took a boat from the quay. He had Carly with him.'

'Oh my God. I didn't know she was here,' she lied, 'you don't think he'll hurt her, do you?'

'No,' he hesitated. 'No I don't. I'm sorry, Josie, but I think this must have been planned. I think something's going on between the pair of them. She was leading him as if she knew where they were heading.'

'Oh, I see,' she faltered, sham tears brimming her eyes. She shot Theo a furtive glance. He looked relieved she hadn't let on she didn't give a damn about Jem's love life. She understood Theo wouldn't want her to reveal anything about their relationship. It would muddy the waters. His superiors might conclude Jem's actions were the retaliations of a wronged husband and put Theo in the firing line if blame was being apportioned.

'I've been upstairs to Jem's office,' said Josie, for Mike's benefit. 'He's cleared out the safe, and look ... ' She opened the door to the booth, revealing Treeve, slumped and bound.

'Treeve ... Oh God,' shouted Mike. 'What's he done to him?'

'It's okay, I've checked. He doesn't seem to be injured, but I think he's been drugged. I tried to wake him but was frightened to do anything else until you got here.'

Finally, Theo spoke. He looked shaken and Josie understood the implications of all this must be dawning on him.

'Mike, go and get something to cut those ties off.'

Mike retreated to the car.

As soon as he'd left, Theo closed the door behind him and grabbed Josie's hand.

'Are you okay? I was worried sick he'd hurt you.'

'He didn't hear me come in,' she lied, 'it was fine, I kept out of sight. I just wanted to know what was going on, that's all. I had a feeling he was up to something, that's why I called you.'

'You were right to. The little shit has got someone to take the boat out, pick up the gear as planned, but then drop off only about half of the consignment to my boys. God knows where the rest is.' He paused, looking through the door at Treeve. 'I suppose Sleeping Beauty here might know something when he comes around.'

Theo stepped into the booth, moving towards Treeve as if he intended to beat him back to consciousness but instead ripped the tape from his mouth.

'I doubt it,' Josie, cut in quickly, 'I think he's been there ages from the smell of him. She pulled a face and pointed to the patch on his jeans. I think Jem tied him up and had someone take his boat. My guess is, he doesn't know anything about it. If he did, Jem would have got rid of him properly. He hasn't been with him long, and I can't see him bringing a local fisherman in on any double-cross. If Mike doesn't know anything, nobody does. My guess is it's some outside team. There have been a lot of private phone calls at home lately. I thought they were from you, but if you're saying not, then it must have been his new pals.'

'Yeah, you're right,' Theo agreed, taking on board her logic. 'This is a professional job. Jem probably planned it from the off. There has to be someone else pulling the strings. He's not got the brains to do this on his own. I reckon he's been cosying up to someone else all along.'

Josie smiled to herself. *Hook, line and sinker*, she thought.

'Did Jem have any bags with him when you saw him on the quay?' she probed, casting the net that would trap him.

'No just a holdall, not big enough to have the drugs in, not all of them anyway.'

'Didn't he have the suitcase, the one I said was missing, I assumed he took it from the car?'

'What car?'

'The Aston, it's outside, didn't you see it on your way in?'

'No, I didn't. I was too anxious to see you.'

He dropped her hands and sprinted out of the door, brushing past Mike as he returned with some wire cutters and set about cutting Treeve free.

With both men busy, Josie walked to the other end of the room and texted Ross;

Mike and Theo here now. Jem's on the run. Has Carly with him!

***

Ross watched the BMW drive up the alley at speed. He recognised Mike in the passenger seat and guessed Theo was the driver. He knew he had to call this in the minute Josie said Jem had Carly with him. He immediately made the call to the station to say he'd been tipped off by a reliable source there was a drug deal going down at Fielding's club and that Feilding had taken Carly Taylor as a hostage. A call came back from his superintendent within minutes confirming the local station had been alerted along with headquarters and the National Crime Agency who would be sending down a team by helicopter as soon as the intel was verified. The local boys had been instructed to do nothing other than monitor the situation from a distance until backup arrived from Camborne. A separate team were being deployed to Sennen to intercept the drugs. Until then, as the senior officer on the ground, Ross was to take interim operational control but basically do nothing. He knew that wasn't going to happen. For the first time in ages, he felt like a real policeman again

Theo and Mike were inside but that wasn't to say they'd hang around for long. He needed to do what he had to do before the glory boys from the NCA pulled rank and he lost control of the situation. They would want to be the ones who made the arrest. They'd have plenty of questions for Theo. He was on their list of high-profile professional crooks who up until now had managed to avoid the limelight. They'd be all over this like a rash. He'd had dealings with the National Crime Agency before on other cases, and they'd shared information at various times about Fielding and his connections. He knew they'd be wetting their pants with excitement at the prospect of getting Jem, or better still Theo Morgan, in an interview room, miles away from his city-slick brief. Things had gone beautifully to plan up until then and he had no intention of letting it go left field now because they wouldn't get there quickly enough.

Keeping to the shadows he crept along the dimly lit side street from the quay into the alley. Morgan was standing by Jem's car with the boot open. Ross took his chance.

'Police! Put your hands behind your head and slowly ... slowly mind, walk back towards me.'

Theo paused for only a second before doing as he'd been told.

'Okay, okay, no problem. What is this?'

'You'll know soon enough. Keep your hands where I can see them,' Ross shouted. 'I need you to step to the side, Mrs. Fielding.'

'Now get on the floor, face down, Mr Morgan.'

'How the hell do you know my name?'

'Because Mr. Fielding told us all about you. He's the one who tipped us off about the cocaine, about your hidey-hole in Sennen and about the drugs you're here to pick up from his car. The whole plan, in fact. Now, do as I said and get on the floor, face down.'

'That prick, I can't believe he's gone and sold us out to you lot to save his own neck. Well, you'd better do a good job hiding the little shit,' mumbled Theo, lying face down on the ground, straddled by Ross.

'We won't be hiding him. He's not under witness protection. In fact, we've no idea where he is. He's done this with no prompting from us. He must be getting brownie points from elsewhere, along with protection. It doesn't get better than this as far as we're concerned. One of your lot grassing for free.'

Ross knew Theo would be certain now Jem had changed

allegiances and planned the whole thing. Pulling the cuffs from his back pocket Ross knelt, yanked Theo's hands behind his back and was about to cuff him when he felt the cold, steely weight of a gun barrel behind his left ear.

'Get up!' shouted Mike.

'I'm police,' Ross said, fumbling for his warrant card, 'you really don't want to do this. My men are blocking the exits, so there's no chance of you getting away. Look Mike ... it is Mike, isn't it?'

'Mr. Morgan, what do I do?' Mike's voice had an air of desperation about it. Ross knew it could be riskier than self-assurance in the wrong circumstances. Animals were always at their most dangerous when cornered.

'Put the gun down, Mike.' It was Josie's voice. 'This is not you. Who would you be doing this for? Jem is gone. He's left you, just like he's left me to clear up his mess. You wouldn't be helping Theo; the police already know who he is from Jem. All you'd be doing is making matters worse. Isn't that right, Theo?'

There was an agonising moment of hesitation.

'She's right; chuck the gun, mate.'

SIXTY-NINE

Piran had left the band packing the gear away into the van and cadged a lift to Penzance off one of the caterers from the wedding venue. He needed to see Carly. He had something important to tell her.

He'd walked around in a daze for weeks after that first time, only coming to life when he'd plucked up courage to ask her out. Since then they'd met in secret a couple of times a week. It was always the same routine. She texted him to say the coast was clear and he'd head for the club. He always went via the side alley, up the fire escape. There was a light above the door she turned off when she knew he was coming to signal it was safe. If Jem was staying overnight, the light stayed on. Between meetings, they communicated by text.

He told no one about them, how could he? He could do without the relentless ribbing he'd get from his mates if they found out. A couple of them had been to watch Carly dance since Jack's stag and hadn't stopped talking about it. He hadn't been again. He didn't need to. The Carly who danced was different from his Carly, the one he was in love with.

That was what he wanted to tell her; he loved her, and he'd decided not to go to university after all. He'd seen a job advertised in the Cornish Packet at a new swanky hotel opening in Carlyon Bay on the outskirts of St. Ives. He'd gone for an interview and got the job. It involved teaching the tourists to sail and surf. The wages weren't great, but accommodation came with the job; a mobile home on-site and he'd agreed with the manager at the interview he could earn extra playing guitar in the hotel restaurant in the evenings.

He dreaded telling his mum and dad, especially Mum, who

he knew would hit the roof. She was already on his case, questioning him about who he'd been hanging around with lately, why she never saw him and whether he had a new girlfriend? He'd seen her smelling one of his shirts earlier that week before putting it in the washing machine, checking for perfume. She wouldn't find any, Carly didn't use it.

He'd bought a kebab from the place opposite the train station where he'd been dropped off. He was starving. The tiny bites of finger food at the wedding buffet had barely touched the sides. Mum had been eager to get him out of the house early. She and Treeve had been acting odd all day, and when she'd asked him if he could drop Livvy off at her friend Lilly's for an overnighter, he knew something was up. She'd been grounded for weeks.

If he had to guess he'd bet Mum had finally decided to give Treeve the old heave ho. It had taken her longer than he'd thought it would. He'd sensed the man was on borrowed time since he'd ditched the job with his grandad to work for Jem. He hadn't told his mum about the night he'd seen Treeve manhandle Carly's dad at the club. It wouldn't bring John Taylor back.

Personally, he'd be glad to see the back of him. Treeve being around would make it difficult for him and Carly, given what had happened.

He headed down the side alley lifting the lid of a green wheelie bin to throw in the last of his kebab. The gig had been booked for months, and the band had a room at the venue overnight. Carly wasn't expecting him. He thought he'd surprise her.

The place was in complete darkness, and he guessed everyone had left. The woman who used to live there, the one who managed the place, had moved out recently. It was one of the reasons he worried about Carly. It meant she was sometimes on her own there with Jem. It wouldn't be a problem anymore if they could live together. She could carry on working at the club if that's what she really wanted, although he hoped she'd be persuaded not to and would get a job at the hotel with him or maybe start painting again. She could do portraits of the visitors; they loved that stuff.

He sent her a text;

Change of plan, outside on the fire escape.

The light above the door was off. He headed up the fire escape watching his footing on the slippery aluminium steps. He knocked at the door gently at first, then when there was no response, a little harder; still nothing. Although the curtains weren't drawn, there was no light coming from Carly's bedroom. *Perhaps she was asleep?*

He retraced his steps back to the alley where he rooted around by the wall for a stone to throw up to her window. He couldn't see a bloody thing in the dark as he fumbled among discarded fag butts and takeaway food wrappers. He hoped he didn't grab at anything worse. He turned on his torch, pleased he'd finally thought of it, and found a few granite chippings from around the bin.

He aimed one up at Carly's window, listening to it clatter then tumble onto the sill and back down to the ground by his feet. He tried a second, then a third; nothing.

He looked down at his phone again. What if she'd gone home to see her mum? He hadn't thought to ask if she was working tonight. She'd started to visit since her dad died. He hadn't thought of that; typical, just his luck she was home in St. Ives and he was stuck in Penzance. He'd have to get a taxi, and it wouldn't be cheap this time in the morning if he could get one at all. His best chance was on the main road by the quay.

He was disappointed but his news could wait another day. He was knackered and his bed was calling him. He headed down the alley towards the cut at the back of Mermaids leading down to the promenade.

He scrolled his phone for a Penzance taxi firm's number.

He rounded the corner just as Ross was about to take the gun off Mike.

He looked up from his phone.

'Dad, what are you ... '

The force of the bullet ripping through Piran's shoulder span him around. His phone flew from his hand as he fell.

Ross heard the gun clatter to the ground as Mike stood back.

'Piran ... my God Piran,' Ross shouted, running towards his son.

***

Josie had to think quickly. Picking up the gun she pointed it at the two men.

Theo was on his feet. 'Josie, what are you doing?'

'Both of you in there,' she said, gesturing with the gun towards the back entrance of the club.

'What?' said Theo incredulous.

'In there, then in the booth,' she said.

'We've got to get away,' said Theo.

Josie ignored him. 'Tie Mike up.'

'Josie?'

'I said tie him up.'

'With what?'

'I don't know, his shirt, his belt, anything, just tie him up.'

Mike didn't protest. He huddled in the corner of the booth next door to Treeve's. Josie could see his hands shaking. He was clearly in shock.

Theo looked Josie in the eye for a long thirty seconds. When she didn't flinch, he turned to Mike. 'Take your belt off, mate.'

Mike undid his buckle. Sliding his belt from its loops with a swish he handed it to Theo, who gestured for him to turn around. Theo then proceeded to bind the man's hands behind his back before pushing him face down onto the bench. Reaching up, he tore down the bamboo blind from the booth window. Ripping the pull cord free, he bound Mike's feet, winding the excess cord around the belt.

'Now you and I both know if you tried hard enough, you could break free of this,' Theo said into Mike's ear, yanking the cord tighter, 'but you're not gonna do that. You're gonna stay there like a good lad and wait for the police. We'll get you a brief and see you right as long as you keep your mouth shut, understood?'

Mike nodded with a groan.

'Right, satisfied, now can we go?' Theo said turning to Josie who had looked on mesmerised as he'd hog-tied Mike with a proficiency suggesting it wasn't the first time he'd performed the rodeo trick.

'*We're* not going anywhere. A boy's been shot. He might be dead. You've tied Mike up like I asked, now run, catch your plane, have a happy ever after in Barbados. I want no part of this. I'll say you tied up Mike then overpowered me. Just leave the gun and the drugs and go.'

Theo turned to face Josie. 'But Josie?'

'I said go ... while you still can. This place will be crawling with police soon.'

Theo didn't need a second bidding. Turning his back on Josie, he made a run for his car, no doubt heading for the airport as planned. He made no attempt to try and persuade her to go with him, and she knew she had made the right decision to choose Loveday and freedom over a lifetime of looking over her shoulder with a man whose first priority would always be himself. She knew deep down what kind of man he was, and had the tables been turned, he would have sacrificed her in the blink of an eye just as he had all those years before.

***

Ross cradled Piran as he watched Theo speed away in the BMW. He radioed for backup and an ambulance.

It's DI Ross Trenear. There's been a shooting; my son ... he's been shot. The shooter's still at large.'

Josie ran towards him. 'No he's not, he's tied up in the club.' Ross looked bemused.

'Trust me, it's safe,' she said unloading the gun and placing it down at his side. 'Is he gonna be alright; what can I do to help?'

'You can call Karenza and tell her to get here quickly,' he said before returning his gaze to Piran.

'You're alright, son, grip my hand. Look at me, keep looking at me.' Piran was drifting in and out of consciousness. He was mouthing something. Ross put his head to his. 'What is it, son, what do you want to say?'

Ross lifted him and felt his back. There was blood there and a rip in Piran's jacket where he guessed the bullet had exited.

Josie called Loveday.

'Loveday put me on loudspeaker so Karenza can hear.' Loveday did as she asked.

'Is Ross okay?' Karenza asked, clearly agitated he hadn't been the one calling.

'He's fine.'

'And Treeve?'

Josie knew she had to tell Karenza about her son, but the woman kept butting in.

'Fine too. The paramedics are on their way but he's already coming round. He doesn't remember a thing but I need to tell you ...'

'And Jem, have they got Jem?' Loveday asked.

'No, he made a run for it. He took a boat from the quay, and ... '

'What ... what is it?'

'I'm afraid he's got Carly with him.'

The two women began to rant and rave on the other end of the line.

'Both of you please just shut up for a minute,' Josie shouted.

They fell silent

'It's Piran. He's been shot.'

***

Within minutes there were police cars and flashing lights everywhere. Soon Mike was sitting in handcuffs in one of the police vehicles; the drugs being loaded into large clear plastic bags for analysis by the time the NCA team arrived by helicopter into Penzance.

Karenza and Loveday arrived as the paramedics loaded Treeve and Piran into the ambulance.

'The paramedics say he'll be fine. The bullet went straight through the muscle in his upper arm. They'll check for shrapnel because the forensics team haven't found the bullet yet, but they think it looked clean. He was so lucky, Karenza,' he said, touching her arm.

'What happened, what was Piran doing here?'

'I don't know, love. He walked around the corner from the side alley. I didn't have chance to ask him what he was doing there. Look, you go with them in the ambulance. I need to stay here. I need to get my story straight.'

Ross turned to Loveday. 'Josie's been taken to the station to give a statement. Don't worry, as a witness, not a suspect.'

He watched as a tide of relief washed over her battered face.

Karenza stepped up into the ambulance. She was thankful Treeve was okay and in safe hands, but had to admit to herself the only concerns she'd had whilst waiting had been for Ross. It was his voice she'd wanted to hear. She knew whatever happened to her from here on in, it wouldn't involve Treeve. That part of her life was over.

Her son lay pale and bloody, hooked up to a drip. She gripped his hand.

'Oh, my love. What have I done, what were you doing here?'

Piran's lids fluttered open.

'Carly ... where's Carly?' he mumbled

Karenza remembered what Josie had said about Carly and Jem.

'She's safe, don't you worry, she's safe,' Karenza lied.

'But you don't understand ...' he slurred, the drugs starting to take effect.

'What is it Piran ... what are you trying to tell me?'

'I love her ... I love her Mum so bad it hurts.'

SEVENTY

Carly slowed the boat until they were virtually drifting then cut the engine.

The moon cast an oily slick across the liquorice water, and Jem was struck by how quiet it was now the town was out of range. He didn't like quiet, it unnerved him.

'We must go,' he said, pointing to the engine.

Carly didn't move; her hands folded neatly in her lap, her face, a China doll mask.

'We have to go!' Jem said, raising his voice now; exaggerating each word, still uncertain whether she could hear him or not.

Steadying himself, he gingerly picked his way to the rear of the dinghy, clambering past the holdall at his feet. He felt at odds with this environment. He wasn't a good swimmer. His heart pounded, and the coke wasn't helping. He'd have gone easier on the gear if he'd known what lay ahead.

The boat swayed from side to side as he manoeuvred his way to where Carly sat. He reached out to her, trying to pull her to her feet in an attempt to swap places, but she wouldn't budge.

What was wrong with her; she wasn't helping him. She wasn't moving towards the front of the boat. She wasn't doing a damn thing she was told.

'Carly, move so I can get to the engine. We need to get away, we haven't got time for this,' he snapped.

She stared at him blankly, eyes glassy and cold.

A gust of wind ruffled the surface of the water and whipped her hair across his face, blinding him for a second. The sea was getting choppy, and the boat began to rock. Jem edged past her, plonking himself down by the motor.

Once up, he expected her to move to the front and take her

seat so they could get the hell out of there and back to terra firma, but although she made her way towards the bow, she didn't sit down. Instead, she stood, legs wide apart, shifting her weight from one foot to the other. Jem gripped the seat of the dinghy, his stomach heaving with every sway as water began to slop over the side.

'Fuck!' he yelled.

Carly's coat slipped from her shoulders. He could see the contours of her exquisite body through her flimsy summer dress. She seemed oblivious to the cold.

He looked down and shivered; his leather loafers were soaked. The damp night air penetrated his clothes, and his flesh crept with the jittery sweat of the drugs he'd taken earlier.

'Carly ... Carly, sit down, sit down ... you're going to tip us over!'

She took no notice. Lifting her arms, head tilted back, a tumble-weed of red hair whipping in the wind; she swayed.

Jem held on for dear life; sweat blurring his vision. He had no idea what to do. If he started the engine, she'd go overboard.

Dropping to his knees, he crawled towards her; hands numbing, as he felt his way through freezing water along the splintered deck. Feeling for the hem of her skirt he used her body to pull himself up, gripping her shoulders; trying to force her down into the boat, but she remained rigid; rooted to the spot.

'Carly ... sit down. You're gonna kill us both.'

With one swift twist of her body, she grabbed him, pulling him close; her arms icy against his skin.

He tried to free himself but her vice-like grip tightened, pinning his arms to his sides; making him sway with her. Try as he might, he couldn't wriggle free. Partnered in a strange dance; A rhythmic reel, back and forth, back and forth, their combined weight was now at the front of the boat. The water lapped in as their sway quickened, building faster and faster to an unrelenting frenzy until finally the boat lurched and they toppled into the water.

Jem felt his head go under. He frantically gasped for breath, but as the cold water engulfed him, he felt the sensation of dropping like a stone. He opened his eyes. Above him, through the blackness he could see the distorted shape of the moon and was conscious he needed to kick his legs and swim upwards, towards it, but try as he might, he couldn't.

Looking down, he noticed something wound around his body, around and around, binding him, cocooning him, strand after strand from his feet to his chest, like a reel of red cotton. Only his head was free to twist and turn. It was hair, he thought, the beautiful red hair he'd lusted after, and dreamt of spreading over Carly's naked body. He tried to shake the image from his head. The coke, it must be the coke, messing with him.

His lungs burned, and agonising pain corkscrewed through him. It had only been seconds since he'd fallen into the water, but it felt like minutes; long, desperate, chest-throbbing minutes. Then, out of the corner of his eye, he thought he saw a flash of silver as something muscular and slippery touched his legs. He imagined the brush of a cold grey cheek and a shutter of translucent skin, flashing across lidless green eyes.

A high-pitched ear-piercing note exploded in his head, making his ears ring as a blood-red mist flooded his eyes and water filled his lungs.

This is the worst trip I've ever had, he thought, as he imagined a sinuous black tongue reaching deep down into his throat, curling its way into his gut.

Then, just as the last drop of life trickled away from him into the blackness, he felt something he had never felt before that warmed his soul and filled his heart with soaring joy; love. Pure unbridled, unconditional love.

SEVENTY-ONE
Six months later

Meg Trembath sat down at her kitchen table with a cup of freshly brewed tea and a piece of buttered toast to read the article in *Cornish Life*. She looked down at the face of Carly Taylor. It was not a photograph but rather a photograph of a painting; a self-portrait painted some time ago by the girl. The article said there was going to be an exhibition of her work at Tate St. Ives by way of recognition of her talent, following the publicity she'd attracted.

For that lovely child to have been made to suffer yet another ordeal was terrible; just terrible. Thank heaven she'd survived. Meg still woke at night in a cold sweat, heart pounding, remembering the day her grandson Charlie's dog had fallen down the shaft. She remembered how when the rescue team pulled the girl up, she'd felt her head swim; a dreadful pulsing in her neck and her legs folding beneath her. The next thing she knew, she was being propped up in the back seat of a police car with a blanket around her shoulders, Charlie and his dog, Ginny, beside her.

The piece in the magazine said Carly had been unable to call for help. The police told her as much at the time. She, like everyone else, had thought the girl stumbled down the shaft by accident. When she'd learned the truth; that someone had thrown her down, leaving her for dead, she'd been horrified and cursed the monster who'd done such a wicked thing. The authorities had never caught the culprit, and it left an uneasy feeling in the community.

More recently, the girl nearly drowned, like her father only months before. She'd been rescued by trawlermen along with the body of local businessman, Jem Fielding. It had been a terrible shock for the men, seeing his mangled body tumble with the rest of their catch onto the deck. He'd been practically cut in two by the plastic fishing line wound tightly around him, cutting into his skin and stopping his circulation, making it impossible for him to swim to the surface.

The article commented this was a fate suffered by many marine mammals these days as a result of all the plastic floating about in the sea. *Those poor dolphins,* Meg thought.

The fishermen spotted the dinghy adrift with the girl half-drowned inside. By some miracle, she was alive.

Fielding had been identified as the same man seen getting into a dinghy with Carly, and it was suspected he'd been instrumental in her kidnapping before. Infatuated with the girl, he was also thought to be the mastermind behind a massive drug deal uncovered by local police. Several arrests were made. There was a picture of Ross Trenear of Devon and Cornwall Police with his wife Karenza and two teenage children. He'd been commended for his part in bringing the criminal gang to justice. *It was shocking,* she thought, as she ripped out the page to show her daughter when she called in next week.

Meg recalled the statement she'd given to the police after the girl was found, confirming she'd seen nothing suspicious. She hadn't told them quite everything, of course; she hadn't told them the thing which played on her mind since; the sound, or rather the lack of it.

At one point, there had been absolute silence. The woods had resembled a huge natural cathedral, the trees vaulting above her head, muffled in reverence. It reminded her of when she'd stood in her daughter's garden on the day of the solar eclipse when nature's cacophony ceased; the birds fooled into thinking night had come.

Meg took her plate across to the sink to swill it under the tap. She looked up at the little crayoned drawing blue-tacked to the front of the fridge, made by Charlie one afternoon just after Ginny's rescue. She smiled at the little brown dog sitting in the woods, her name spelt out in irregular capitals. Beside Ginny was a fire engine, and then to the side, sitting on a mound, was a girl with long red hair who she took to be Carly Taylor. She looked out from the drawing, her bright green eyes framed with spiky black eyelashes, wearing the same serene smile she wore in the portrait in the paper, but the funny thing; the thing she'd always thought strange, was Charlie had given the girl a fish's tail; blue and green, hanging over the edge of the mound. She'd assumed he'd drawn the girl as a mermaid to add some extra drama to the picture; after all, pinned next to it was another of his drawings of Ginny being chased by a T. Rex.

She'd asked; 'What an earth is a mermaid doing in the woods?'

He'd looked up at her and said, 'Singing, of course, Nanny, didn't you hear her singing like this?' Lifting his eyes to the ceiling, he let out a high pitch note like the ring made when you ran a wet finger along the rim of a crystal glass.

Looking at the face of the mermaid brought to mind a poem she'd learnt in school many years before. *Half fish, half fallen-angel,* she thought, as she dried her teacup.

SEVENTY-TWO

Piran flinched as he untied the Auntie Lou from her mooring and jumped on board. His shoulder was healing well, but he still felt the occasional twinge. He couldn't complain. His surgeon had told him had the bullet hit one inch to the left it could have nicked his subclavian artery, and he could have bled to death or lost the use of his arm for good.

'Good to go, Grandad,' he shouted to Gil Martin at the helm.

'Alright boy. Got a good feeling about today, fine weather and a bay full of fish just waiting to be caught.' Gil had bought the Auntie Lou from Treeve. He'd been glad to sell her. It gave him a bit of money to make a new start up south where he'd headed after the police had finished their investigation.

Since Karenza had taken over the management of the pub, Gil had a lot more time on his hands. He'd forgotten how much he missed the sea. The night of the heist had rekindled an old love; one less demanding than it had been in his youth when his livelihood depended on it. Now, he was a fair-weather fisherman and it gave him the excuse to spend more time with his grandson.

They headed out from St. Ives, casting the mackerel lines out behind them; dropping anchor off the Gurnard's Head. It had turned into a scorcher, and Gil settled back in his seat to catch forty winks. *A half-hour kip in the shelter of the cove while they waited for the fish to bite was just what the doctor ordered*, he thought as he closed his eyes.

After watching the lines for a while, Piran took Gil's lead and made himself comfortable on deck. Plugging in his earphones, he scrolled through his playlist, dozing as the boat bobbed with the gentle current. His mind, as usual, drifted to Carly and an image of them as kids invaded his thoughts. Carly, running, copper hair streaming out behind her, the sun licking at his neck, as he struggled to catch up. Carly, hopping across the rocks, arms outstretched for balance, eventually plonking herself down to dangle her fingers in a shallow rock pool. Kneeling on his t-shirt to avoid the scratch of limpets, he joined her. On their stomachs; heads touching they thrust their faces close to the crystal water as they fished for translucent shrimps with cupped hands. He felt the hairs on the back of his arm stand on end as he let her lick the salty water from his fingertips.

He remembered how he'd felt that same tremble when she'd taken his hand and led him upstairs that first night at the club. How he couldn't sleep when he got home. When he'd finally dropped off, he'd been plagued with nightmarish images of himself drowning in deep, dark water, bubbling with the squirming bodies of hundreds of slimy sand eels. How he'd woken the following morning exhausted; hair damp and a brackish taste in his mouth as if he'd been tumbled by a wave.

Suddenly, Mr. Brightside was replaced with a piercing ring that made him wince with pain. He pulled the earphones from his ears, thinking there was something wrong with his iPhone, but the sound persisted, a high-pitched ringing he couldn't shake. It lasted only seconds, but he must have shouted out because he woke Gil.

'What is it boy, are you alright? You look white as a sheet.'

'Yeah ... I'm okay, Grandad,' he replied; the noise subsiding, 'it's just my phone playing up.'

An hour later, they lifted the anchor and made their way back, pulling up the lines and landing the mackerel as they went.

'I told you it was gonna be a good day, didn't I, boy?'

'Yeah you did,' Piran replied, absentmindedly. He wasn't thinking about the catch. All he could think about these days was Carly and all the times they'd made love since that first time.

SEVENTY-THREE
Carly

I'm sitting in the studio at the back of the gallery, sorting out the brushes I need to put the finishing touches to the mural I've designed. It's for the dance studio, soon to open in the basement of the club, now owned by Josie and Loveday.

I've taken great care to get the portraits of the women just right, and I'm pleased with how they've turned out. They look content and happy, glowing with confidence; an inspiration to the women who'll go there to get fit. They won't, of course, know the real significance of the painting; the secret behind the smiles or the event it commemorates.

To the ladies Josie puts through their paces, they'll appear a group of everyday women, just like them.

I've painted myself naked; arms cradling my pregnant stomach; a reminder to mums-to-be that exercise is good for baby. I've drawn myself further along than I am, and as I look down at my little bump, I can't wait for that heavy roundness to come.

Walking to the other side of the room, I unclip my paint-daubed dungarees. Gathering them from the floor and rolling them into a ball, I thrust them into the canvas bag on top of the brushes. Sitting back on the chair, I wriggle into my clean jeans. They won't fit for much longer; they're already snug. I pause as they reach my ankles.

I'm pleased with the tattooist's work. I couldn't have done better myself. He's managed to create something beautiful, and it makes me happy.

The iridescent blue and silver scales covering both my legs to the top of my thighs, glisten, as I point my foot and tilt my leg sideways. He's succeeded in covering up the scars; the ones made when I etched Jem's name and the words full of pain and hate. The words written on the shells.

Two new words are now written in their place. The delicate green letters curve and twist like ropes of seaweed. I read once how Native American women tattooed their inner thighs with hunting scenes before giving birth, so their emerging offspring would see only nature's beauty as they entered the world. These will be the first words *my* child will see; words I once despised but have grown to understand. The words that bound us, women, together through necessity; forged us in Sisterhood.

SACRIFICE and **RETRIBUTION**

Pulling up my jeans, I pick up the bag and walk through into the gallery where Mum is busy filling the gaps left by the paintings released to the exhibition at the Tate.

'What time will you be home, love?' she asks.

'Not late, Piran's picking me up. We thought we might go and choose a cot this afternoon.'

***

Alice smiled as she watched her daughter leave. She never tired of hearing her voice; the way her words trembled like music in the air. It was a voice worth waiting for. Her only regret was that Carly's father wasn't there to hear it; he'd have been so proud.

THE END

A LETTER TO MY READERS

Thank you for taking the time to read *A Sisterhood of Silence*.

Cornwall has always attracted its fair share of smugglers; those willing to battle with the treacherous coastline and the customs men to avoid paying duty on continental goods.

In centuries past, French lace, brandy and tobacco would have been the contraband brought ashore. The locals would have largely turned a blind eye believing the only victims to be the revenue men. In the words of Kipling's poem, 'A Smugglers Song';

'Them that asks no questions isn't told a lie.
Watch the wall my darling while the Gentlemen go by.'

The drug smugglers and human traffickers who plague our coastline today have little in common with the 'Gentlemen Traders' as they were known. The unscrupulous organised crime gangs who capitalise on the misery and misfortune of others should not be given the benefit of our silence and the Cornish community is rightly outraged these groups are targeting our beautiful county.

I wanted to write a story about a community of women fighting back. I set my story in the home of buccaneers, Penzance, and created a modern-day pirate, Jem Fielding as my antagonist. West Cornwall is steeped in legends, none more evocative than the Mermaid of Zennor. I decided to make one of my Sisters a modern-day mermaid. Carly Taylor, like the legendary Morveren, uses her feminine wiles to get her man. She is the archetypal silent assassin.

I have always been fascinated by the schizophrenic character of the windswept Cornish peninsula my family has been lucky enough to call home for generations. Occupied by a cast of reluctant bedfellows, city-slick escapees and us locals who carry the remnants of our myth-ridden history etched on our backs like tattoos, it teeters between the bucket and spade domesticity of modern-day tourism and a superstitious past, riddled with Pagan traditions.

The resultant clash of cultures and sensibilities causes friction, resentment and drama. My aim, through my writing, is to explore what happens when these divergent worlds collide to expose a darker reality at odds with the picture-perfect landscape. Whilst I was lucky to enjoy a fantastically satisfying career as a lawyer I cannot now imagine anything more joyous than being able to sit at my desk and write knowing others might read and connect with my words. Cornwall has captured the hearts and imaginations of countless wonderful writers through the decades; their vivid images now woven into its rich tapestry. If I can add one colourful stitch I will be happy.

Would you like to read more of my work? Then visit my website www.cornishcrimeauthor.com to join my list. You will be given the opportunity to become a member of my readers' club and receive free downloads, sneak previews and fascinating insights into the characters and places featured in my novels. These goodies are exclusive to members and currently include a **FREE** novella in the **CORNISH CRIME SERIES,** *THE ROSARY PEA What's Your Poison?*

I look forward to meeting you there and on **Facebook** (www.facebook.com/julieevansauthor).

A final request...

If you've enjoyed this book I would be so grateful if you could leave a review on Amazon.

As an author, it is a great thrill to know someone has enjoyed your work, and it will help other readers find my books.

Thank you.

Julie

Printed in Great Britain
by Amazon

19242932R00169